BLACK RUST

a novel by

BOBBY ADAIR

Website: www.bobbyadair.com
Twitter: www.twitter.com/BobbyAdairBooks
Pinterest: www.pinterest.com/bobbyadairbooks
Facebook: www.facebook.com/BobbyAdairAuthor

Mailing list for new book alerts:
www.bobbyadair.com/blackrust-subscribe

Report typos:
www.bobbyadair.com/typos

Cover Design and Layout

Alex Saskalidis, a.k.a. 187designz

Editing & Proofreading

Kat Adair
John Cummings

eBook and Print Formatting

Kat Adair

Foreword

Writing this book—the first in a new series—was a bit of an adventure.

It was supposed to be easy. I'd been kicking around an idea and writing on and off for about a year. Between other books that I'd written, I'd managed to get it about halfway done. So, when I put Black Rust up for pre-sale, I was confident. It would be easy to finish up.

Such are the dreams of naive men.

Literally, the day after I set the pre-sale up, the day after I'd committed to publishing in 90 days (actually ten less because some retailers want the manuscript early), Kat (the missus) finally got around to reading the first chapter.

She was mortified.

Crap.

It's worth mentioning, she's got a low mortification threshold. She thought Dusty's Diary would end my writing career. (She likes to joke that when we met on eHarmony, they didn't have a compatibility checkbox for the "f-word.")

She got a couple of readers and my editor, John, to read the first version of Black Rust. John's usually quite blunt, and while he didn't say he hated it, he hated it.

So there I was, my back-burner masterpiece detested, my pet bunny stomped.

It was a sad day, a sad day with a deadline attached.

Anyway, I moped for a few days...maybe weeks. I went shopping on Craigslist for ugly old cars to restore...I'm not mechanically inclined. Kat and I kicked around some ideas. I wondered if I could ever recapture the true joy of flipping burgers and bagging French fries to pay my rent, and eventually decided I liked writing better than doing that.

Then, as it regularly does, an inspiration sparkled into a concept and I wrote out a few chapters to see what it looked like. Kat and John both read and liked it (or pretended to, sometimes its hard to tell which). Those chapters grew into this book. And I made the deadline.

I'm proud to say, I like it. I hope you do, too.

— Bobby, June 2016

Chapter 1

I knelt behind a rusty stove and peered into the mist between the pine tree trunks, looking for the glow of flames in the distant dark. The slightest of breezes shushed through the needles on the branches sixty feet over my head.

To my left in the waist-high undergrowth lay an upturned bathtub. Beside that, a dishwasher and then a coffee table, all in line along a worn footpath that I knew from experience arced into a full circle. With most of the path out of sight in the night forest, I guessed the circle was maybe two hundred feet in diameter, the largest of two or three concentric circles. The outermost circle was always lined with the big stuff—refrigerators, couches, patio Pepsi machines, and occasionally the rusty hulk of a car.

The next circle might be lined with microwaves, desktop computers, a stand mixer or two, dining room chairs, and end tables. The innermost circle would be laid solid with the surplus detritus of a million devolved lives—silverware, toasters, knickknacks, eyeglasses, anything shiny or jingly.

The three rings made up the boundary of a post-apocalyptic Stonehenge, constructed by diseased cretins to worship the gods who'd come before them and whose descendants still walked among them. Whatever passed for logic in their deficient brains often led them to create simple, pagan religions with crude, open-air temples, almost always incorporating the discarded, inexplicable tools of their lords.

Lords like me.

Laughable, I know.

The closest I came to being a god was that I was a reaping Lucifer, stealing the souls of their faithful and flushing them down to hell. I liked that picture of myself. I liked it a lot. But it wasn't me. I was more like a lethal high school bully, an armed mall cop, a death camp guard. Sure, we had long, euphemized official titles prescribed by the laws that made our services legal. But nobody used those titles. Truth be told, I got paid by the head for snuffing violent dimwits. So maybe *exterminator* was the best name. It was accurate.

Christian Black, the exterminator.

I smiled at the thought of it.

Most people called us Regulators.

Other Regulators, the ones who knew we cheated, called us Front-runners.

I looked down the line of deteriorating appliances and saw Lutz standing behind a tree trunk that had no hope of concealing all of him. His foot was propped up on a water heater lying on its side, and he was fumbling with the video recorder attached to his assault rifle.

"Lutz."

He looked over at me.

I cocked my head in the direction of the glow, in the direction of the chanting of jibber-jabber syllables I suspected did little more than keep the degenerates' mouths busy.

He nodded. He heard them, too.

Even without the spotter drone intel that had led us to the scene, we both knew what was going on — a ceremony for the moon, or the stars, or maybe the fog, since that's pretty much all they could see in the air tonight.

And a sacrifice.

Of course, they were sacrificing one of their own.

If they were just dancing, chanting, and burning a pile of brush, Lutz and I wouldn't be here.

Speaking softly into my headset, I said, "You go left, I'll head straight in so we can catch them in a crossfire."

"No," Lutz replied, still panting from the effort of the hike we'd taken to get so deep into the woods. "I'll go straight. You circle 'round to the right."

I looked into the shadowy trees to the right knowing the ground opened up to a cornfield in that direction—the spotter intel had provided us with a wide view of the area. I wished for the hundredth time I'd been able to replace my night vision goggles after they'd gone on the fritz a few months back. But like everything worth spending a dime on these days, used NVGs were hard to find and expensive to buy. New, they were impossible to get.

"Okay," I whispered, knowing I shouldn't have wasted the breath on telling him to take the longer path in the first place. He was unashamedly lazy and had been eating his way toward a heart attack since before I was born.

I stood up and walked quietly over the thick mat of pine needles, doing my best not to rustle the bushes and doing my damnedest to stay away from the poison ivy.

"Watch out for all the shit on the ground," said Lutz.

Something pathetic buried in Lutz's ego needed to pretend he knew more about what we were doing than I did. "Thanks, Detective." Pure sarcasm.

His breathing grew labored. He was moving through the underbrush. "Must be some houses close by."

"How's that?" I asked.

"They wouldn't carry all this shit out into the woods this far."

"I've seen it before."

"Doubtful."

Yeah, of course, you're right. More sarcasm, even if it was just in my head.

I was following the curved arc past a row of rotting nightstands and easy chairs, having lost sight of Lutz. I crunched through a layer of dry twigs as I tried to gauge my progress. From overhead, I heard the whispery buzz of drone rotor blades. More than one was up there. They were moving in close for a good view of what their operators knew was coming: bloody slaughter, video to sell to the internet voyeurs—the violence pervs who got their rocks off on that sort of thing.

Everybody got a payday when degenerates died.

"I see 'em," Lutz told me.

"Sit tight." I stepped between a cracked flat-screen television and a terracotta flowerpot and made straight for the glow of the fire. "I'll be in position in a minute."

"Dancing," whispered Lutz. "Naked. Got some streaks on their skin. Blood, I think."

Blood. That's what the report from the spotter had said. "You see the kid?" It was always a kid who drew the short straw when the d-gens decided their imaginary god wanted a sacrifice. Usually it was a young girl.

"Can't tell," said Lutz. "Lots of blood. I think they've gone cannibal. I hate this kind of shit. Know what I mean?"

No answer required. I knew exactly what he meant. I'd heard about a thousand versions of why he hated "this kind of shit." I'd heard it through my earpiece. I'd heard it over donuts and coffee. I'd heard it over beers. I'd heard when he explained it to me over the sound of the music blaring in the car. And it didn't matter how high I turned the music up, Lutz spoke louder. It was some kind of hater-mouth magic to always be the loudest goddamn thing around.

And it wasn't the kind of shit they were doing they he hated. He hated *them*. Simple. Straight-up. Period.

Now, I don't have any love for them myself. Nobody who can still do simple addition in their head has any reason to like the d-gens even though most of them are nonviolent and useless. Most of them wouldn't raise a finger to harm another human, but most of them won't raise a finger to feed themselves, either. That turned into a problem for the rest of us. When the disease came and worm-holed their brains, they'd pretty much ruined everything for everybody.

Exaggeration? I think not.

I was a kid when it all happened. I could have grown up to be a doctor spending my afternoons on the golf course and my summers in the Bahamas ogling tanned girls half my age and drinking myself into a stupor by the pool. Instead, I spend long hours every damned day hunting violent degenerates through the woods and through the crumbling suburbs, so I can pay my rent on time and dream about getting out of debt.

Looking at the light through the trees and trying to get a measure of how far away I was from the fire, I wasn't paying attention to where I was putting my feet, and I got tangled in bramble. "Dammit."

"What?" Lutz asked, instantly panicked. That was his way, always expecting the worst.

"Be cool," I told him. "I'm fine."

"We need to hurry this along," he said. "How close are you?"

"Does it matter? Do it yourself if you can't wait." It was a threat more than permission. Lutz didn't trust himself to take twenty-three d-gens on his own. Sure, he had a thirty-round magazine and another half-dozen mags on his belt, but in the trees, as close as we'd need to get before we had clear shots at them all, he'd miss, and half or more might get away. Or they might rush him. He was too old and too slow to run away if it came to that. His only choice would be to kill 'em all or die.

That's why he'd paired with me—not because we liked each other, but because I was a killer.

Twenty-three d-gens at pistol range? Not a problem.

Mostly not a problem because I'd be using an M4 on full auto and I could swap an empty magazine in just over a second. That, and I carried two Walther PPQs with fifteen-round magazines. With those, I could kill thirty of anything within fifty feet of me before I needed to reload.

Good? Yeah, I'm that good.

In his nasally voice, Lutz said, "I see the kid."

I froze. "The kid? Live?" That's not what the intel said. That's not what the pictures showed. Or kinda showed. The damn fog had made everything hard to make out from the perspective up there.

"A couple kids." Lutz's hate was trying to override his good sense and telling him to pull his trigger.

"Dead or alive?"

"I think there's one on the fire."

"Calm down," I spat as I yanked my foot free and started to run. I'd worked with Lutz long enough to know he was about to do something stupid, and I didn't even have eyes on a d-gen yet.

That was bad. Lutz might get injured—no big deal. Lutz might get sidelined—big deal, as that would have a negative impact on my income. Lutz might get killed—he had all the spotter contacts, which he made a point of never sharing with me. So a dead Lutz meant I'd be back to scraping by like all the other suckers without any inside info. To hell with that. I had debts to pay.

"Do you have your video on?" I asked Lutz in order to get his mind out of his hate for a moment and into the land of rational thought. Just like me, Lutz had a digital video recorder. Mine was on an elastic strap on my head, pointed forward to record my kills. His was mounted on his rifle. It was legally required for Regulators, but more importantly, video met half the documentation obligation we needed to get paid for our kills. Two videos from separate points of view, not of the kills—that would be near impossible—but of the whole scene, fulfilled the government requirement. That was the main reason Lutz and I worked together rather than alone. No Regulator worked alone. At least none who made a living at it.

"Damn camera!" Lutz was frustrated again. He wasn't keeping his voice down.

"Lutz, turn on your video." It was an order, but I tried to keep my voice unemotional to keep him calm.

"I think my batteries are dead."

"You're fucking kidding me." No more calm. "Change your batteries. Quick! Before they see you."

I heard breathing and frustrated grunts in response. I didn't know if he was changing his batteries or beating his camera with his fist. With Lutz, it could have been either.

Speaking slowly, I said, "You need to read the VC Act. I'm too far away to get a solid view of the proof."

"Can't."

I burst through a stand of thick bushes and stopped. I had a view of some of the d-gens but too many tree trunks were in the way. Still, I could tell they were dancing aboriginal-style around a bonfire, naked, streaked in glistening blood, with two live children off to the side, held in the strong grip of an older woman.

On a spit, over the fire, the bodies of some toddlers were cooking.

Motherfucker! They were planning a goddamn smorgasbord.

I dropped to a knee to get out of view as my heart gushed blood through my veins so hard I could hear it rushing through the capillaries in my eardrums.

I flipped my cam on and pointed my head toward the clearing while I whispered into my headset, "I am Christian Black, Independent Degenerate Regulator number 77379, and Franco Lutz, IDR number 14634. We've witnessed approximately twenty-three degenerates engaged in violent or cannibalistic behavior. In accordance with the H5N1 Brisbane Strain Prion Mutation Violence and Cannibalism Act, sections three dash two and seven dash two, IDR Lutz and I will attempt to terminate the offenders under verified Sanction Case Number—"

Shit.

I didn't have the Sanction ID, which should have been relayed from the Degenerate Oversight Authority Office through the spotter drone and down to my phone.

I fished in my pocket to get my phone. No cellular signal out this far, but I did have the direct Wifi connection with the spotter drone, which had provided the data on the pending sanction when we were parking the truck before hiking into the woods. I'd taken the precaution to dim the brightness on the screen down to the lowest level, a habit I always used in the field. I keyed the phone on and the screen instantly blinked to life, displaying a red flashing pending notification over the Sanction Certificate.

Pending? What the hell?

I had to be looking at the wrong case. There was a dead toddler cooking on the goddamn fire. Lutz saw it. The spotter drone had to have seen it.

Lutz shouted through my earpiece, "They heard you!"

Chapter 2

I looked up from my position, still squatting behind a bush, too far out for a clear shot at any more than a few of the degenerates.

Some of the dancers had stopped. A woman—a young, blonde-haired d-gen—was staring into the dark, right at my position. Only, she couldn't have been staring at me. With the light of the fire ruining her night vision, she had to be seeing nothing but black.

A rifle shot cracked.

"Dammit, Lutz!" He should have waited for me. I raised my rifle and started to run.

Lutz answered me by squeezing his trigger and emptying what sounded like a full magazine into the dancers.

D-gens screamed.

Lutz yelled.

I heard the sound of his pistol shooting.

D-gens were running in all directions up ahead and their shadows were strobing black through the trees, making it impossible to tell exactly what was happening.

I lost sight of the blonde, staring woman. I couldn't see the two kids.

Lutz yelled something I couldn't make out and I feared he might have a d-gen's teeth at his throat.

I burst into the clearing, planted my feet, leveled my M4, and started shooting at a handful of d-gens who were charging Lutz.

The degenerates all tumbled to the ground at his feet.

He looked over at me with a silent pistol in his hand.

"Reload!" I shouted at him as I aimed and shot at other d-gens.

They were standing, running, attacking us, or already on the ground, trying to die.

They fell.

They screamed.

They scattered. But not fast enough.

I shot down three running into the woods on the far side of the clearing. One crawling away got a bullet in the back. Two more were in the trees but still visible. I dropped them both.

And just that quick, it was over.

No d-gen was on his feet though many were still moving.

I scanned the ring of light around the fire, looking for anything that might still be a danger. Once you started shooting them, they tended to take a violent dislike to you. Go figure. You couldn't leave any alive. That's just the way it was, regulating degenerates. "Lutz. You okay?"

Lutz grumbled.

"Are you hurt?"

"No, goddamn it." Futzing with his pistol, Lutz stepped over a writhing d-gen to get closer to the fire. "You get 'em all?"

"All I could see."

Lutz looked at a d-gen squirming on the ground near him. He holstered his pistol, switched out the magazine in his rifle, aimed, and pulled the trigger. Nothing.

He was shit for taking care of his weapons.

He hadn't run the magazine dry. He had a jam.

I scanned the dark forest for movement. Over the groans of the dying and wounded, I listened for the sound of anything running, either toward me or away.

Lutz got his weapon unjammed and fired a round through the skull of the d-gen at his feet. Then he methodically and quickly pointed his rifle and finished off every wounded degenerate on the ground. "There. I killed more than you." Lutz crossed the clearing, stepping over bodies, focused on something that had his interest.

I was certain he was wrong on the count, but said anyway, "Good for you." I heard a noise in the cornfield, coming from the edge of the clearing. I looked but couldn't make out anything in the dark. I reached into my pocket to fish out my phone, hoping. "When I tried to get the Sanction ID for the mandated recording the case was still pending. They never approved the sanction."

"The hell they didn't."

Lutz stared at me as I pulled out my phone. Only the crackle of the fire and chirping cicadas made any noise. I activated the device and looked at the screen, reading the details slowly, trying to confirm a mistake.

No mistake.

Lutz saw the truth on my face and ran to the other side of the fire for a look at the roasting kid.

I cautiously stepped in that direction for a clearer view. Evidence of the dead toddler would undo the sanction mistake. The cops would flip the sanction to active. Lutz and I would get paid. No problem. Pretty much.

Lutz came to a stop, staring. "These aren't kids."

I took another step to get a view of what Lutz was seeing —carcasses on a spit, legs splayed, tiny torsos split open, roasting, crusted in black. I saw claws on feet but no fingers, and snouts, not flat faces.

"They're raccoons or dogs or something," Lutz whined, looking up at me, worry drenching his features.

Raccoons?

What the hell?

The d-gens are barbecuing little forest critters, not children?

And where were those two kids I saw? *Thought I saw?*

Lutz looked up.

I did, too.

A white spotter drone with flashing red LEDs, a pregnant Frisbee the size of a trashcan lid with a half-dozen little rotors around its circumference hovered over the tops of the trees at the edge of the clearing. It had led us to the kill site. It had gotten us into what was looking like a mess.

Two more white drones, a little farther away, floated higher in the night sky. They were smaller—the voyeurs spying, recording video, witnessing.

"These d-gens aren't cannibals," Lutz muttered. "It's a dirty kill."

A dirty kill.

One year mandatory in a work camp, per head.

Every Regulator knew that. It was the wrinkle in the law that kept men like Lutz from joyriding through the d-gen neighborhoods and shooting down every one he saw because it satisfied his hate and filled his billfold.

He looked at me and made a show of fumbling with his gun, raising it for the cameras on the drones to see, as he said too loudly for normal conversation, "My gun jammed. I only got off a couple shots." He pointed into the darkness, arguing his defense for an invisible jury. "Into the ground. Over there." He looked at me. "This is your dirty kill. You're fucked."

Chapter 3

I scanned the sky. The drones were usually white or neon orange, something easily spotted when they needed to be retrieved after an unexpected battery failure. The color didn't help a lot through the spotty fog, but the flashing LEDs mounted on each did.

Three. That was the count—one spotter, two voyeurs.

One was already buzzing back toward town to get in range of a functioning cell tower to download gigabytes of video showing juicy, two-fisted, blood-spewing slaughter, the kind the violence fetishist would view a million times before midnight. Every insomniac cop in Houston would see an easy arrest and a quick conviction. Other Regulators would salivate at the chance that one of their own might be charged, might run, and give them a chance at a big payday. Fugitive Regulators might bring in ten thousand a head.

"Give me your rifle." I reached a hand out to Lutz as I watched the flashing LEDs in the sky.

"What?"

"Give me your gun, dammit!"

Lutz stepped back.

I spun on him. He was afraid. He was putting the pieces of our situation together, just not fast enough. Mostly he was a dipshit. "You've got a night vision scope on that thing." I pointed at the sky. "I need to take down those drones before they get out of range—now give me your goddamn rifle."

Lutz fumbled with the clip attaching his gun to his harness.

"Hurry," I told him, taking the rifle as soon as it was off his harness and handing him mine to hold. I raised his rifle to my shoulder.

"You can't shoot the spotter," Lutz protested.

The spotter drone, shiny white composite, looking every bit like a flying saucer with its spinning propellers invisible against the night sky, was hovering about eighty feet up, over the trees, past the edge of the clearing. It was a fat goose of a target, hanging stationary in the cold, still air.

"It's a federal offense," Lutz explained in a weak voice he knew was spilling out of his mouth more to cover his ass than to stop me from taking the shot.

Pussy.

I pulled the trigger.

Pop. Pop. Pop.

Plastic cracked and metal pinged instantly after the noise of the shots.

The drone spun, flipped, and power-dived into the trees.

"Goddamn," Lutz whined. "We're screwed now."

"The spotter drone is the only thing that can get bandwidth out here. It's the only one of the three that can send anything back to town. The voyeur drones when they're out this far just float around on autopilot trying to catch some good video. Dammit, Lutz. Don't you know how any of this works?"

Lutz looked like he wanted to punch me. People don't like having their ignorance thrown in their face.

I scanned the sky for my next target as I told him, "You said your spotter drone friend checks our video feeds and cleans them before they go back to the dispatch center.

That's what you told me, Lutz, to justify the share of our bounties we pay your guy. If that's true, then as far as the cops know, we haven't broken any laws, yet."

"Then why'd you shoot down his drone?" Lutz snapped.

"Precaution." I trained Lutz's rifle on the voyeur drone. "We'll work out a deal with your buddy. Pay him for the drone." I pulled the trigger and sent a volley of three more bullets into the sky. The second drone shuddered from the impact but didn't fall. I'd hit the drone with maybe one bullet, but probably missed twice. *Damn! No time to screw up here.* I fired again. The drone dropped.

It was going to be hell finding these things in the trees.

"Just to double check," I said, "you got a cell phone signal?"

Lutz dug his phone out as I trained my sights on the last drone skimming away over the treetops. It was pretty far away.

I fired to no effect. "Shit."

Lutz looked up. "It's getting away."

I bit back a response and fired again. "Crap." The drone flew on. I futilely emptied the magazine.

"No cell phone signal." Lutz held his phone up for me to see, just about ruining my night vision in the process.

"Good." I slapped his hand away. The light from the fire was bad enough. Seeing the bluish light-shadows left on my retina by Lutz's phone, I blinked and cursed. "We need to get that other drone. How long do you think before it gets a signal all the way out here?"

"We're a good thirty miles from town," said Lutz, finally taking a productive part in solving the problem. "Most of those drones cruise at about twenty miles an hour. You can probably get a signal ten miles from town."

Doing a little basic math, I said, "He might be an hour from getting in range of a cell tower." I leveled the rifle at the trees and scanned the forest through the night vision scope. I wasn't looking for anything in particular, I was just looking, evaluating the situation, taking all the unknowns off the table, looking for threats because my adrenaline was pumping at full bore.

Lutz looked into the darkness. "The old highway is the fastest way back."

I looked across the field of brown, shoulder-high stalks of corn, waiting for harvest. "Shit."

"What?" Lutz froze.

A woman was out there in the corn, long blonde hair hanging straight over bare shoulders. She was staring at Lutz and me. Or most likely she saw the fire and shadowy figures around it. But I knew I was kidding myself. That was an optimist's view.

I was tempted to pull the trigger. Hell, we'd already killed a couple dozen. Why risk letting one go who might be halfway smart—smart enough to give an eyewitness account of us actively working to destroy the evidence of our crime.

She turned and ran.

Did she see me pointing the rifle at her?

I looked for another few seconds, knowing I could take the shot, knowing I could hit her—knowing, but doing nothing. Even through the rush of save-my-ass urgency, I'd made enough mistakes for one night. I lowered the rifle. "The drone doesn't need to follow the roads. No onboard pilot. The operator sets the GPS coordinates and—"

"GPS doesn't work for shit anymore," Lutz told me.

"I know."

"Then they can't autopilot. They have to—"

"Dammit," I shot back. "They adjust. Just like we do. We get the coordinates and go two blocks northwest or—"

"That's not right, we—"

"Goddammit, Lutz! I don't want to argue with you about this shit. They adjust. Just because we don't have enough nerds anymore to keep the GPS system running right doesn't mean we don't have enough smart video drone operators to figure out where to send their drones. Maybe they have a software fix. Maybe they do it on the fly. I don't know. I don't care. Shit! They always show up, just like us. We use the GPS coordinates we get from your spotter. They probably get them the same way."

Lutz just looked at me and for the moment had nothing to say. So I ranted on. "Those video drone operators are probably front-running just like us. Your guy is selling the same information to them before it goes out on the public network. You ever wonder why the video drones always show up on time to record, no matter how quick we get to a job?"

Lutz didn't answer.

He knew.

"There's a charging station," said Lutz. "Just off the highway. It's got a hardwired network link back to the city. Maybe fifteen miles from here."

"As the crow flies?" I asked.

"Yes."

"How far for us?"

"Twenty. Maybe twenty-five miles."

"If he goes there, and it makes sense that he would—" I looked at Lutz. "Make sense to you?"

"It'll be the fastest way to upload."

I shoved Lutz's rifle back into his hands as I took mine back. "We need to get to the car and catch that drone before it gets to that charging station. We've got forty-five minutes." I ran into the trees.

"What about the two drones you downed?" Lutz asked, as he lumbered after me.

"Doesn't make a difference if we can't get to the one that's flying back. We can come back for them."

Chapter 4

One of the few things Lutz excelled at was driving.

He owned a beast of an old box-shaped Mercedes that he drove like he was on a racetrack. It was black, three kinds of ugly, and built like an awkward tank that might roll over sideways as easily as forward. Lutz had paid someone to mod the 416 horsepower engine so it would pull over 600. When he first told me that, I figured it was pure braggadocio. Of course I'd thought that. Lutz was the type to tell such stories. Then I rode out with him our first night together. That was seven months ago. If anything, he'd underestimated the horsepower. The clumsy-looking black beast was ungodly fast.

And beast it was, whatever color the machine had been when it was new—back when I was still playing with matchbox cars—that layer of paint was long gone, scraped off or sprayed over. Every angular piece of metal that had once been smooth or square, wasn't. Every window was covered with metal rebar welded to the body. And on the front, a sturdy brush guard protected the engine from impacts. Through the years, there had been many.

Lutz raced the beast up a dirt road pushing speeds that defied physics, at least my intuition of it. At every curve, I just knew we'd slide into the trees, but Lutz kept the Mercedes on the gravel. I didn't look over at the speedometer. I didn't complain. As much as Lutz didn't like me, he trusted me to do my part when the shooting started. As much as I didn't like him, I trusted him to drive.

My belt was buckled. I had his rifle in my hands again, as I scanned the sky through the windshield, looking for a tiny flash of red LEDs.

The tires rumbled over an old cattle guard across the road and Lutz smashed the brake pedal to the floor as he maneuvered the beast up an incline and around a tire-squealing corner. He accelerated as the tires found the old asphalt of a narrow country road. "Anything?" he asked, not taking his attention off the road in front of us that was illuminated by the bright headlights.

I looked through my side window and then leaned over to look out Lutz's side.

The engine revved loudly.

"Nothing."

We raced through a few fast miles before Lutz had to swerve the SUV off the road and into a steeply sloping ditch to avoid a giant piece of farm equipment that had been rusting in the road for what must've been a decade. Once past, he gunned the engine, rolled up the side of the ditch and took the Mercedes airborne for a fraction of a second before we bounced again onto pavement. He laughed.

I laughed, too. Why not?

Another mile passed before the road widened and I saw dilapidated gas stations and abandoned fast-food joints. We'd reached the highway. Lutz used most of the road to cut a turn onto the entrance ramp. The wheels protested loudly on the pavement and the Mercedes leaned way over to the driver's side. Lutz righted the vehicle and straightened us out on the incline up to the highway lanes.

A d-gen ran across the road right in front of us, so close I threw a hand to the dashboard to brace for an impact that frankly would have been minimal. Six thousand pounds of Mercedes reinforced with a huge steel brush guard would mow down any single d-gen. But it was moving fast, and just as I realized he was going to make it across without being hit, Lutz swerved onto the shoulder and caught the d-gen dead center on the hood.

The Mercedes lurched but didn't lose momentum. The body banged under the floorboards and the Mercedes bounced a wheel over the body.

"Fuck 'em," Lutz yelled, checking his rearview mirror as we raced ahead.

I looked back to see a sack of broken bones, formerly in the shape of a man, rolling and skidding on the asphalt. No doubt, dead.

A dead d-gen in the road didn't worry Lutz.

It didn't worry me, either.

Lutz wasn't worried because his hatred for the d-gens blessed him with a clear conscience whenever one died as a result of his doing.

As for me, I was like most people—I had a hard time seeing degenerates as human, that is as long as I didn't look too closely when I was busy killing them.

Neither Lutz nor I had a worry about the legalities of hitting a degenerate with the car. A driver couldn't help it when a stupid deer ran in front of his vehicle. It was much the same with a d-gen. No law was broken. And nobody gave much of a shit about it.

The world had a lot of that in it these days—not giving a shit.

Chapter 5

I saw nothing but black sky and silvery twinkles above.

Where are those damn red LEDs?

Apparently getting nervous as the ramifications of everything sank in, Lutz said, "We should run."

"Run?"

"One year mandatory for each dirty kill," Lutz told me like I didn't already know it. "I did maybe half of 'em. I can't do twelve years in a work camp. Not at my age."

Twelve d-gens?

Lutz might have shot six or seven. I'd had to kill the rest to keep them from killing him. Or maybe just because my blood was running hot and I liked pulling the trigger. I wasn't sure. It all happened so fast.

"You want to do ten years in a work camp?" Lutz asked, as he swerved the speeding car onto the shoulder to get around a derelict semi tractor-trailer. "What if they pin all twenty-three on each of us? They do that, you know."

I knew. At least I'd heard talk about it. Rumors are as good as facts when you're nervous.

I looked for the drone's red lights. It had to be up there.

Lutz rubbed the sweat off his face. "It's four miles more, maybe. Just off the highway."

Thinking about what lay ahead, I asked, "By that old mall?"

"Tall building right by there," said Lutz.   "Five or six stories.   Cellular phone antennas all lined up on the roof. None of 'em work."

Five or six stories wasn't tall by Houston standards, but way out here it was.

I knew the building he was talking about.   That's to say I'd seen it a dozen times when Lutz and I chased sanctions into the piney woods northwest of Houston.   Like every other building—short or tall—out this way, most of the windows had broken out long ago.   Some of the structures were sagging under the weight of roofs crushing frames of rusty metal and rotten wood.   This one was still sturdy, probably.   If it weren't structurally sound, it wouldn't have a drone charging station built on the roof—made sense to me.

That was important because I'd soon be running through it to get to the roof just as fast as I could.   If that drone we were chasing arrived and docked, it'd take only seconds to get a connection and start downloading the incriminating video.

With the destination and a plan in mind, I urged, "Get us there as fast as you can."

Lutz pressed the pedal to the floor, the engine revved. The beast sped faster.   "Three years for shooting down that spotter drone. That's on you."

Are we still talking about this?

I was working to cover my ass and his.   He was busy divvying up the blame.

Where are those damn red LEDs?

"We should go to Old Mexico," he told me.   "Get a gig doing security for a cartel boss.   Maybe those Camacho brothers. I bet they'd hire a couple of gringos."

We were driving over a hundred miles an hour, a risky speed on roads that hadn't seen any maintenance in twenty years.

"There is no Old Mexico." I pointed at a green exit sign with its weathered white letters barely reflecting our headlights through the tall grasses growing around it. "Is that where we get off?"

"Next one." Lutz told me. "You've been there, to Mexico. You know people."

I huffed but said nothing. Going on the run into a failed state with Lutz in tow was just about the last thing I wanted. Chasing the Old Mexico dream, a dream I knew didn't exist, wasn't on my list.

"I've seen the pictures," he said. "Beaches. Palm trees. Girls."

Poverty. Lawlessness. Shortages worse than here, unless you worked for one of the cartels. And plenty of people down there who wanted me dead.

I pointed up the highway. "If we get the drone, we can shake this. No arrest, you hear me? We've got a good thing going here."

"Canada, then." Lutz looked at me to gauge my interest. "We head north. Get there in three or four days."

"Across Oklahoma?" I laughed. "Kansas? They're as bad as Mexico. We'd never make it. You'd need to go around the long way. Run up through Denver, maybe. Or head east and go up on the other side of the Mississippi."

"So, Canada?" Lutz turned the wheel slightly and took his foot off the gas as the Mercedes rolled onto a long exit ramp.

I pointed across the highway at the black silhouette of a building standing next to the old mall. "There."

Still no damn LEDs.

If that drone had already docked and had downloaded its data, maybe I'd have to try for Canada with Lutz.

Lutz careened around a turn at the end of the ramp to run the SUV across an overpass.

"When we get there," I told him. "Get me as close to the door as possible. "I'll run inside and get up to the roof. You might be able to get a cell signal and call your spotter friend if you can. We need to find out how much video made it back through the network."

"He'll be pissed about his drone," Lutz told me.

"We'll pay him for it."

"I can't afford that."

"How can you not afford half a drone?" We'd been making a lot of money working together.

"I got bills." Lutz bounced the Mercedes over a curb into an expanse of old asphalt surrounding the mall. His voice turned angry. "You know that. I got kids to pay for."

Yeah, a dozen. Because you're so in love with your DNA, you can't imagine a future without your progeny there pissing in the gene pool.

Just like everyone, Lutz was trying to beat the odds. And the odds had been badly skewed since the Brisbane strain of H5N1 burned its way through the global population back when I was just learning how to spank it to Internet porn. Seven percent of everybody died. That doesn't seem like a lot when you figure ninety-three percent of the population survived. But a nearly one-in-ten kill rate puts the kind of scare into people that changes the world. Every precarious social institution shattered. States collapsed. Wars festered. Treaties were forgotten. Churches dissolved and new religions formed. Then more people died. And that wasn't even the worst of it.

It was that damned Easter egg the virus left in a gene called PRNP that remade the world.

Like ninety-nine point nine-nine-nine-nine percent of everybody in the world, I'd never heard of PRNP and in a year of guessing wouldn't have come close to landing on the right answer.

Everybody with a normal PRNP gene knows what it is today, and they know a mutated PRNP gene produces protease-resistant prions. Very few have any understanding of what that means, but we all know the words because we hear them everywhere.

"Mommy, why are there so many mental degenerates in the world?"

"Prions, honey. Now go to bed. Be a good girl and stay quiet or the prions will turn your brain into a hunk of Swiss cheese."

That's exactly what happens, one gene mutates, it produces a misshapen protein, the protein rots holes in the brain turning it into spongy Swiss cheese and eventually—a long eventually—kills.

It doesn't take much of an education to guess that a brain full of cheese holes doesn't work as well as a normal brain.

Degenerates have Swiss-cheese brains.

How all of this relates to Lutz's excessive offspring problem comes down to math. If a man and a woman with normal PRNP genes have a baby, it's born normal. But the Brisbane strain of H5N1 and its descendant strains became the most common influenza strains on the planet. Unfortunately for us, they all infect many species of birds and all humans. Almost all those strains mutate the PRNP gene. In short, we all catch some strain of that flu eventually. Some of us recover with no gene mutation. Over ninety-five percent of us get the Easter egg.

So, having a kid is a matter of rolling the dice and hoping to win against really shitty odds. Produce twenty kids and one might grow up normal.

It doesn't take a genius to figure out that a one in twenty normalcy rate is the road to extinction for humans.

Out in the feral d-gen population, a baby has a fifty-fifty chance at being born with normal genes. They all catch the flu. For the half born with the mutated PRNP gene it doesn't matter. For the half born with a normal gene, ninety-five percent mutate because of the flu. So of all the babies born to the d-gens, roughly one in forty has a chance to grow up normal.

It's not intuitively obvious to anyone who's uncomfortable with word problems, but d-gens ultimately produce most of the babies who grow into normal, intelligent adults. It's true because there are so many more d-gens than normal people in the world.

As distasteful as the thought is, they are the hope for our species. Not to mention Lutz's hope of having a normal little version of himself born into the world.

And that's why killing otherwise healthy d-gens of childbearing age is a really bad thing.

Chapter 6

As the Mercedes was rolling to a stop, I swung my door open and jumped out. I adjusted Lutz's rifle at my shoulder and took a peek through the night vision scope for a glimpse into the building's lobby.

Nothing moving.

I leaned back into the car and laid a hand on my rifle, which was pointed at the floorboard and leaning on my side of the console. "Use it if you need it. Don't muck up my gun. Call your buddy. I'll be right back down."

I stepped away from the Mercedes and scanned across the sky, once without the night vision scope, once with. It was always possible the drone was up there, and I hadn't seen the flashing LEDs. Too far away. Too dim. Burned out. Disabled intentionally. Anything was possible.

God, I hate that phrase.

It's damned disempowering when trying to formulate plans to save your ass from a work camp.

I ran up the stairs in front of the building, crossed under a pretentious portico, and jogged through a metal framework that a decade or two ago had held panels of glass to separate the building's air-conditioned lobby from the humid mosquito soup outside. I paused and used the night vision scope to scan what I could see of the first floor, looking for dangers and looking for a stairway door. It wasn't uncommon to find individuals or clans of d-gens in these old buildings. I guess they liked having a place to call home just as much as a normal person did.

The thing with the d-gens this far outside the city was that you never knew if they were going to be hostile or not, territorial or not, deadly or not. The ones who filled the rotting suburbs and fed from the troughs tended to be predictable.

Maybe a regular meal schedule makes mammals lazy.

I spotted a door hanging from a rusted hinge and saw through the gap.

I hurried across the lobby and stopped outside the door to peek inside the stairwell. It wouldn't do any good to surprise any d-gens bedding down there. Startled animals don't always run away.

Seeing nothing at the bottom of the stairs, I went in and started to climb.

The stairs were fairly clear, which told me I was on the right path. The stairwell had probably been used by the maintenance personnel when they came out to repair the charging station on the roof.

Sneaking and stepping, quiet in the dark, I made my way from floor to floor, around a landing and back up again, thinking about the problem, thinking through the solution—get the memory cards from the three drones, disconnect their backup batteries so the locator transponders wouldn't function. Maybe dispose of the remains in a pond somewhere and get back to Houston to spin up a good lie to fit whatever facts had found their way back to the bureaucracy.

So many of life's speed bumps could be smoothed over with a well-told lie.

I just needed to get that last drone.

At the top of the stairs, I found a hollow steel door with a chain running through a hole big enough to stick an arm through. The chain looped back through the stair's handrail. A padlock held the chain together and kept the door mostly closed, but closed enough to keep me from squeezing through the gap.

Crap.

The maintenance people must have had trouble with d-gens sneaking up onto the roof and messing with their equipment.

I looked at the lock and chain for a moment, mentally inventorying my equipment, wondering if anything on my person could break the lock or chain.

Shit. Nothing.

Shoot the lock? No. That only worked in old movies.

Did Lutz have something in the car? Probably. How quickly could I run down five floors and get all the way back up?

I looked at the door again. It was in sad shape and banged all to hell. The paint had long since flaked away, leaving only layers of rust. The chain and lock, though, were in good shape. I'd not be breaking those without tools.

But the door—

The rusty hinges had to be in worse shape than the surface.

Why not give it a go?

I took two steps back to the edge of the landing and threw myself at the door.

I'd surely have a bruise wrapped over a sore shoulder in the morning, but I felt the door give. I guessed at least one of the old hinges had bent. I stepped back and slammed the door with my shoulder a second time.

The top hinge broke away, and the door leaned out.

I slammed into the door a third time, and the middle hinge broke away, leaving the door hanging on the chain and one hinge.

I climbed through, got a foot hung up, and tripped as I tumbled out onto the roof.

Getting quickly to my feet and panting from the exertion, I looked around and saw old cell phone antenna clusters standing up on three sides of the building's roof. A much newer construction stood at the roof's center, a cylindrical metal framework twelve feet tall with two layers of docking stations running around the circumference, with one layer for the large spotter drones at about shoulder height. The ring above that was made up of smaller docking ports for private video drones, and those operated by corporate farms and work camps in the area.

Jogging over to the charging cylinder, I circled it, seeing two big white spotter drones, dormant and charging. Neither of those concerned me—the only spotter drone that contained video of my crime was sitting in the trees fifteen miles west.

No other drones were docked.

Good? Bad?

Hell, how was I to know?

I ran to the edge of the roof and looked east in the direction of the city, and I scanned the sky.

Where's that damn drone?

Chapter 7

"All I'm sayin' is the last video image transmitted by my spotter drone shows your golden boy Christian aiming his rifle at it. Then I lost the signal." Ricardo was not happy.

Lutz couldn't gauge whether Ricardo was angry enough to do something vindictive. "Are you recording this?"

"If I was, would I tell you or would I lie about it? It's a stupid question, Lutz."

Lutz tried a half-truth. "We saw your drone go down."

"Shot down," Ricardo clarified, "by that new guy you run with. You know how much drones cost these days? Parts aren't easy to come by, and I've got to pay for it out of my pocket because you morons will be in a work camp."

"What?" Lutz took offense. "After all the business we've done. You're gonna throw me to the cops over one goddamned drone?"

"The low-res signal went straight through to the clearinghouse." Ricardo paused, adding a bit more clarity. "The police have it."

"You cheese-brained asshole!" Lutz yelled into his phone, no longer caring if he was being recorded. "What do I pay you for?"

"You pay me to send you the coordinates of the good kills before I send them to the clearinghouse so you and your partner can get there before anybody else. And I did that. I always do my part."

"No," Lutz snarled. "I pay you a premium price to not only send me the coordinates but to delay the return video feed so you can make sure nothing incriminating ever gets through to the police. I pay you that because I don't want to get fined and I sure as hell don't want to go to a work camp. If all I wanted was to front-run kill coordinates I could pay any dumbass spotter for that."

"You watch your tone, Lutz." Ricardo's voice turned acid. "I can give the police a lot more than they have right now." He paused, giving Lutz a chance to understand the threat. "You could wait for approved sanctions like everybody else but because I front-run the sanctions to you, you get them before they finalize. You know you can't pull the trigger until you have an ID on an approved sanction. Everybody knows that. This sanction got cancelled. I never sent the ID through the spotter drone to you guys. How the hell was I supposed to know you were going to go in there and kill the whole herd anyway?"

Lutz wasn't listening now so much as thinking through the implications of what Ricardo had already told him. "Did all that video go out? Do the police have everything?"

"They have the low-res feed from my drone," answered Ricardo.

"Why didn't you intercept?" Lutz was thinking this would rile Christian up and push maybe push him to murder. Then it was down to Old Mexico for blue water and cheap whores. Who cared about the stories he'd heard about the cartels? Lutz knew how to take care of himself.

"I didn't intercept because I didn't think you morons were going to kill them. I thought you were done for the evening. I have other guys out there, Lutz. You're not the only one who pays for the services I provide."

"You screwed us," said Lutz with a lethal edge in his tone. "I can run. You know that. But I don't know what Christian will do. He did all that work for those cartels down in Mexico. You've heard the stories. He's a wicked bastard."

The phone went silent. Ricardo drew an audible breath, but still sounded confident when he said, "I didn't know you guys were going to go through with it, that's why I stopped monitoring your feed. I was trying to find you another job while you were all the way out there. Do you know where my spotter drone is?"

"We can find it," said Lutz.

"Look, if you can bring me the drone, maybe I can fix this. I've got a video guy, we used him on that thing last year."

Lutz knew exactly which thing Ricardo was referring to— that thing was the reason Lutz had suddenly found himself without a partner and had to team up with Christian. That problem had been expensive to get out of. "You better make me a good price."

"Just bring in the drone. Do it quick. If we get the video altered and out to the cops before they get into the office in the morning, nobody will ask any questions. The low-res will look incriminating, but we can alter the high-res to make you look innocent."

"Will it be good enough to get the kill sanction retroactively reinstated?"

"For enough money, my guys can give you a video of Joseph Stalin humping Mother Teresa."

Lutz ignored the attempt at humor. He was too stressed for the silliness. "There were two video drones on the scene."

"That's shitty luck," said Ricardo. "Might be there's nothing I can do."

"We're working on that problem."

"What does that mean?" asked Ricardo.

"One of those drones is down in the woods. We'll have the other one in a minute."

"How do you know they didn't already upload their videos?"

"We don't," Lutz told him. "You need to find that out for us, you understand?"

"That's not what I do."

"You're doing it this time," Lutz commanded. "I'm not going to get screwed on this. We'll be at your place in a few hours."

Chapter 8

Before seeing anything, I heard the familiar whispery buzz of a drone's spinning rotors.

I looked away from my view of Houston ten or fifteen miles to the east and ran back to the charging tower. Just as I was rounding the structure, looking in the sky for the drone I expected to see there, I saw it maneuvering to line up with the dock.

Surprised into action, I smacked the drone with the barrel of Lutz's rifle, sending it colliding into the charging station's framework. The drone bounced away and hit the roof, throwing up small stones where the spinning rotors ran through loose gravel. It rose back into the air as I reached out and grabbed one of its rotor arms. I spun it around and smashed it into the tower's frame.

Two of the drone's rotors stopped instantly. Pieces of plastic flew. I smashed the drone twice more into the framework before throwing it to the ground and stomping it.

It was dead. I hoped.

The cameras were busted off. The rotors had come away. The rotor arms were cracked or separated. The drone's electronic innards were exposed.

Breathing heavy from the brief fight, I dropped to a knee beside the carcass and dug through, looking for the memory card and the wires to disconnect the transponder from the backup battery.

Chapter 9

Having run down the dark stairwell, out through the lobby, and back to Lutz's Mercedes, I opened the rear door and tossed the expensive piece of drone junk into the back.

"What the hell?" Lutz looked over his shoulder, frowning. "Get that outta my car. That's evidence."

"Can't leave it here." I hurried around to the passenger side door, unclipped Lutz's rifle from my harness and passed it across as I got into the seat.

"Why not?"

"Don't be stupid." I thumbed to the highway. "Let's get going. We can ditch it in a pond or river. Hell, somewhere in the woods. Anywhere except at a charging station where it'll be spotted by the next drone coming to the dock."

Lutz put the Mercedes into gear and turned in a big loop over the rough asphalt, heading back toward the highway entrance ramp. "I talked with Ricardo."

About time you gave me his name. "Ricardo's your spotter?"

"One of 'em."

"It was his drone we shot down?"

"*You* shot down," Lutz snapped.

"Grow up." It didn't matter that I shot the drone down. Lutz's trigger-happy fuckup had sparked this fiasco. "Let's just fix it, okay? We can point fingers later."

Lutz bounced the Mercedes over a curb to get onto the frontage road that ran along beside the highway. "Ricardo wants his drone back."

"Maybe we can sell him the other two for parts. Did he say whether any of the video got through?"

"The low-res."

The low-resolution version.

"Incriminating?" That was the answer I wanted most of all. Was I on the hook? Was there video evidence enough to put me in a work camp?

"He's got you aiming the rifle at the spotter drone."

"But he didn't forward that part of the video, right? I mean, that's your deal with him, right? He intercepts the video and edits out any incriminating snippets before the police see, right?"

"Supposed to be the deal."

I glared at Lutz. I didn't like where this was going.

"He didn't intercept anything. The sanction was never approved so he ignored our feed and surfed porn or something. The cops have all the low-res video—the whole feed until you shot down the spotter."

Lutz's dumbass move to start shooting before we had a confirmed sanction was bad. Now his buddy's failure to hold up his end of the bargain had just made it a lot worse. Life was hard enough, trying to straighten it out past my own mistakes, but the weight of other peoples' catastrophes was getting hard to bear.

Chapter 10

We didn't say much of anything on the drive back to the site of the slaughter.

What were we going to talk about that was productive?

I wanted to pistol-whip Lutz, and he wanted to cover his ass. That much was evident to me in the way he emphasized it was me who shot down the drone. He just couldn't understand I was taking action to save both our asses. It served to double-down on my conviction that corruption was indeed his only talent. If not for that, he'd be a penniless transient one step ahead of a work camp detail.

I took advantage of the silence to think through my options. Unfortunately, I couldn't come up with any that didn't intimately involve Lutz. Well, there was one—ditching him and getting out of Houston. But what then? Move out to Lubbock and sharecrop my life away on a dried-out dirt clod farm? Go back on the road until I lucked into a place to land on my feet? That would make me a transient, too. Romantic? Sure. But the realities of going on the road with no money and no car in a world full of people who'd lost any inclination to charity two decades ago would be hard. And could I find work? The only job I was good at involved pointing a gun and pulling a trigger. Only two kinds of organizations hired people with those skills: governments and cartels. Well, glorified rent-a-cop jobs, I guess. Bodyguard gigs.

Maybe there were a few I wasn't considering.

With a federal arrest warrant chasing me, getting a legit paycheck was out of the question.

With my debt to the Camacho brothers still outstanding, getting work on the bad side of the law would be putting my neck into a slowly closing noose. Once back in criminal circles, my name would get back to the Camacho brothers, and they'd send somebody for me.

What did that leave me? Skip off to Canada? Try for Europe? Asia? They were all as tumultuous as the USA and not open for immigration, at least not for the likes of me.

Lutz stopped the Mercedes on the dirt road near where we'd parked earlier in the evening.

I got out and trudged through the underbrush, passing between the tall pines, using a map on my phone to keep moving in the right direction.

Lutz bumbled along behind.

When we passed between an old riding lawnmower and an overturned dining table—part of the outer circle—Lutz asked, "Do you know where it is?"

"I can pick the direction to the downed drones from where I was standing in the clearing."

"You sure?"

"Does it matter if I'm sure?"

"Yes. I don't want to spend all night in the woods."

"You'd rather rush back to town and turn yourself in?" I asked. "You want to go to a work camp?"

Lutz huffed.

When we got to the second of the concentric circles, Lutz came to a stop beside a precariously standing highchair. "I don't see the fire."

"It's burned down by now." It was a simple deduction. I knew it. He had to know it. He was being difficult. I turned to face him. "I don't know what your deal is, but we're both in this together, you know that, right? It's not just a picture of me aiming a rifle at a spotter drone that mysteriously crashed two seconds later. If the cops have that picture, then they've got the low-res pics of the whole extermination."

"Not necessarily," Lutz argued. "Those low-res cameras on the spotters only send back a pic once every couple of seconds. Bandwidth restrictions. Ricardo told me."

"So what?" I asked. "Are you honestly hoping all the incriminating shit you did happened between pictures? Is that it?"

Lutz shook his head. "Ricardo didn't say the cops had anything on me. Just you raising your rifle at the drone."

"*Your* rifle," I snapped, trying to put some solid guilt in his mind.

"Maybe the drone wasn't snapping pics at the normal rate," said Lutz. "Maybe it had bird shit on the lens. Maybe it was covered with condensation.   Maybe it was too far away. Maybe the fog was too thick."

"Is that the way you want to play it?" I asked. "You want to hope that maybe you're safe because Ricardo didn't describe in detail every image passed back to the police? Are you willing to bet your life on it?" I stepped up close to Lutz, eye-to-eye. "What are you—fifty, fifty-five? If they toss you in a work camp for this, say you get the max, one year for each dirty kill, twenty-three years and another handful for the drones we downed. You'll never breathe free air again. You'll die babysitting soybean-picking d-gens in a work camp."

Lutz pushed his face close enough that his big hooked nose was nearly touching mine, and I could taste the onions on his breath from what he'd eaten for dinner. "I'm not going to a work camp."

Raising my fists and trying to beat some sense into a well-upholstered old man in the woods wasn't going to help the situation.   I stepped away, deescalating. "Let's find the drones, get the data cards, dispose of the evidence, and get the spotter drone back to your friend Ricardo. Once we're at his place, we'll see what was passed back to the cops. Okay? He'll be able to show us everything. Then we'll know where we stand. Right now we're just two pissed-off boneheads standing in the cold forest, thinking the worst is gonna happen. Let's do what we need to do here and get back to Houston. One step at a time. You okay with that?"

Lutz buried his face in his hands, rubbed his skin, and clenched his fists over his eyes as if trying to squeeze all the night's bad choices out of his head. He dropped his hands and kicked the highchair, sending it clattering into a tree. "Shit!"

I stepped away to give him room for his tantrum and looked around in the moonlight, seeing only pine tree trunks, underbrush, and the long curved line of artifacts disappearing in the fog.

Lutz jumped over to the high chair, picked it up, and beat it against a tree trunk until it came to pieces in his hands. Still, with more frustration than he could bear, he turned and glared at me, panting.

I pointed at a folding table nearby and said, "There's plenty of shit. Break as much as you need."

Lutz shook his head and looked at his feet, snorting as he breathed. "Let's find the damned drones."

Good enough.

I led through the trees and Lutz stomped along behind, cursing under his breath, berating himself, and second-guessing.

Once at the edge of the clearing, I saw the fire had burned down to a pile of embers and flickering logs. Everything seemed different. Was it the change in light, the relative quiet?

I raised my weapon to my shoulder and scanned through the dark. "Get your rifle up."

Lutz grunted and came to a stop beside me.

"Look through your night vision scope. You see anything in the woods?"

Lutz did as told. Thank God. Unfortunately, emotion usually won out over pragmatism with him.

"See anything?" I asked.

"Trees."

I walked into the clearing, stepping over bodies, gazing across the cornfield, looking for anything out there that wasn't corn. I had a thought about the kids we'd seen, the live ones. I hadn't shot them. I was sure of that, but I didn't recall seeing their bodies either. I looked over the corpses on the ground. "You shoot those kids, Lutz?"

"No."

"I'm not trying to pin anything on you. I don't know what happened to them."

"I didn't shoot any damned kids." Lutz huffed, lowered his rifle, and walked over to warm himself by the big pile of embers. "The raccoons are gone."

I looked at the fire. The spit that had held the carcasses of the animals had indeed disappeared. "Coyotes?"

Lutz shook his head. "They'd be afraid of the fire, I think. Degenerates would be my bet."

That disappointed me, because as we were racing back to the kill site, I'd fostered the unrealistic, yet pretty sick hope, that in the frantic aftermath of the kill, we'd mistakenly identified the carcasses roasting over the fire. I'd hoped we'd find that they weren't animals but dead children, and their little corpses would convert our dirty kill into clean profits.

It was maybe the most repulsive glimmer of hope I'd ever felt.

That didn't stop me from looking around the fire for the possibility of finding partially eaten body parts, whether of children or other d-gens. It wouldn't matter. If we could prove cannibalism, then the kill sanction could be reinstated —Lutz and I would be off the hook with a very good night's work behind us.

"What are you looking for?" Lutz asked.

"Wait." I looked across the clearing again. "Something's very wrong here."

"If you tell me you don't remember where those drones are I'm gonna—"

"No." I pointed at the ground around the fire. "Look."

Lutz glanced at the ground but didn't really look at it.

"No, really." I started counting bodies. "Some of them are gone."

Exasperated, Lutz said, "They were all dead. C'mon. Let's get on with this before another drone shows up." He looked at the sky.

I looked up too, but saw only the glow of the moon through the thinning fog. No red LEDs. "Either they weren't all dead, or somebody took some of the bodies."

A mean laugh bubbled out of Lutz's big belly.

"Count 'em," I told him. "There were a lot more here than this."

"Doesn't mean shit to me," said Lutz. "We can't get paid, so who cares?" He looked at the trees and pointed. "Over there? Is that the direction where you shot that drone?"

I nodded. Lutz was right. Mostly. The count of bodies on the ground didn't matter. There were no signs of cannibalism. No dead children. I was wasting my time on pointless curiosities. I took a long look at the trees, got my bearings, and started into the woods. "The two drones can't be far."

Chapter 11

With three disabled drones rattling in the back of Lutz's Mercedes while the stereo blared hillbilly fiddles over a discordant gospel choir, Lutz raced south down old residential streets and along narrow thoroughfares. The music was his favorite — gritty and despondent. Not quite right. Blaring it was his way of telling me he didn't want to hear any more of my talk about possibilities and responsibilities, about what we needed to do, what we needed to plan.

He was afraid. His venal life was clumped on the side of a swirling toilet bowl and he wanted to hide in his beer tunes while he pretended the water wasn't washing at his feet.

We all have our teddy bears.

Just as well. I needed time to think through the eventualities, because if things started to go bad once we got where we were going, we might not have a lot of time to sit around and debate. We'd have to act.

A faster route could have been taken to get us where we were going, but we were avoiding the highways now that we were close to town. The police, maybe the military, and especially other Regulators could be out there already, looking for two bonehead Front-runners.

We didn't know if we were on their radar yet.

Best not to be seen if being seen might lead to getting shot.

We passed a communal feeding trough, fifty feet long, running down the center of the street, and spotted a few more down the road ahead of us. Lutz slowed the Mercedes. Degenerates by the hundreds shared the houses near each feeding trough because they had the good sense not to want to walk too far three times a day for their free meals. That meant the decrepit houses behind the thick trees on both sides of the road were full of d-gens, and though we were in the wee hours of the morning, some degenerates were out doing whatever stupid shit kept them occupied.

Wandering into the road was one of their favorite hobbies.

All we needed was to hit one at a bad angle and unfortunate speed and get a broken femur stuck through the radiator. Unlikely? Sure, but weirder shit has happened. Then we'd be stuck, or more to the point, Lutz would be stuck with a car full of vandalized drones. Incriminating evidence that couldn't be explained away.

We neared Highway 10 somewhere near Katy, I think. Generic sprawl had made it hard to tell one of the endless suburbs from the next before Brisbane had flipped the world on its head. Now with all of the road signs and landmarks decomposing and being eaten by a slow tsunami of vines and shrubs, it was nearly impossible to differentiate.

Lutz drove the car off the road we'd been traveling for a mile and pulled into the parking lot of a shopping center. Of course, in this part of town, all the businesses had long since closed. Many of them had plywood over the windows, hammered in place by owners optimistic enough to want to preserve what they were leaving behind, thinking one day they'd return, reopen, and thrive. Oh, the futility of optimism. On other storefronts, only the broken metal window and doorframes remained. No hindrance to scavengers and vandals, but anything worth stealing had been stolen long, long ago. And bored teenagers didn't kill their free time with vandalism anymore. It was too much work to find anything that time and weather hadn't already battered.

We crossed a street and drove along the backside of another shopping center. I looked closely at each back door we passed, thinking we had to be nearing our destination.

Lutz cut the wheels hard left and stopped the Mercedes at the base of a ramp that ran up to a rolling metal door on the tall back wall of a store that hadn't seen a customer in twenty years.

I turned the volume down on the music and pointed at the metal door. "Your spotter friend?"

Lutz nodded, picked up his phone, and dialed.

A moment later he had someone on the line. "I'm here. Open up."

A few more moments passed.

The door rolled up, flooding us in yellow light.

Lutz drove in.

Chapter 12

As the door came down behind us, an angry-looking Hispanic man directed us to park beside four other vehicles by a wall in the cavernous, well-lit space.

"Is that Ricardo?" I asked.

"No." Lutz pulled the Mercedes up facing the wall.

"Is this Ricardo's place?"

Lutz killed the engine, turned to me, and leaned on the console. "Ricardo is one of my guys. My spotter," he emphasized. "When this is done, if you buddy up to him and try to front-run sanctions and cut me out, I'll kill you."

It took about two blinks of an eye for me to pull one of my pistols and jam the barrel up under Lutz's jaw. His eyes went wide because he'd seen the pistol coming. He just hadn't had time to react. That didn't stop him from reaching for a weapon, though.

I pushed the barrel into the meaty part at the top of his throat, hard enough I knew it hurt. "Don't."

Lutz's hand stopped.

I leaned in close enough again to smell his oniony breath. "You listen. Don't threaten me. If you got something to do, then you fuckin' do it. Understand?"

Lutz nodded as much as he was able given the barrel of my pistol pushing up under his jaw.

I lowered my weapon. "We got a good thing going. We both make good money. I'm not going to screw it up to steal one crooked spotter."

Lutz leaned back in his seat and rubbed the underside of his jaw.

I couldn't tell if it was fear, respect, or a craving for revenge I saw in his eyes.

"If you don't trust me," I told him, "then let's wrap up this business with the dirty kill, get our asses off the hook, and split. You go your way. I'll go mine. There are plenty of Regulators around you can partner up with."

Lutz mulled his response, ginned up his courage, and said, "Don't you ever—"

I ignored him, got out of the car, walked around to the rear, and leaned against the back window, not caring that caked red dirt was getting on my clothes. A night of tromping through the woods and killing degenerates had already left a pretty good layer of crud on me.

The Hispanic man who'd let us in had turned his back and was walking across the floor toward the far side of the building where a multilevel structure of offices or apartments had been built along the wall. The building was a big empty warehouse under a corrugated steel ceiling thirty or forty feet up. Besides the relatively small structures built against opposite walls, it was empty. From the ceiling over that empty space hung various items—nets, sheets, punching bags, obstacles for what was flying through the space, drones, weaving in and out, up and down, racing along a course that was visible to them but hidden from my view.

A deep voice said, "Everybody wants to be the best drone pilot."

I turned to see a wiry, tall man with shaggy red hair coming toward me. He looked very familiar. "Everybody?"

⹁ pointed at the structures against the far wall. "I rent some other spotters."

"You rent to them?" I asked, trying to figure out where I knew the tall man from. "You own this place? The spotter business must be good."

"I've got the whole shopping center," he told me. "I squatted back when there was still unclaimed real estate to squat on."

"I missed that boat," I grumbled. I was too young in those days and didn't know shit about anything when Brisbane took both my parents. "I pay rent. Where do I know you from?"

"Basketball probably." He glanced into the car to see Lutz.

I looked over my shoulder at Lutz, who was still in the driver's seat. I said, "He's pouting." Looking back up at the tall man, it clicked. "You're Ricardo George. You used to play for the Rockets."

He extended a hand to shake.

I put my hand out to be engulfed by his and introduced myself. "Christian Black."

"You're the mysterious partner with the skills." Ricardo made two pistols with his fingers and pretended to squeeze off a few shots.

I turned and opened the rear door of the Mercedes. "Sorry about your drone. I shot it. Sorry."

Ricardo leaned over to look inside. "You got money?"

"To pay for the drone?" I asked.

"You did shoot it down."

"I don't want to buy a new one. If you can fix it, I'll pay for whatever you need."

Ricardo straightened up and didn't look pleased. In fact, he looked like he was contemplating a violent response.

"Or I can buy you a new one," I told him. "And we've got these two others. Maybe there are some parts you can use. Maybe you can sell them to your tenants."

Black Rust

"After I have some time to look at those video drones, I'll let you know. All this stuff is hard to come by."

"Isn't everything?"

Ricardo grinned. "That's why it's expensive."

"More expensive because they have bullet holes?" I asked, trying to gauge where this whole thing was going.

Ricardo shook his head. "I don't do business like that. You'll pay me a fair price, but I don't think the price will be the problem."

That made me curious. "If the money isn't the problem, what is?"

"You need to pay me tonight. Cash."

Shit. One more goddamn complication.

I didn't know how much Ricardo would want for his drone, but I knew I had enough cash in the safe at my house to cover it. I just didn't want to burn off an hour and a half driving to get it. Time was going to turn into a problem. Still, keeping Ricardo happy was high on my priority list. He had the video containing the evidence that could get me locked up in a work camp or set me free. "I've got the cash."

Ricardo smiled. "Good."

"Why tonight?" I asked. "I can get my hands on the money and bring it back here, but it'll be a pain."

"I need my money tonight because you might be in jail tomorrow."

Crap. That wasn't encouraging. "Is the video that incriminating?"

"There's an arrest warrant out for you."

Chapter 13

I stood. Lutz sat in a rolling chair. Ricardo sat at a long desk in front of a bank of monitors, six sets of three. Each of his drones had three cameras with wide-angle lenses mounted on the bottom to provide a three-sixty view. Six sets of monitors meant six drones in the air. One set of screens was conspicuously black. All of the other screens were alive in shades of black and green from the night vision cameras being used. Some of them displayed real-time, sharp video feeds from those drones close enough to the city to get a broadband signal. Others—those further out—cached their video and sent back only low-resolution, low-frame-rate images. Those screens were choppy and hard to watch.

The video Ricardo played for us looked like that—the one that showed me murdering dancing degenerates. Due to the angle of the video, Lutz was mostly blocked by the trees. So though he showed up at the end of the choppy video, right before I took his rifle and aimed it at the drone, the video showed little direct evidence of Lutz killing anything. And depending on what got back to the police from the two dead video drones in the back of the Mercedes, Lutz might get off.

Most of the guilt was on me.

Without looking away from the wall of video monitors, Lutz told me, "You should run."

Run?

That would get Lutz off. Based on what we'd seen so far, if I disappeared, he could spin whatever story he liked, pin it all on me, no problem for him.

And why not take the whole rap? What difference would it make? Ten years in a work camp? Twenty years? I couldn't do a single one.

Still, he might be right.

If I ran, I'd have other problems. I could get no legal jobs. I could get no illegal work—the Camacho brothers problem. Avoiding a slow death in a dirty back room somewhere down in what used to be Mexico was high on my list of wants.

New identity? Sure. That would be fine for a job in a factory or for babysitting toddlers, but getting a new Regulator ID with a fake identity wouldn't fly. Regulators were akin to law enforcement, and they received the same degree of scrutiny prior to hire, the kind of scrutiny my background couldn't suffer.

I'd already spent too much money on the bribes to get my current ID. Then it had taken a long time before I started making a real profit on the deal, which only happened after I hooked up with Lutz. Would I be able to find a Lutz 2.0 in the next city I fled to?

What about staying? Lutz and I had a good thing going. We were banking a mountain of cash. If we could keep it cranking another year without killing each other, I'd save enough money to pay what I owed the Camacho brothers.

Then what?

Too far in the future to think about. Too many obstacles.

I looked at Ricardo and asked, "What do the video operators have?"

Ricardo shrugged. "Enough to get a warrant."

"Don't play coy," I told him. "The sanction was never approved. A kill went down. That's all the cops needed to issue a warrant. You know that. The video from your spotter drone was enough. The video from the voyeur drones is just the icing, the confirmation. I need to know what went through the network back to their operators."

"A warrant is just the start of your sentence," Lutz whined. "Once they arrest you, it's over. They toss you in the can, and then they convict you. *Everybody* gets convicted. Then it's a work camp."

"You're shittin' me." I had no doubt Lutz was exaggerating.

"Maybe things were different where you came from," said Lutz.

There was no law where I came from.

"He's right," Ricardo told me. "You prove your innocence before they pick you up, or forget it."

"They don't investigate?" I asked.

Ricardo and Lutz both laughed.

It was a naive question but one I should have known the answer to. I'd been outside the reach of governments for so long I was guilty of remembering them how they used to be when I was a kid. At least back then they went through the motions of administering a judicial system.

"If I were you," said Lutz. "I'd run."

Ignoring Lutz's squawk-bird repetitive bullshit, I focused on Ricardo. "You sold the location of the kill to the video voyeurs. You know who they are. Have you talked to them?"

Lutz got up and headed toward the door. He muttered, "I gotta pee."

Shaking his head and showing me his empty palms, Ricardo said, "I don't front-run kills to those guys. They can't be trusted."

"That's bullshit." I yelled it. I shouldn't have, but I was tired, and I was getting frustrated.

Ricardo stood up and looked down on me. "If I were lying, I wouldn't be offended, but I'm not lying, and I *am* offended. Now you can apologize."

Ricardo stood a head taller than me. He was twenty years older, but solid. I put a hand on one of my pistols.

The door opened on creaky hinges, and Lutz stepped through.

Ricardo cocked his head toward Lutz.

What? I turned away from Ricardo. "Stop."

"No." Lutz didn't look at me when he responded.

"You better stop and answer a question."

"You didn't ask me anything." Lutz pulled the door to close it.

"If you make me come after you—" I left the threat there.

Lutz put on a defiant face and stopped.

"It's you. You're selling the locations to the video operators."

Lutz didn't answer.

"You fucker." It was the best I could come up with at the moment.

Chapter 14

I apologized to Ricardo.

Lutz took his leak, came back into the room, and took a seat. "Don't get pissed at me because I know how to make a buck." Apparently having his dick in his hand had convinced him that indignation was the best response.

Lutz irked me for a lot of reasons. Him making more money off our work than I did only served to strengthen my animosity. He was becoming a less and less palatable partner. Making no attempt to hide anything I was feeling toward him, I said, "We need to know what your video drone guys have, which means we need to know who they are—don't give me any shit about keeping it private. Until we know what they've got, this is *your* ass on the line just as much as mine."

Ricardo added, "He's right about that."

Lutz looked at me with suspicion. He turned to Ricardo. "You got pen and paper?"

"I live in the twenty-first century." Ricardo made no move to check any of the drawers under his desktop.

"People with real lives still use real pens and real paper." Lutz huffed and took out his phone, turned his back to me to block my view, and went to work with his thumbs. He glanced over at Ricardo. "I'm sending you their contact info."

Ricardo shook his head, disappointed.

After Lutz finished, Ricardo spun around in his seat to look at his screens. He pulled up his email client and opened Lutz's email on a screen three feet wide.

I laughed. "I guess it's no secret now, Lutz."

Ricardo spun back around in his chair and looked at Lutz, daring him to say something.

Lutz chose to keep his mouth shut.

"I know who these guys are," said Ricardo.

"Will they deal with us?" I asked.

"They're scammers, but everybody likes to get paid," he replied.

"Can you find out what they have?" I asked. "Find out what they want?"

He looked at Lutz, and told me, "I can make a better deal than he can."

"Have they posted any of their videos yet?" I asked.

"I haven't seen anything," said Ricardo. "Maybe that's because they're still trying to figure out what happened to their drones. They're like me—they've got to keep a lot of drones in the air to keep the cash flowing. That's the game. Everybody loses a drone from time to time. Everybody's got a guy they know who'll go out and find the downed ones. Nobody loses sleep over it. Maybe these guys both think their drones dropped out with a battery problem. Maybe they never saw the low-res, low-frame-rate pics come back across. Maybe they don't know anything. Or maybe they saw what was coming, and now they're both waiting for the HD video to come through so they can plaster it all over the Internet or sell it to a reality TV show. That's how these guys make their money. A lot of people like watching d-gens die. More gore means more money. A lot of people hate degenerates, and a video of dirty kills and guilty Regulators will generate an ass-ton of traffic, especially with as many as you guys shot tonight."

People working a morally ambiguous angle to make a buck? Sounded like the kind of people I'd always dealt with. "If we can bribe these guys, will they give us the video they've got?"

"They'll give you a copy," said Ricardo. "But a copy of the low-res is all you need, even if they decide to take your money and throw you to the cops."

"How's that?" I asked.

"We've got the high-res on the data cards from those two video drones you dropped." Ricardo looked at Lutz then back at me. "If you're going to stay in Houston, then the smart thing to do is alter the three high-res copies—mine and the other two—and feed them back to their respective owners. Oh, and we'll have to alter your gun cam video as well."

"So," I said, "you're saying we alter the high-res copies so they jibe with the low-res copies but still provide exonerating evidence."

Ricardo nodded. "Like maybe showing cannibalistic behavior or showing them attacking you before you fired. Everybody has the right to defend themselves."

"And you can make that happen?" I asked.

"Pay-offs to Lutz's two video buddies—" Ricardo's grimaced at the mention of the two, "pay them for their lost drones, finding some video guys in the middle of the night, paying them to get out of bed and making it worth their while to work through the night and get this all done by morning—"

"How many video guys?" I asked.

"Six," answered Ricardo. "It's a lot of video to fix in not a lot of time.

"That's bullshit," Lutz whined. "Stick a dead kid at the beginning and the rest is justified. Easy."

Ricardo shot Lutz a glare that made me think he might jump up and punch Lutz in the face. "Sure, but the kid has to be the same kid from five different angles, and you have to show some kind of cannibalistic act. Or just murder would do. So, it's not just a body, unless maybe you alter one of the animals on the fire. Then it's not just at the beginning. What happens to the body after you kill everybody? Does it just disappear? Or does it lie there the whole time like the rest of the corpses? You got to use your brain and think when you're constructing good lies and manufacturing evidence. That's why you run through the woods and shoot d-gens in the middle of the night instead of sitting at a desk in an air-conditioned office, Lutz, because you're not smart. Now be quiet unless you've got something intelligent to add." He looked back at me. "This all needs to be wrapped up before too late in the morning. Then you gotta pay them to stay quiet about it. Then you gotta pay me to put it all together. Everybody's got to get paid."

I nodded. I didn't have a problem with it. "How much?"

"A hundred thousand."

Lutz choked, turned red-faced, and coughed before he sputtered, "You should run, Christian." He apparently still thought I was the only one on the hook here.

A hundred thousand was a whole lot of money, nearly a quarter of what I'd put away in the seven months I'd been working with Lutz. But if I paid the cash and it bought me another year with Lutz, I'd earn enough money to pay my debt. One hundred thousand was a setback, but it wasn't the end of the world. I looked over at Lutz.

"This is on you," he told me. "I don't have that kind of money."

"What do you have?" It was a challenge as much as a question. He needed to come up with something.

"I've got debts," he said. "I've got bills."

"It's a lot of money," said Ricardo. "But if you can't do it, you can't do it. Pay five thousand for my drone and I'll send you on your way."

"Five thousand for a crashed drone?" Lutz snapped. "That's ridiculous."

"Don't pretend you know what a drone's worth just because it's more than you want to spend," said Ricardo. "Pay the man or go to a work camp."

"Lutz," I asked, "what can you do? How much can you kick in?"

He put his elbows on his knees and buried his face in his hands. In a weepy voice, he said, "I can't. I've only got three, maybe four thousand. I gotta run."

I sighed. It wasn't unexpected. I told Ricardo, "I can cover it."

"You?" he asked. "By yourself?"

"I've got the cash." I looked at Lutz. "You owe me. When this is all done, you're paying me back your half."

Lutz didn't look up. He didn't say anything. He nodded with his face still in his hands.

"It's got to be tonight," Ricardo reminded me. "You've got to get me the cash. None of these guys are going to take a risk on credit. Not on *your* credit. They don't know you."

"I've got the cash." The money was in my house, stashed in an old gun safe. "Will you get your guys working on the video while me and Lutz go get the money? Might take a couple of hours. Will you take the credit risk?"

"I'm a gambler." Ricardo leaned back in his chair. "Leave the data cards and the wrecked drones with me. You go get the payment and bring it back." He sat forward and pierced me with a hard look. "These guys will start work on my good word. If you don't show back up here with the cash, I'll pay them to protect my reputation, but I'll put a bounty on your head that will get your ass hauled to a work camp, sure as shit. You understand me?"

I returned Ricardo's stare. I'd been threatened by harder men than him, and I already had a bounty on my head big enough to get a dozen Christian Blacks killed in a dozen, horrifically slow ways. "You're going to make a fat profit on this. Do your part. I'll do mine."

Chapter 15

It's interesting how cities lay themselves out—an art district here, a bar district there, restaurants clumped around this intersection or down that street. Industrial parks and factories on this side of town, Asians in one part of town, Hispanics in another, whites racing each other out to the suburbs and wealthy people taking the biggest houses with the best views, most preferably, close to other wealthy people.

When the Brisbane strain came, property flooded the market as owners and heirs died or turned degenerate. Property values cratered like never before. The crash affected every neighborhood and every city in every country. Supply and demand. Some people made the move from little houses in bad neighborhoods to bigger houses in nicer neighborhoods with no impact to their family budgets. Others didn't go, locked in by sentimentality to their home or an ill-considered responsibility to a contract with a bank that wouldn't be around in another few years anyway.

As Brisbane's spongiform encephalopathy started to degenerate the mental faculties of a larger and larger percentage of the population, d-gens wandered away from their homes and went feral out into the woods. Some of the mentally diminished banded together in single houses, clans of the simple-minded feeling comfort in being close to others of their kind. Mortgages and every other kind of debt went unpaid and uncollectable. The economy, locally and globally, followed the real estate market's tumble into a black hole.

For many people, the collapse of the monetary system was the end of the world.

But money is just money. People still needed to eat. They still needed a place to live. As much as modern Americans thought they could throw a few beans and seeds in the lawn and start an instant farm to feed the kids, the ones who didn't eventually starve realized they were better off producing something else of value to trade for food.

A new system emerged to replace the old.

A cynic might say the only difference was that the paper money got a new color.

But there was more.

In the US, part of the new economic system came from a decision on how to handle improved properties, anything with a house or a building, especially those within the borders of the old cities. Anything that didn't have a living owner with any kind of claim under the old system was legally open to squatters.

That created a gold rush for anyone willing to take responsibility for a house, a block of houses, a neighborhood, a mall, an industrial park—anything they thought they could control. Of course, the words *responsibility* and *control* weren't sufficiently clarified in the rush to redefine property rights, so squatting eventually came down to the act of simply filing a claim form with the new bureaucracy and either living in or hiring an agent to live within the borders of any contiguous piece of real estate—that's how Ricardo came into possession of his shopping center.

Every knucklehead quickly figured out that a warm body could be dropped on any piece of property to lay claim to it whether the property was a one-bedroom apartment or a depopulated county in Nebraska. So by the time I was old enough to have to pay for a place to park my pillow, everything with a roof and a couple of walls was already owned by somebody else.

In a city with a million houses either vacant or full of indigent d-gens, I still had to pay rent.

With no need to be downtown, where most normal people lived among the highest concentration of police and military, I rented in the suburbs, the part of the city with the highest concentration of my customers—d-gens.

I lived in a mostly deserted golf course community surrounded by a tall wall with a gate that functioned well enough to keep stray degenerates from wandering in. My house wasn't a gem. Well, it had been at one time. In fact, it was what most people would call a mansion built right on one of the golf course's greens.

Time had not been kind to it.

A giant old pine had fallen on one end of my mansion, guillotining a three-foot gash through the roof and walls, cutting a third of the house away from the rest. The open roof let the critters, crawlies, and rain through, making most of the house uninhabitable. I stayed in what had been a maid's quarters over the garage, far from the end of the house that had suffered the assault by the tree. My little suite was self-contained with its own kitchenette and bathroom. Not spacious, but it was all I needed—the electricity was dependable and the water ran almost every day.

What more could a civilized man want?

After forty-five minutes in the Mercedes, Lutz drove past an impressive stone sign that pretentiously told passersby that they were entering a special community of beautiful people who lived in shiny houses that sat on carpets of grass so thick and monochromatic green you might expect to see naked forest nymphs napping under clouds of butterflies.

But that was thousands of yesterdays ago, before Brisbane.

Now the bushes and vines growing around the big stone sign obscured the name of my community. In fact, I had no idea what the place had been called back when people cared about such things. I'd found it from a set of semi-accurate GPS coordinates after I answered an online ad for the rental.

Far ahead of us, the road that ran outside my community's wall widened into a roundabout at a T-intersection with a non-functioning fountain at its center. It had been built at the gated entrance to appeal to the egos of potential homebuyers. Now it was a stinking concrete pond that manufactured mosquitoes by the pound.

Parked on the far side of the roundabout, off the road and in the trees, sat a black SUV that wasn't normally parked there. One got used to the derelict vehicles that sat along the roads usually traveled. At least I did. Anything out of the norm raised my hackles.

I pointed down the road and told Lutz, "Don't go to the gate at the roundabout, drive past the entrance."

"Is there another way in?" Lutz asked, perturbed. He was often perturbed, though I guess at the moment he had plenty to be perturbed about. The thought of a work camp life had loomed over us since we first saw those raccoons on the spit.

"Down on the south side, but we won't be going in that way."

"You're running?" Lutz asked, making the wrong guess. "Now that you've promised to pay Ricardo."

"No." I clipped my rifle to my harness in preparation to get out of the car. Was that the police in the black SUV, already here, staking out my place, or had the Camacho brothers finally found me? Or nothing at all?

Maybe that.

But I hadn't managed to stay alive so long by taking a complacent attitude toward little things that didn't seem right.

"What then?" Lutz put a foot on the brake pedal to slow.

"Don't," I told him. "Faster. Through the roundabout. Don't make it look like you're worried, just in a hurry."

Lutz groaned. "How do I do that?"

"Speed up, dammit." We were nearly there. "Do it!"

Lutz put a foot to the gas pedal.

I slid down in my seat and raised the tinted window on my side just enough to hide from anyone in the SUV who might have an interest.

The Mercedes lurched right into a turn, following the curve of the roundabout.

I watched the SUV between the pines. We passed within feet of its front bumper, and I saw nothing but black inside. It could have been empty, but it didn't feel that way, and that was what mattered to me.

"What now?" Lutz asked, coming off the roundabout to drive south on the boulevard outside the wall.

"There's a cut-through in the median up here. A quarter-mile."

Lutz took his foot off the accelerator.

"No," I told him. "Keep going. Don't slow until we're almost there."

"I don't see it."

"I'll tell you when."

"What do I do when we get there?"

Knowing I only had a few seconds to give Lutz instructions, I quickly gave him the code to the keypad on the door of my house. I said, "When you turn up here, slow way down, but don't stop. I'll hop out. After that, you head back to the gate. You know the gate code, right?" He almost always picked me up at my house before we went out on jobs, he had to know the gate code, but you never know with Lutz.

He nodded.

"Once you're in, go to my house and—"

"Who was that back there?" Lutz interrupted. "The cops? You think it was the cops, don't you? You want me to go to your place to get arrested."

"No," I told him. "The warrant is out for me. When you get inside my house, go up to the second floor." He'd never been inside before, so he needed instructions. "Go to the right at the top of the stairs. Way down at the end of the hall around the corner and past the laundry is my room. It's at the end. Go inside. That door's not locked. There's a black case under the bed. Grab it and come back to pick me up."

"Where?"

"I'll call you when you get outside again."

"What if the cops stop me? What do I tell them?"

"Dammit, Lutz. Make something up. You're good at lying. We don't have any more time. Get the case. If the cops are on your ass when you leave, and I can't get to you, take the case to Ricardo. Got it?"

Lutz grumbled something.

"Got it?"

"Yeah," he yelled, "I got it."

Lutz braked and turned the Mercedes into the cut-through.

I swung the door open, and as soon as we were moving slow enough, I jumped out with rifle in hand and I ran into the trees.

Chapter 16

I watched Lutz's taillights shrink as he drove the Mercedes back toward the roundabout at the entrance.

Checking in both directions up and down the road, I didn't see another car or anyone else moving. I figured I'd slipped away undetected. I ran across the street and made my way through the weeds and bushes to get to the eight-foot stone wall that surrounded my neighborhood. The wall wasn't a formidable obstacle to anything determined to get in, but it served to keep most d-gens out.

Well-hidden from the road, I followed along the wall for a bit. Rustling through the shrubs and vines, I found a tree growing right next to the wall, cracking the lower cinderblocks with its roots. Using the tree's branches like a ladder I climbed, and in a matter of moments I was over, coming down in someone's backyard.

With the wall at my back, I knew I wasn't more then a hundred feet from the nearest house. I was completely concealed by the forest that looked every bit like the wild woods Lutz and I had done our dirty business in earlier that night. Two decades prior, I'd have been slinking on a lawn of green grass bordered with colorful flowers, shaded by a handful of regularly pruned trees. Lawn mowing and maintenance had been a commodity service in those days. Now it was a luxury well beyond the means of the residents in my neighborhood.

I made my way quickly through the trees, and came upon a house that seemed to be empty. No surprise, most of those in the neighborhood were vacant. The seven-person partnership that owned the community—probably some of the original residents or their heirs—charged rents much higher than anywhere else around. They still believed the price bought them exclusivity from the wrong kind of people.

How'd I get in? Long story.

I did not, however, pay the higher price for the exclusivity. A system of solar panels provided electricity when the lines were down—as they often were—and a system of cisterns throughout the neighborhood kept water in the pipes. Those were the reasons behind my choice.

Once at the street, I got my bearings and took off at a quick pace, weaving through the trees just off the road. No point in making myself needlessly visible as I suspected the Regulator in the SUV at the front gate had a partner waiting at my house.

With no intent to come to my place from the front, I took a circuitous route down several blocks, between houses, and finally onto an oblong meadow that had once been the fairway for the golf course's eighth hole. A herd of deer froze when they spotted me. After a moment of evaluation, they bolted into the trees.

I jogged down to the end of the meadow and slowed as I walked through the knee-high grass on the eighth green. At the remains of a metal fence that bordered my yard, I stopped.

Across a murky pond that used to be a swimming pool, I scanned the back of the house and looked for movement in a cave that used to be a vast, covered porch. Now it was laced with giant spider webs and humming with a nest of wasps or bees. I never ventured close enough to find out which. For that matter, I never got near the pool either. A snapping turtle the size of Ricardo's spotter drone had taken up residence there after one of Houston's frequent floods.

Taking care to keep myself hidden in the trees, I skirted the stained-concrete deck around the pool and made my way toward the roots of a tall pine that had fallen on my house many years before I'd moved in. The tree hadn't broken when it fell—the saturated ground had given way, and the roots had let go. Now, much of the root system was sticking up in the air, and the trunk of the tree lay angled like a ramp through the first floor on the backside of the house. It stuck out through the second-floor wall in front.

I stopped and listened as I peered into the darkness through the windows I could see.

I heard no unusual sounds coming from inside the house, but I did hear agitated voices. I listened longer and realized they were coming from out front—arguing. One of the voices belonged to Lutz. There were at least a few others.

I climbed onto the downed tree's trunk, balanced on top and walked up, using protruding, leafless branches to keep myself steady.

Halfway up the wall on the first floor, I passed from outside to inside through the three-foot gap cut when the tree fell. I continued up until I reached the second floor. I couldn't immediately step off the tree, as it had come down through a couch that didn't look safe to plant a foot on. I moved on past the couch and got a little higher. With a clear spot to my right, finally, I hopped off the trunk and landed in what had been a loft overlooking the foyer. When my feet hit the old carpet, the rotted wood beneath gave way and one of my boots slipped through up to my ankle. I fell forward onto more solid flooring.

In the room beneath me, pieces of the ceiling disintegrated and made just enough noise in hitting the floor below to bring the argument outside to an ominous halt.

Damn!

I rolled farther onto the loft and came to a stop, looking between the posts on the railing and seeing out one of the giant broken windows on the front of the house. I had a view down a sidewalk from the front door to the street. There I saw Lutz, facing three armed men I didn't recognize, backed by two beefy steroid junkies carrying cudgels shaped like short baseball bats.

The armed men were Regulators. No doubt.

But three working together?

Maybe they specialized in catching bounties on regular criminals like me instead of exterminating rogue d-gens.

Unusual.

And here already? Front-running assholes.

The two brutes with the dull eyes standing behind the Regulators were d-gens—the worst kind—representing what I believed was the most god-awful idea to percolate through any greedy bastard's brain in a generation.

D-gens of a certain stature and beastly temperament, who could follow basic commands, were sorted out of the state preschool system early on and trained for placement as muscle for the military and the police. Bully Boys, that's what they called them, old slang, repurposed. The first crop of Bully Boys had gone to the Army six or seven years ago. The police started utilizing them a few years later for riot control. I'd heard rumors they were now available for use in the private sector. I just hadn't seen it, not until that very moment.

None of the three Regulators were looking at Lutz. Their eyes were fixed on my house. They'd heard the noise I'd made.

Before any of them moved, I pulled my rifle up, evaluated, and aimed.

One of the Regulators had in his hand the black case I'd sent Lutz to fetch. He was in the center of a rough arc arrayed in front of Lutz. He was farthest in the street and a little behind the other two Regulators who were both up on the sidewalk, closer to Lutz. A bullet in the middle guy's forehead would buy me a few fractions of a second while his two buddies looked around to see what had happened to him. Those smidgens of time would be all I'd need to take them both out. As for the Bully Boys? I could harvest them last. They wouldn't understand quickly enough what was happening to take any action. Besides, they were trained for taking orders. They weren't any good at deciding on their own. At least that was the rumor.

At this range, where my targets were standing, pale faces against a dark background, all stationary, I wouldn't miss.

But three dead Regulators in front of my house, with the high likelihood a drone of some sort was up above getting the whole thing on video, it wouldn't be a work camp for me if I got caught, it would be a death sentence.

And that made me miss Mexico a little bit. It was nice not having a government around with its overbearing rules about when I could and couldn't kill somebody.

The Regulators were looking at one another, and their lips were moving. They were conferring in hushed voices.

Run out the back?

No. I was a gambler. I already had chips on the table, and I knew what some of the cards were.

Without a doubt, Lutz had told them I lived in the apartment over the garage, at the far end of the mansion. The guy with my black case in his hand, no doubt was thinking he had something valuable. He wouldn't risk coming into the house after me. He had his payday already. The Bully Boys? They were wild cards.

Two of the Regulators started toward the house with their Bully Boys on their heels.

Chapter 17

Alone now with one Regulator, Lutz figured it was time to push back. "Let me see the warrant."

The Regulator looked at the black case, hefting it, jostling the contents. "What's in it?"

"None of your business," Lutz snapped, knowing from the weight of the case it had to be filled with every dollar Christian had ever earned. "Let me see the warrant."

Holding his gun on Lutz, the Regulator bent at the knees and laid the case on the curb in front of Lutz. He straightened up and took a step back. "Open the case."

Lutz looked down at the worn black box. "It's locked."

"You have a key for the lock," the guy insisted.

"No. I don't."

The guy looked up and scanned the sky. "No drones." He looked back down at Lutz with a mean smile and said, "None on the way. Don't need drone evidence to haul in criminals."

Lutz understood the threat. No drone overhead meant no proof. The guy could tell the police anything. Or, he could dump Lutz's body in the river and not spend another worry on it. Lutz nudged the case with his foot, and he looked at the lock. It wouldn't be hard to open. But it wasn't the lock that worried him, it was Christian's wrath. Lutz looked up and scanned the sky. "You can't always hear them, you know. They don't always have those little lights on them."

The Regulator glanced up.

Lutz decided he'd rather take the chance with the Regulator than with Christian. He kicked the case off the curb. It landed in the road at the Regulator's feet. "I'm not opening it. If you open it, then you're a thief. If you take it, same thing."

The Regulator knelt down again and lifted the handle, checking the case's weight. "Why'd you come here for this?"

"Where's your warrant?"

The guy ran his hand across the case. "Doesn't look very sturdy." He rapped on the side with his knuckle. "It's made of wood, I think." He stood back up. "Where's Black?"

"I told you I haven't seen him in days."

"You tell me where he is, and I'll cut you in." The Regulator tried to make it sound sincere.

"There are already three of you. What do I get, a quarter share? No thanks."

"All you have to do is tell me where he is. We do all the work. A quarter share is fair."

Lutz thought it over. It was tempting, but when he looked at the other Regulators, he saw men just like himself, and he knew a man like him would never give up a quarter share of a bounty plus whatever was in the case. The best he could hope for would be a thank you and a fuck off.

"I see how it's going to be," said the guy, losing patience and standing back up. He lifted a booted foot and stomped on the side of Christian's case. "I'll see for myself what's inside."

Lutz shook his head. "I'm not threatening you right now, but I wouldn't do that if I were you."

"Sounds like you *are* threatening me." The guy stomped down harder.

"You know anything about Christian Black?"

The guy chuckled and looked at the house.   "I know where he lives. I know he's your partner."

Lutz laughed. "You don't know where he came from?"

"We've picked up our share of bad boys.   It makes no difference to me where your buddy came from."

The guy stomped the case again.   Wood cracked.   Old vinyl wrapped over the top tore.

"It'll make a difference when you do find out."

Encouraged by his success, the guy stomped a few more times before the case broke open.   Still keeping his weapon pointed at Lutz, he knelt down and pulled away a piece of broken wood to look inside. "What's this?"

Chapter 18

I suppressed a laugh as I snuck down a short hall past what had been the original owner's home office and walked into the master bedroom. The case I'd had Lutz fetch — my decoy case — was packed full of old money, legal US tender from before Brisbane turned the world economy on its head. All of that old cash was worthless now except as tinder or toilet paper. I'd used food coloring to dye it all red so that it might, at the quickest of glances, look like real money. The outside bills on each bundle were real, though. Again, at a quick glance, it looked like a lot of money.

The front door of my house opened, and I heard the sound of a voice whispering orders, but the voice was too far away for me to make out what was being said. At least one of the Regulators was coming inside with his Bully Boy.

I took care as I crossed the floor in the master bedroom. The roof on this end of the house leaked terribly and there was plenty of rot through the floor and walls. I went into the master bath — a spa really — with marble and glass enough to make a decadent Roman proud. The faux gold fixtures, though, were all flaking as the metal beneath corroded. Funky mauve wallpaper was peeling off in sheets.

At the far end of the bathroom, I slipped into a cluttered closet that was bigger than my room at the other end of the house, including its bathroom and kitchenette. And the closet was just one of two, a his and a hers. All that space for clothes. How could anybody have time to wear so many different garments?

I quietly worked my way around a boxy island containing shelves that stood in the center of the closet. It had been a home for shoes, hundreds of pairs, many sitting right where the former owner had left them, collecting dust. Some were now homes for mice. Others had been shredded into nesting material. Silverfish and roaches were ingesting anything their simple little systems could turn into turds or egg cases for their young.

Did I mention everything about my house was big?

Not big enough to keep me hidden from four searchers for very long, but big enough to buy me the time I needed.

They'd start their search by working their way down to my quarters at the other end, slowly and carefully, checking rooms as they went. At least that's how I'd do it.

That could eat up several valuable minutes.

Clumsy feet clomped quietly on old wood. A Bully Boy was on the stairs, giving away the presence of his Regulator.

Bully Boys had their uses, I guess. Stealth surely wasn't one of them.

I shoved aside a smelly old chair piled high with clothing that hadn't been worn in two decades to reveal a large gun safe bolted to the floor. Inside, I kept some weapons, but mostly the safe protected my savings. The only question I needed to decide as I spun the combination was whether to take all the cash now or just enough to pay Ricardo and a cushion for unexpected expenses.

Both choices were full of risks.

Now that I was a fugitive, even though temporarily, Regulators and police would be coming to my house to find me. They'd search. One of them might find the safe. It was a rusty relic that looked like it had been in the house since before humanity tripped on Brisbane and stumbled down the stairs. The only thing new about the safe was the locking mechanism. I'd paid a good bit of cash to have the lock refurbished on the inside—people capable of that kind of work were hard to find these days. On the rest of the safe, I left the patina. I wanted it to look like it hadn't been touched by anything but rust over the past twenty years. I wanted it to say to anyone who saw it that going to the great trouble to crack it open would lead them to find nothing valuable enough to make the effort worth it. And it would take a great effort. Nobody carried with them the kind of tools they'd need to break into my safe.

Back to the question of the cash, then.

I swung the door open on well-lubricated hinges.

Take it all? Big risk. That much cash on me would be a death sentence if I were captured by Regulators or the police. It was enough to tempt anyone to knock me off and dispose of my body. Of course, the hundred thousand I was going to carry out with me to pay Ricardo was probably enough to get me killed, too.

So, I had a risk that could only be avoided by not getting caught.

Still, the idea of taking it all with me at once seemed bad. I took a conveniently sized canvas bag, stuffed in a hundred thousand, and then took another fifty just in case. I silently closed the door and locked the safe. I scooted the clothing-laden chair back in place.

I tiptoed to the closet door, through the master bathroom, and took a peek into the bedroom as I listened for noises down at the other end of the house.

Furniture scooted around and doors were being opened and closed noisily down by my room. I heard soft, sneaky sounds, too, coming from elsewhere in the house. One or both of the Regulators were quietly searching for me under the noise of the Bully Boys.

Smooth, but not smooth enough to force me to kill them.

I passed through the expansive bathroom and slipped into the master bedroom. A pair of French doors opened off the master bedroom to a private, second-floor deck over a walled garden on the side of the house. I knew the deck's planks were rotted, and the garden beneath it was so overgrown with vines I'd risk getting tangled if I tried to make my escape that way.

I'd have to leave the way I came.

I snuck out of the master, down the short hall, past the study, and stopped before crossing the loft.

Bully Boys were still ransacking my room. Clearly they were meant to be a distraction. I scanned the darkness across the loft and listened. I didn't like not knowing exactly where the sneaky, quiet Regulators were.

Thinking the floor might be sturdier along the wall, I worked my way around the edge of the loft, testing the boards with my toes before I put all my weight into a new step.

Leaves crunched from somewhere below.

I froze.

They crunched a second time.

One of the Regulators was in the room below, far down at the other end where it opened up to the kitchen.

I didn't hear a sound from the second guy.

Moving quietly, tracking the Regulator downstairs by the sounds he made, I reached the tree trunk I'd used to climb to the second floor. I stepped onto it as I craned my neck to scan what I could see of the sky for a drone. I didn't hear one. I didn't want one to spot me making my break, but that was not my primary concern. Not thirty feet away from me, on the floor below, was a man with a gun who wouldn't have any qualms about shooting me.

I took several quick steps down the tree trunk, reached the house's back wall, and leaned out for a look.

Shit!

One of the Regulators wasn't fifteen feet away, at the edge of the covered patio, weapon at the ready, staring over his shoulder at my snapping turtle pond. His Bully Boy was at the edge of the swimming pool, leaning over, concentrating on something in the water.

I gulped and pulled back inside the house, holding my breath.

I waited for a breath, a second breath.

No reaction from the guy outside that I could hear.

He hadn't realized I'd peeked out at him.

The sound of a foot squishing into something rotten and damp told me the guy downstairs was getting close. Momentarily, he'd be able to look up through the gaps in the broken ceiling above and see me standing on the fallen trunk.

I couldn't go out through the back of the house without taking a big risk on somebody getting shot, which is to say, I wasn't going to take that risk. If I went out the back, I'd have to shoot that guy. Then I'd have to shoot them all.

Have to?

I guess.

The all-or-nothing logic was stuck in my brain, and I was too short on time to come up with a shooting solution that didn't end up with all of them dead.

Alternatives?

Only one.

I turned and walked up the trunk angled through the house, squeezing my way around branches, trying not to make noise on the old bark, and trying to move as fast as I could.

The guy below sensed or heard something because he started to run across the floor.

A few seconds later I heard his feet hit the stairs.

Through the noise of stomping boots on the steps, I gave up all efforts at silence. I pranced up the trunk, dodging branches, long and broken.

From behind me, outside the house, I heard a rustle. Twigs snapped. The second Regulator was coming.

One of them called out.

Through the gap in the second-floor wall torn by the tree, I saw the ground below and it looked much too far for a jump.

Being out of options, I spied a bare branch angling down. It looked thick enough to hold my weight.

I leapt.

I hit with my chest and wrapped my arms over the branch as bark crumbled off the wood and I slipped, scrambling to keep a grip until I came to a stop, grasping bare wood, feet dangling.

Looking down at flat ground between trees, I saw that I wasn't that high and I dropped to the dirt.

A thick mat of pine needles cushioned my fall and muffled the sound.

I jumped up and ran through the trees to get away from the house.

Twenty minutes later, I was back in Lutz's passenger seat.

With no legitimate right to hold him, the Regulators had to let Lutz go.

Lutz glanced over his shoulder at the broken case full of useless bills in the backseat. "You hoard worthless old money like a d-gen. You know you're not going to fool Ricardo with that, right? That Regulator saw through your charade, even in the dark."

"That's okay." I looked behind us at a car I spotted far down the road. "Don't go directly to Ricardo's. Just in case. Take the long way."

"We can't go there at all. You can't give him that."

"It's okay." I reached into my bag and took out a stack of hundred dollar notes—new currency, the good stuff. I showed it to Lutz. "I've got Ricardo's payment. All of it."

"Where'd you get that?"

"I have a stash."

Lutz ground his teeth and snorted as he bit on angry words he wanted to speak.

"Spit it out," I told him.

"You sent me in as a decoy."

"Yeah."

"I could have been killed by those assholes."

I shook my head. "You weren't." I didn't elaborate. I knew the situation had been risky for Lutz, being my diversion, but I also knew he wouldn't have stepped up to take the risk on his own, even with his freedom on the line.

He'd taken ownership of the idea that going on the lam was an easy out. That made him afraid to take any responsibility for fixing the shit we were in.

Chapter 19

Lutz stewed most of the way back to Ricardo's.

I used the quiet miles to think through a question I probably should have asked much earlier in the night: Was everything what it appeared to be?

I had ten bundles of a hundred one hundred-dollar bills—a hundred thousand dollars in my bag to give to Ricardo, and the money was fanning my suspicions.

Could the dirty kill have been a setup? Was Lutz smart enough to conspire with Ricardo to scam me out of my savings? I didn't think Lutz was that clever but I knew his sense of morality could be bent far enough that he wouldn't be bothered by taking every penny I had.

Maybe Lutz had run a similar game on his last partner and that's why he'd wound up dead. That was three dead partners for him in as many years.

Enough to worry anybody.

By the time Lutz pulled the black Mercedes through Ricardo's loading dock door, I was feeling a little bit paranoid and was entertaining fantasies of jumping out of the car with pistols drawn, ready to lay down some red mayhem.

Lutz parked, and we got out of the car.

My pistols stayed holstered.

Drones raced through the cavernous space, buzzing around the obstacles hanging from the ceiling, but no one had come to the big empty floor to meet us. I took a glance at the cars parked near ours. All the ones from earlier were present, as were two more—one of those a four-wheel-drive pickup, the other a Jeep. Both were rugged and dented, exactly the kind of trucks a Regulator might drive.

I nudged Lutz on the arm and nodded toward the two trucks.

He looked at them and looked back at me like there might be something wrong with me. "What?"

"Those two weren't here before."

"So?" Lutz took a few steps toward the stairs that led up to Ricardo's office.

"They don't worry you?" I asked, striding to catch up as I scanned for dangers.

"I'm not afraid of ugly cars."

Sometimes I wanted to punch Lutz. I grabbed his arm, stopped him, and turned him around to face me. "Those don't look like Regulators' cars to you?" Maybe I was indulging my paranoia a bit too much.

Lutz heaved a pained sigh as he looked the Jeep and the truck over again. "Could belong to the governor for all I know."

"Dammit, Lutz, don't be stupid. You know what I mean."

Lutz yanked his arm out of my hand and started walking away from me. "Could be."

"Why are they here?" I asked.

"Don't know."

"It doesn't worry you?"

"I don't have a bounty on my head."

Lutz was right about that. But what went on in his brain that he couldn't see his turn was coming?

"We're not the only Regulators Ricardo does business with," said Lutz. "Houston is a big town."

"Before we go up there, let me ask you a question."

Lutz stopped and turned to look at me. "What?"

"Why were we sent out on that job tonight?"

"I'm too tired to play a game. Ask me what you want to ask me."

I took a hard look at Lutz's face. I wanted to catch the lie when it happened. "Those weren't kids being cooked on that fire. Why were we sent out there to kill those d-gens?"

"Oh, goddammit!" Lutz spun around and stomped away. "Shit like this happens. How many times do we show up to find something other than we expected? How often do we find nothing at all?" Lutz glanced over his shoulder at me. "You coming? Or you wanna stand down here and make up stories to tell yourself?"

Chapter 20

Ricardo was in his desk chair, spinning away from viewing his monitors to look at us as we came into his control room. He casually asked, "You have the money?"

I pointed vaguely. "Whose cars are those?"

Ricardo's mood turned suspicious. "Why do you ask?"

"There are a couple of cars down there that weren't there when we left," I told him. "Who do they belong to?"

Ricardo looked at Lutz and then back at me. "Don't come in here and pretend you're a policeman with questions I have to answer. Do you have my money?"

"If you want the money, you'll answer my questions."

Ricardo deliberately stood and raised himself to his imposing height so he could look down on me.

He stood a dozen paces across the room, so I wasn't worried that he could do anything besides look intimidating.

"We had a deal." Ricardo's face was hard. His words weren't angry, but they weren't nice. "I'm holding up my end. Nothing in our deal was contingent on me answering stupid questions that might come up. If this is your way of backing out, then get the hell off my property and enjoy being on the run because that video is going to the police unaltered. Now, are you going to pay me or not?"

I didn't want to part with my money in what I suspected might be a scam, but I decided it didn't matter whether I got my answers before or after I paid. If it turned out I wasn't satisfied with Ricardo's responses, he wouldn't be alive to stop me from putting the money back in my bag.

Holding Ricardo's eye, I walked over to his desk, took ten bundles of bills out of my bag, and stacked them messily in front of the array of computer monitors. "A hundred thousand."

"My faith is restored." Ricardo smiled. "Why are you worried about those cars?"

I stepped back from the desk.

Lutz said, "He's paranoid about Regulators."

"Wouldn't you be?" Ricardo shrugged. "He has a bounty on his head."

Pointing again toward the parked cars, I said, "The Jeep and truck out there, they look like Regulators' cars."

Ricardo laughed and went back to his seat. "Those belong to a couple of fellows who fetch downed drones for us."

Lutz laughed in that mean way he does when he's torn between feeling amused and feeling that perverse satisfaction he gets from seeing someone else embarrassed.

I thought about shooting Lutz. Just because. Well, not just because. The more time I spent with Lutz, the more I found myself fantasizing about putting a bullet between his eyes. Talking to Ricardo, I said, "What happened tonight with the sanction? Why'd you send us out there?"

Ricardo's brows knit as he steepled his fingers and he propped his elbows on the arms of his chair. "That sounds like an accusation."

"Tell me about the sanction."

"You know I don't assign Sanction IDs, right?" Ricardo looked over to Lutz. "Does he know what we do? Does he know how this business works? Or is he just a stupid trigger boy?" Ricardo turned back to me, put on a disappointed face, and then returned his attention to his computer screens. He started typing.

It took thirty or forty seconds, but one of the screens flashed to a different view. Ricardo pointed. "This is my raw footage."

All I saw were treetops in fog with glimpses of a pale dirt road down on the forest floor. "What am I looking at?"

"I'm showing you what I saw."

"This is from your spotter drone?" I asked.

Ricardo nodded.

I noticed immediately how sharp the picture was. The video was high resolution. "This wasn't what was sent back through the air, was it?"

"It came off the memory card you took out of my drone. My drone arrived at the scene seven minutes ahead of you." Ricardo leaned over and pointed at the road down between the trees. "You two will come up this road. Keep an eye on it when the drone gets more altitude."

The road disappeared, and the video showed only trees slide by below through thick bands of fog. The fire in the clearing came into view as did the celebrating d-gens. The fog grew thick again, and it was hard to make out the details of any of the individuals.

I focused particularly on the animals on the spit over the fire, trying to match the count with the number I recalled from seeing them in person, but with the fog, it was impossible.

The drone ascended, and the fire grew dim. Momentarily, the barely visible strand of the pale-colored road came into view at the edge of the screen.

I said, "I don't understand."

"In a moment," said Ricardo, "You'll see Lutz's piece of shit come down the road."

"It's not a piece of shit," Lutz protested. "It's a Mercedes."

"Lutz's piece of Mercedes," Ricardo goaded.

I put a finger on the screen as though touching the image of the fire might help to clarify it. "The timing doesn't make sense to me. How did they even assign a pending sanction off that video? I can't see anything incriminating." And that seemed for the moment to answer a very important question. I was being conned by Ricardo, maybe with Lutz's help.

"Take a deep breath," Lutz told me, his hand suddenly on my shoulder.

I shrugged it off and stepped back, ready to raise my rifle and start shooting holes in people. "What happened?"

"They didn't assign the pending sanction based on the video." Ricardo pointed at me. "Take out your phone and check the Sanction Certificate. You'll see the time. Compare it to the time on the screen."

I took my phone out of my pocket, asking myself if Ricardo's guys had time to alter the video, asking myself which bits of evidence I was seeing were real and which had been altered. I keyed my phone and opened up the app to look at the sanction. The big red cancellation letters virtually stamped across the screen taunted me with the evening's mistakes.

"After you check that time," said Ricardo. "You need to take your SIM card and battery out. They can track you by your phone."

Shit! I forgot about that. We all did.

I checked the time. The sanction had been assigned nearly forty-five minutes before the time the spotter drone arrived on the scene. It appeared that it wasn't Ricardo running a scam on me. I really was in trouble.

Apparently seeing the change in my expression, Ricardo said, "You see?"

I stared at the canceled sanction on my phone. "It took us what, Lutz, thirty minutes to get out there after you got the call?"

Lutz shrugged. "About that."

"I contacted Lutz after I got the coordinates from the police," said Ricardo. "I had a drone relatively close, and I tasked it to go. That's the one you shot down."

"But that's not how it usually works," I protested. "You find the d-gens when they're up to no good, right? That's how the spotter drone system works. Then you send video back to the police, they assign a pending sanction, and as soon as they're satisfied with what they see, they assign the ID."

"Mostly right," said Ricardo, "but you know as well as I do that I usually contact Lutz or someone like him before I alert the police. That way when the sanction goes out to the Regulator network, you guys are already on your way or pretty close."

"Front-running," muttered Lutz.

I didn't need a primer on Front-running. "What I don't understand is how the sanction was assigned before your drone arrived on site."

"Anonymous tip," said Ricardo. "Somebody from one of the corporate farms said the d-gens were out in the woods killing kids."

"So, there could be dead kids out there," I said, conflicted over the hope I could go back out to the site and find some toddler corpses to prove my innocence.

Nobody said anything about that. Maybe Ricardo and Lutz saw the dilemma the same way I did. It was hard to wish for dead kids, even if they were d-gens.

I had to ask myself whether going back out to the site of the kill before any cops went out there later in the morning would be a good idea. Maybe when the sun came up, a more thorough check for bodies of cannibalized children would turn something up.

Ricardo, seeming to read my thoughts, was ready to crush those hopes. "I asked my video guys to give every frame a thorough look before they altered anything. They only had to find one body on the video before you and Lutz showed up. It might have been enough to put you in the clear."

That's not what I wanted to hear. I sidled up to Ricardo's long desk and asked, "Do you mind if I sit?"

He shook his head.

I seated myself in front of a pair of monitors with video panning past an overgrown neighborhood somewhere in the suburbs. Another of Ricardo's spotter drones at work. "So nothing on the video to clear us. Your guys are working on it, at least."

Ricardo said, "They're working on it and they—"

"They'll finish it," Lutz cut in, "right? You have the money."

Ricardo looked over at Lutz and didn't answer him but instead turned back to me. "There was a woman there we think was normal."

"Wait. What?" I leaned toward Ricardo. I hoped he wasn't telling me we'd murdered a citizen. If that was the case, we'd have to run. No choice.

"Not all of them were d-gens around that fire. One was a normal woman."

Lutz made a noise that sounded like a prelude to tears.

Chapter 21

Ricardo got out of his chair and walked to the back wall of his office where a bank of cabinets stood. He opened a drawer, rummaged through the contents for a moment and retrieved a pill bottle. He took a second to examine the label before saying, "Hey, Lutz."

Lutz looked up from the mental movie of his world coming to an end.

Ricardo tossed him the plastic bottle as he came back toward his desk.

Lutz caught the bottle and looked at the label. "What's this?"

"It'll help you stay calm," answered Ricardo. "Complimentary, on the house." He pointed to a worn couch, also against the back wall. "Go lay down. The adults have grownup stuff to talk about."

Lutz's face turned red. He threw the bottle at one of the computer monitors. The cap popped off, and pills scattered. "Don't treat me like a cheese-headed degenerate."

Ricardo looked down his nose at Lutz for a moment before turning back to me.

"Did we kill her?" I asked, trying to guess which of the d-gens by the bonfire had been the normal one.

Ricardo shook his head.

What?

Ricardo used his keyboard and mouse to find a place on the video. When the image froze on the screen, he pointed to a blonde woman standing by the fire, staring into the forest.

From the angle of the video, I was able to see her face. "I remember that woman. She got away across the cornfield."

Lutz stepped up and leaned over Ricardo's shoulder.

Ricardo grimaced at the smell and leaned back. "Man, get a toothbrush!"

Lutz put a fat finger on the screen, right over the blonde woman's face. "She's naked and streaked with blood just like the others. She's not normal. She's a d-gen."

Ricardo pushed Lutz back, and he resituated himself in front of his keyboard. He started the video. "Watch."

The camera slowly changed angle as the spotter drone that filmed the video drifted over the trees. There was no sound, but it was perfectly obvious when the first shot was fired because every d-gen around the fire jerked and turned. In the seconds that followed, d-gens ran and charged Lutz's muzzle flashes.

It was clear to me now, just as it was at the time, that he was in trouble, and likely would have been killed by the d-gens had I not been there. I saw the image of myself from the back as I stepped into the clearing, rifle blazing as d-gens dropped in every direction. It was also obvious that if one of the high-res videos hit the network, a warrant would go out for Lutz, too.

Of all the people in the wide view of the clearing, only one person did not move, the blonde. She stood with arms half raised, a look of horror on her face, paralyzed. The Christian Black on the screen, having shot every d-gen attacking Lutz and every d-gen who'd had the courage to come at him, started working on downing the rest, shooting systematically around the clearing, from left to right.

The girl's head snapped to her right as she came alive to the realization a bullet would soon find her. She stumbled to

Bobby Adair

her left, bent over and picked up a droopy canvas bag, and crouched as she ran for the cornfield.

"Watch the bag," Ricardo narrated.

"Lots of 'em collect shit," Lutz muttered.

The girl tripped and sprawled onto the scrubby grass. Her bag spilled its contents.

I watched the girl for anything unusual. All I saw was the initial paralysis and then the ducking. It wasn't typical d-gen behavior. D-gens didn't understand bullets. They didn't know to duck.

Crawling on her knees in a rush for the corn, the girl scooped her treasures back into her bag, got her feet beneath her and ran between the nearest stalks, creating a wake in the corn that indicated the path she followed off the screen.

Ricardo stopped the video and looked at us, nodding. "See?"

Lutz snorted. "That doesn't prove she's anything."

Ricardo looked at me.

I shrugged. "Could go either way."

Ricardo turned back to his computer and backed the video up to the point where the girl fell and her bag spilled. He stopped it there with one frame burning on the screen.

The girl was down, mostly. An elbow and forearm were planted in the dirt, as was the side of her face and her chest. Her hips and legs hadn't yet hit the ground. One arm was stuck out in front, hand open, fingers splayed as the bag got away and some of its contents were caught mid-tumble: a shoe, what looked like a pair of jeans, something light-colored halfway out—maybe a blouse—and a brilliantly glowing little rectangle.

I leaned in close for a better look. "Oh shit."

"Uh-huh," confirmed Ricardo.

Lutz leaned in and shared the smell of his dinner again. "What is it?"

Ricardo pushed him back. "Cell phone."

"No." Lutz stepped back and dodged left, then right, as though the fact was in the air and trying to catch him. "A glare from the fire."

"Wrong color of light," said Ricardo. "My video guys are looking at this at a level of detail you wouldn't understand."

To help Lutz accept the only conclusion, I said, "D-gens don't carry charged cell phones."

"And look at her arm." Ricardo pointed. "Tattoo."

How did I miss that?

D-gens never had tattoos. Nearly all of them showed signs of mental degeneration before they were old enough to go to kindergarten. By the time they were mature enough to want a tattoo they were too far gone to understand what one was or how to get it.

Lutz shook his head and muttered silently before he stepped up to me, blocking out Ricardo. He glanced down at the pile of my money that was still on the desk. "Canada. That's plenty of money to get us there and get us set up."

"That's Ricardo's money," I told him.

Lutz glanced over his shoulder at Ricardo. He looked back at me and exaggerated a slow look at the money.

I'm pretty sure he was urging me to kill Ricardo and take the money back. But maybe that was just me reading too much of Lutz's unpleasant personality into his intentions.

Speaking slowly, he said, "We should go to Mexico."

As much as going to Mexico or Canada was still an option, it wasn't an option I was willing to exercise with Lutz as a traveling companion. His only value to me came from the contacts he had in Houston's graft market. He'd be a burden anywhere else. That, and I didn't intend to take part in the robbery he was clearly hinting at. I'd made a deal with Ricardo—that money on the table was now his. I put a hand on Lutz's shoulder to nudge him out of my way. "You're getting too worked up to think straight. Take one of those pills and go rest on the couch." I didn't say it kindly.

Lutz's face showed a desperate sadness as he stepped out of my way.

Ricardo was at his keyboard again, opening up an email. "I just got this in from Blix—she's a hacker who rents one the apartments on the other side of the building."

I looked at the screen. "What is it?"

"Blix ran a facial recognition program on the girl." Ricardo looked back at Lutz to emphasize just how wrong Lutz's desperate guesses were.

"And?" I asked.

Ricardo clicked an attachment, and a document filled the screen as it opened up. He leaned back and pointed at the glowing monitor.

I stepped behind Ricardo for a full view, seeing some type of identification paper I wasn't familiar with. It held a picture of the blonde girl—I was pretty sure it was her—younger, clean hair, not as lean as she looked in the video. I read aloud, "Sienna Galloway.   Five-Six.   Green eyes. Behavioral Conditioning Specialist at Blue Bean Agriculture, LLC."

"Blue Bean?" Lutz asked as he headed for the couch. "That big farming outfit? They own half of three goddamn counties out there. She works for them?"

"Makes sense right?" Ricardo answered. "All of those d-gens you killed were wearing Blue Bean dog collars."

"What?" Lutz didn't believe it.

"She's the only one who wasn't."

I didn't believe but I kept my mouth closed.

Ricardo rewound the video again to a point where a clear view of several of the d-gens wearing collars on their necks could be seen. Ricardo stopped the video. "See?"

How did I miss that?

Ricardo said, "All those d-gens were Blue Bean Farms' workers. Every one except the girl."

Neither Lutz nor I had any response. Somehow, with all that had been going on, that detail never stuck with either of us.

"There's a phone number here." Ricardo pointed at Sienna Galloway's information sheet.

Time to get back on task.

Having already disassembled my phone, I came back around to my place on Ricardo's desk. "Can I use your phone?"

Ricardo opened a drawer that contained a half-dozen phones among other random pieces of junk. "Pick one. A thousand each."

I looked at the phones. *A thousand dollars?*

"Clean," said Ricardo. "Use it for a week or two then toss it. Better yet, toss the SIM card and sell the device."

New phones were impossible to get outside of government, but old phones like these were a dime a dozen. "I'd be lucky to get fifty bucks for it."

"Without a SIM card and an active account, that'd be exactly right," Ricardo confirmed.

I'd already put too much risk on myself by stupidly not pulling the SIM card out of my phone the moment I found out I had a warrant. I wasn't going to risk putting the SIM card back in. I reached into my pocket and took out two thousand dollars and laid the money on the desk. "If I buy two, can I get a third for free?"

Ricardo laughed. "Why not?"

I took three phones, dropped one in my pocket, tossed one to Lutz, and flipped the third open. "I'll need the number off that phone, Lutz, so you and I can call each other."

Lutz grumbled something as he fumbled with his overpriced, used phone.

I looked at the number on Ricardo's screen for Sienna Galloway, and I dialed as he looked on approvingly.

The phone took a moment to connect, but once it did, it didn't ring, it went straight to a generic voicemail account.

"Crap."

Ricardo raised his eyebrows in question.

"Her phone's dead," I told him.

Ricardo looked back at the screen. "It was working when she threw it back in the bag."

I dialed a second time to confirm the result. Still nothing but voicemail. Damn. An expeditiously placed bribe could do so much to remedy my problems. Ten thousand dollars for a few little lies from Sienna Galloway and I'd have flimsy but sufficient proof to keep myself out of a work camp.

Chapter 22

Sienna Galloway sat among tightly packed trees at the top of a red clay bank that plunged steeply down to the river. Fog floated thick over the channel, hiding the soupy, reddish-brown water flowing beneath.

She'd just finished putting on her jeans, blouse, sweatshirt, and boots.   In her hands, she stared at her smashed phone.   While running through the woods she'd tripped and fallen. The phone was beyond repair.

The phone had cost her nearly a week's pay back when the best job she could get with her Ph.D. was at the state nursery, trying to sort the thousands upon thousands of preschoolers by intellectual aptitude, turning the incorrigible ones loose—eventually—and funneling the others into roles of graduated complexity.   The least-complicated jobs for degenerates were often on the corporate farms where they labored at simple, repetitive tasks, many of which had been done by machines back in the days when there was sufficient skilled labor in the country to keep the tractor factories open.

Degenerates with a few more smarts and a degree of social skills were trained to domestic help for those who could afford it. Many wound up in janitorial roles, some in food service.

The brutes—the trainable ones with a penchant for terrorizing their peers—were earmarked for roles that matched their talents. Some went to the military as backup muscle for the regular soldiers. Many wound up with the police, attached to the riot control squads.

Degenerates beating their debilitated brethren into submission, that was an idea the thinking public loved. In truth, they'd have embraced anything they thought might curb the d-gen riots that incessantly plagued the cities.

Sienna hated that requirement of her job, sentencing young boys to a future of progressively worse violence. She believed most of those boys could have been put into productive roles in other places, but she had quotas to fill. The military and police quotas took priority over all others. The quotas that irked her the most were those for the private security firms. Every year, they took more and more boys. Every year they lobbied for a higher priority until, by the time Sienna left, they got whatever the military and police didn't take.

It was a waste of the country's scant semi-intelligent manpower. So many industries that could otherwise be rebuilding America's economy were bridled by a lack of workers.

And most degenerates simply couldn't work.

They sat on the curbs in decaying suburbs, trying to catch rats and scratching their genitals. Wasting their days staring at the empty food troughs in the street, waiting for the trucks to come and fill them. The most their brains were capable of was eating and procreating. Even basic hygiene was too taxing for their minds. They couldn't put a square peg in a square hole if square was the only choice.

Hell, even a chimp could do that.

And a degenerate who couldn't consistently master a simple task was useless to society except in the role of producing more humans.

Unfortunately, nearly every degenerate wound up useless no matter how much aptitude they seemed to start with. For instance, a degenerate who grew into his late teens with the ability to harvest strawberries, pull weeds, and cultivate a field, might — by the time he was thirty — be unable to tell a strawberry from a snail. By the time degenerates were thirty-five they were completely useless in an industrial sense.

That was the spongiform encephalopathy at work. Prions never stopped eating away at the cortex. Few degenerates lived past the age of forty.

Those were all old frustrations that burdened Sienna when she worked for the state.

The offer she'd received from Blue Bean Farms had saved her from that. At least, it seemed to at the time.

She'd been reluctant to accept the offer at first. Blue Bean, like many of the corporate farms, was constantly being fined and continually under federal investigation for their abuses.

But Keith Workman, Blue Bean's CEO, had assured Sienna they were hiring her as a way to become the industry leader in humane farming methods. He'd explained to her that Blue Bean, like so many other businesses in so many industries, lacked the expertise to humanely maintain degenerate productivity. It was that simple. Sienna would help solve that problem by redefining Blue Bean's standard operating procedures and retraining employees to follow those procedures.

It sounded like a wonderful job to help Blue Bean become a better corporate citizen and by extension make the world a little bit better place. Oh, and she'd make a lot more money.

Such are the effects of the rose-colored glasses everyone wears into new employment opportunities.

Blue Bean Farms owned a parcel of land measured in square miles rather than acres. It covered the westernmost parts of Harris County, a corner of Montgomery County, and more than half of small Waller County.

Mr. Workman was notably tight-lipped about operational information, but as near as Sienna could figure, Blue Bean had maybe a few hundred paid employees overseeing the whole operation, and most of those had little to do with direct farm production.

The farm work was supervised by work camp detainees serving sentences that ranged from a few years to life. There were nearly a thousand of those. Stealing from a tradition dating back to Deep South prisons from over a hundred years ago, some of the lifers were selected as trustees. They were armed and given responsibility for keeping the rest of the work camp prisoners in line and to keep them from escaping.

The work camp inmates oversaw Blue Bean's degenerate population, nearly thirty-thousand of them. The inmates were the ones responsible for productivity. They were the ones who handled the degenerates on a daily basis. And they were the ones Sienna most needed to retrain.

Unfortunately, Sienna came to learn that she had no authority over the inmate population. She could only make recommendations to the Warden, a state employee who oversaw the work camp facilities on five separate corporate farms. He spent little time on Blue Bean property. Sienna suspected he and his two-dozen guards spent most of their time fishing and hunting, only showing up in force when an inmate escaped. Even then they did little except drink beer in the admin building while the trustees tracked the runners down.

Despite all that, Sienna tried. She filled out her forms. She cajoled trustees. She pleaded with the Warden, and she continually begged Mr. Workman to back her up in something. That, and she filed whistle-blower complaints with the Texas State Degenerate Oversight Board.

Those complaints went ignored as far as she could tell. And the longer she stayed at Blue Bean, the more she grew to hate her job—as much as she'd hated the previous one at the state nursery.

Sienna realized tears were silently tracing down her cheeks.

She sniffled.

She wasn't a crier.

She wiped her eyes, got to her feet, and scanned the foggy night. She had miles to go to get back to her bungalow in Blue Bean's admin compound, and she had an early meeting with Mr. Workman and the State Inspector. She couldn't be late.

She started walking.

Chapter 23

I turned my attention to Ricardo. "Does Sienna have any convictions or warrants?"

"I can find out," he told me with a smile full of meaning.

I sighed. More money.

He pointed at the screen still showing Sienna Galloway's work identification papers. "I did this one for free. Blix charges me, too."

I pulled another three thousand out of my pocket, wondering if the extra fifty thousand I'd taken from my safe would be enough. I laid the bills on the table. "Three thousand, but that's for everything I might need until this is over."

"Everything?" Ricardo asked, leaning back in his chair and looking at the money. "That's a big risk for me."

"Could be," I said. "Might be this is the last thing I ask for, and then you make a good profit for not a lot of effort."

"Or I end up spending another ten thousand fulfilling pointless requests," countered Ricardo.

"You'll know if they're pointless when I ask," I said. "If so, don't fulfill."

Ricardo looked at the money for another moment before he said. "Okay, but make it five."

"Jesus. I work for a living. I'm not rich."

"Four."

I heaved a sigh and pulled another thousand out of my pocket. "Deal. Find out if Sienna is clean."

Lutz asked, "Why do you care if she's clean?"

Ricardo looked over, "Because he wants to bribe her to back your side of the story, to get you off. If she's a credible, upstanding citizen, it'll work. If she's a screwup like you, Lutz, the police won't believe her."

"Keep it up," Lutz threatened. "You just keep it up."

"Blue Bean is a huge operation," I told Ricardo. "I need to know where to find her out there."

Ricardo typed up a quick email and sent it out. "I'll have an answer in an hour. Maybe less."

"Good."

Lutz said, "If you'd shot her when you saw her in the corn, we wouldn't have to do this now."

"Shoot a citizen?" I asked in a tone that said, "You're an idiot."

Lutz shrugged and pushed a pair of duck lips out from under his mustache. "You saw her, naked like a savage. Nobody'd think twice about one more body. Now you've got a witness on top of the video."

"And a death penalty case," I told him, "that would be investigated because the police get kinda pissed when you start gunning down citizens."

"How would they know?" Lutz asked.

"The same way we figured it out." I had to try to keep from yelling at him. "You saw the video. You know what they would have found when they came across her body—clothes, a charged cell phone, probably a purse, and an ID. Car keys. You know, all the stuff normal people carry around with them, the kind of shit that's a dead giveaway that she's not a d-gen."

"We coulda took the bag," Lutz argued. "We'd just have to go back out there one more time, find the body in the cornfield and pick up the bag. Easy."

"Well," I huffed, "I didn't shoot her, so there's no point wasting time arguing about what we could have done."

"You can still kill her," Lutz told me.

"I don't work like that." Not anymore, I didn't add.

"Bullshit!" Lutz jumped to his feet and marched toward me. "I know what you did down in Mexico."

"You don't know shit," I told him. Outside of me, the Camacho Brothers, maybe a handful of other guys who had no reason to talk, and a whole bunch of people who'd never open their eyes or breathe again, nobody knew what I'd done down there. "Rumors."

"*Oscuridad*," Lutz pushed. "*Oxido Negro*."

"The Darkness?" Ricardo asked, interpreting the Spanish.

"The Blackness," Lutz crowed. "Black Rust."

"What does that even mean?" Ricardo asked.

Lutz glared at me. "Why don't you tell him?"

"It doesn't mean anything," I told him. "It's stupid Mexican boogeyman bullshit. It has nothing to do with me."

"The Camacho brothers?" Lutz threw that one out and stood triumphantly in the center of the room. It was his trump card, one I hadn't known he was holding.

"What does this have to do with the Camachos?" Ricardo asked, warily. It was hard to run the most powerful cartel in the failed states of Central America and not have a widely known name.

With a hand on one of my pistol butts, I stepped up to Lutz and fixed him with a hard stare. "That's who you think I am, that guy the Camachos are looking for?"

Lutz must have seen the killer in my eyes because his words suddenly had trouble finding their way out of his throat.

Black Rust   115

I stepped in bad breath range and leaned closer. "Answer me, Lutz."

He turned his head and stepped back. "I hear rumors." With a few paces' distance between us, he turned and tried to pump up his confidence again. He looked at Ricardo and pointed at me. "I've seen him kill. Hell, you've seen the videos. You know what he can do. Everyone who's seen that stupid TV show, Bash, knows what he can do." Lutz looked back at me. "You didn't learn that shit in a state school, that's for sure."

"Maybe the military?" Ricardo suggested. "CIA?"

The CIA? That agency didn't officially exist anymore, but everybody believed it was still out there, lurking nefariously in the shadows.

"I checked," Lutz told Ricardo. "He was never in the military. I'll bet that dude, Blix—"

"Blix is a girl," said Ricardo.

"Okay, Blix the girl hacker, could get the answer. She'd dig up the truth about Christian Black, if that's even his real name."

Ricardo looked at me with a little trepidation on his face that hadn't been there before. "Information costs money, Lutz." Ricardo reached over and tapped the bills I'd just laid out to pay Blix for info on Sienna Galloway. "Near as I can tell, you can't afford it."

That was satisfying enough. Ricardo was telling me he wasn't going to get any info about me for Lutz. That didn't mean he wasn't going to dig himself. I didn't know where that might lead but no matter where it led, I felt better keeping Lutz in the dark.

Lutz looked at Ricardo with a silent plea stretching his face, but seeing Ricardo was unreceptive, Lutz gave up. He went back to the couch and dropped his weight on the cushions. Talking for his own benefit, he muttered, "You shoulda killed her. You still can."

With that settled, for the moment anyway, I turned back to the bank of computer monitors.

"He's got a point," said Ricardo.

"I can afford a bribe." I pointed at the screens. "Where are you guys at with the video alteration? Will they get it done on time?"

"The girl's a complication," said Ricardo.

"I know."

"It's more than you know."

One more thing. Always one more thing. I seated myself on the desk again. "Explain it to me."

"One of Lutz's friends, one of the video drone operators has a low-res version up on the web. Terrible quality, very low frame-rate. It's more a series of bad still shots. But it gets the point across. He's teasing his customers and getting some traffic."

"Great." Sarcasm, of course.

"You've brought me the high-res version of his video, so you're probably going to be good in that respect, but if the low-res got through, it's possible portions of the high-res did too. That'll be a problem. Like I said, my guys can doctor all the video, but there's going to end up being a couple versions out there in the world—the doctored version we put together and their version, the original, at least what they have of it. The girl becomes important because she can be a witness who says which one is real."

"Or if she's dead," Lutz called across the room, "there's enough doubt that we can get off."

"Those are the choices," said Ricardo. "But if you plan to kill her, then we need to edit her out of the video altogether. If not, then it'll be too incriminating having the lynchpin witness to a dirty kill video turn up dead. You'll get the death penalty without a doubt. Juries aren't sympathetic when you kill a citizen these days, and they don't care if there's a little doubt in the mix. Houston is a hangin' town."

"Can you do two versions of the video?" I asked. "Both fixed so it looks like Lutz and I were justified—"

Ricardo said, "The raccoons are already altered to look like toddlers."

"—and make one version with the girl and one version without. Shouldn't be that hard, right?"

"That's what everybody says about work they don't understand—*it can't be hard.*"

I didn't want to have to, but I reached into my pocket, took out my cash, counted out another twenty thousand and slapped it on the table to make it clear there'd be no more negotiations. "Two versions."

Lutz got off the couch and came over. "You might kill her then."

"I need to keep my options open." That was my straight-up honest answer. If putting a bullet in apparently innocent Sienna Galloway's head was the only way to keep myself out of a work camp for twenty years—who's to say what I'd do?

Chapter 24

Sienna Galloway punched the code into the lock on the gate and let herself through the chain-link fence into the residence compound. After a harrowing night, she was home. Making sure the gate closed behind her, she felt relief. With her phone broken, she didn't know the time exactly, just that it was still early with the sky now turning from gray to blue.

She looked across the dew-covered grass on the slope up to the first of three rows of widely spaced cabins. Sienna's was fourth from the end in the first line of fourteen, all matched. Hers, like all the others, was not large—one room that served as bedroom, living room, and kitchenette. Of course, each had a bathroom separate from the rest of the small house, an adequate front porch, and a decent-sized back patio with a view down the slope, over cultivated fields, and across the more distant forests.

In those first months after she'd arrived on Blue Bean Farms, she'd spent her evenings sitting on her porch, drinking wine with her new coworkers, thinking they were turning into friends. It was a little more than a year ago, and for a time, she felt like she'd discovered an anachronistic oasis, a world apart from the slowly collapsing cities.

But time has a way of eroding illusions from repugnant realities.

By the time Sienna had been in her job six months, doing exactly what she thought she'd been hired to do and meeting nothing but resistance, she'd irritated or pissed off every one of her neighbors, not to mention dozens of others around the company. She was making Blue Bean a better workplace for everyone. They thought she was trying to drive Blue Bean out of business, put them out of their jobs, chase them out of their peaceful little bungalows and force them to go back to the dirty cities to dodge d-gen riots and scrape by with all the other unlucky shmucks.

Dinner invites ceased.

Drinking on the patio turned into a solitary activity of mixing despondence with alcohol to try and blur away the hateful stares from her neighbors.

She crossed the jogging path that ran just inside the fence and saw a pair of runners far down to her right, moving away. They were too far off to identify, but it didn't matter. In fact, it was preferable. Too many of her good morning greetings had been returned with, "Why don't you just quit, cunt?"

Outside of necessary work communication, she barely spoke to anyone anymore.

Rather than follow the path along the fence, she started up the hill, toward the houses across the grass. Her jeans were streaked with dirt, and her shoes were caked with mud. Her shirt was ripped in two places where it had gotten hung up on broken branches as she ran through the woods. She was scraped, and her hair was a fright. She was afraid of what she might see when she looked in the mirror—a suburban d-gen, with no concept of hygiene. And it brought memories of a childhood nightmare that still haunted her on occasion, that of waking one morning to find that she'd lost her humanity to Brisbane's prion disease.

It was a lurking hazard nobody talked about, but everybody feared.

But she was inside the fence now. It didn't feel quite secure anymore, yet it was safer than being shot at in the woods by rogue Regulators.

Sienna passed her back porch, but she had no key to her back door. She'd been assured on countless occasions that a maintenance man would come soon to rekey her locks to match. The more word of her complaints about Blue Bean got around, the less pretend-friendly those reassurances became.

So she fished the front door key out of her bag and crossed between her house and the one next door. At the front corner of her house, she stepped between two bushes to come onto the side of the front porch. She was tired and looking for the shortest path to her front door and then to a shower.

"Christ on a cricket, girl! Where you bin?" asked a shadowy man from where he sat in the dark morning shadows in a chair on her front porch.

Sienna stumbled off the porch, coming down between the bushes.

A man in a plaid western shirt with cut-off sleeves stood up from the chair. The side brims of his straw cowboy hat were scrunched flat against the top, giving the Stetson the look of a ratty canoe upside down on his head. A long-barreled revolver hung in a leather holster on the man's hip. He held a sheath of papers folded in one hand. Sienna didn't need to see his amateur tattoos and bad teeth in the shadows to know it was Goose Eckenhausen.

"Where you bin?" he asked, in his East Texas accent.

Sienna didn't step back onto the porch. She wanted to stay out of Goose's reach. "What are you doing in the residence compound?"

"Ah asked you a question," he persisted.

Sienna took a step back onto the lawn. If Goose made a move, she could run in either direction. She could scream.

Over forty Blue Bean employees—professionals just like her—lived in the residence compound. They would come to their doors if a woman screamed. The most hateful of them might turn away when they saw it was her, but rather than pin her hopes solely on the goodwill of others, Sienna knew most of the women despised Goose more than they detested her.

Goose Eckenhausen was a trustee in the work camp interlinked with Blue Bean Farms. He was a lifer, a serial rapist who'd brutalized victims every time he'd been given a chance at freedom outside the penal system. And it wasn't d-gen women who tickled his fancy, it was normal girls with fully functioning intellects who had the capacity to understand what it was Goose was doing to them.

Sienna tried to mask the quake in her voice with a full measure of authority. "Trustees aren't allowed in the administrative compound."

"There's what you think ya know, and there's how it is." Goose showed off his ragged smile. "Unfortunately, fer you, Boss Man makes the rules. Ah go where Ah need to go. Ah do whut Ah need to do. Now tell me, where you bin ta git all a mess like 'at?"

"You get off my porch." Sienna fished in her bag for her pepper spray. She found it, raised it, and pointed it at Goose.

Goose cocked his head to the side, and he rested a hand on the butt of the gun on his hip. "You got ah meetin' at eighth-thirty with Boss Man and the 'spector." He meant the State Inspector. "Boss Man sent me to make sure ya got these papers signed and to remind you to git to that meetin' on time."

Getting to the meeting with the State Inspector was why she'd tried so hard to get all the way back, despite having followed the degenerates so far on foot the evening before. "What time is it?"

"Told you. Eight-thirty."

"No. What time is it right now?"

"Don't you know?"

"My phone broke."

Goose shrugged. "'bout seven-thirty. Get a replacement phone from Irene before the meetin'."

"I'll be at the meeting." She pointed toward the compound's main gate. Most of the administrative buildings were generously spread over several acres outside the main gate, just a ten- or fifteen-minute walk from her front door. "I don't need a reminder from you to get there and I'll sign the papers when I deem it necessary for me to do so."

"Yeah, well, that's just it. Boss Man thinks maybe since you ain't turned in yer papers for the Bloodmobile, the State 'spector won't be able to put them bad d-gens down."

"They don't need to be put down," Sienna snapped. "They're not bad."

"Says you. But that ain't the way it's gonna be. You can pretend all you want that they gonna wake up one mornin' and start learnin' how to do farm work again, but the Boss Man, he ain't got time, patience, or money to waste on d-gens that's too brain-rotted to stop shittin' in their pants. He ain't feedin' 'em for doin' nothin'."

It was exactly the point that made Sienna angry. "You can't put down degenerates just because they aren't as productive as they once were. That's the law."

"Oh now," Goose smiled falsely as he took a step toward Sienna.

Sienna took another step back and brandished her pepper spray.

Goose leaned against the wall. "I seen 'em myself. Ever' one ah them I put on that list fer you was violent. They was mean. They was hurtin' other d-gens."

"I took every one you listed out of the working population and put them in the training compound," Sienna argued. "My people haven't witnessed any violent behavior."

"Just cuz you ain't seen it don't mean it didn't happen. They all got three strikes. My guys seen it. Them d-gens is all defects. They all need to be on the kill list." Goose leaned forward and his false smile instantly disappeared, and his eyes looked as hollow as a shark's. He waved the papers. "Yer signin' this mornin', fer every name." He stood up straight and smiled through his bad teeth. He turned and walked down the length of the porch to the front steps. "Ah'll wait out here fer ya. You take yer shower, but yer gonna sign before you go to that meetin'."

Chapter 25

I sat in the passenger seat as Lutz drove the Mercedes down another dirt road illuminated in the morning's slanted light. He'd complained through the first half hour of the drive out of town but had run out of steam when he realized I wasn't going to argue with him. We both needed sleep. Griping about how tired we were wasn't going to magically make time for us to get some.

We'd gone to a lot of trouble, and I'd spent a lot of money to get our asses out of a sling. The video alterations were on track to finish up a little later in the morning. Ricardo would soon know how much of the low-res and high-res video of our crime had made it back to the world. Ricardo was hooking me up with an attorney he was acquainted with. Damn, I was putting a lot of faith in Ricardo, a man I'd known for less than twelve hours.

I decided that didn't bother me. If Ricardo chose to screw me, I'd get myself out of whatever mess he put me in, and I'd teach him a lesson in regret. I had a lot of experience helping people learn that lesson.

After a long night of crossing items off a seemingly impossible do-list, all I had left was to find Sienna Galloway and convince her to tell a lie. I'd help her to see that it was her best choice. With her statement to corroborate our version of the video, the Sanction ID would be assigned retroactively, the police would rescind the warrant, and Lutz and I would avoid a work camp.

Back to business.

At least that was our thinking. Maybe the attorney would tell me different. Maybe he'd say everything we'd done was overkill. Maybe he'd say it was wasted effort as a warrant was tantamount to a conviction and that running had been my only option all along. Well, that or a work camp.

Lutz stopped the SUV, skidding the wheels on the dirt road to make some kind of statement that was important to him. He squinted at the bright blue sky through the windshield as he tried to get a view above. "You see the drone up there yet?"

I thought it was pretty obvious I wasn't looking, but I understood Lutz's meaning. I took a glance up through my side window then out through the windshield. "Ricardo said he'd fly it pretty high. We might not spot it." I took the phone out of my pocket. We were well out of cell phone range, but if I could pick up the Wifi signal generated by Ricardo's spotter drone, I'd know it was near.

Lutz copied my action and took out the replacement phone I'd purchased for him. He turned it on and stared at the screen.

Mine didn't show a signal. I got out of the car and looked up.

"I got nothing," he told me. "Not a damn thing."

"Ricardo told us that was a risk." I scanned the sky for the white disk. "When it's high, the signal will be too weak for us to pick up."

Lutz turned off the engine and got out of the car. "Or he's not here yet."

"He has drones in the area," I told him. "One should have beaten us here. Don't you listen?"

"I listen." Lutz shielded his eyes from the morning sun and looked east.

I reminded him anyway, "Ricardo can't legally fly his drones over Blue Bean property. They'll shoot 'em down, and they're within their rights to do it. Ricardo's got to stay up out of shotgun range. He'll drop down from time to time to download some overhead pictures. That's the plan."

Lutz looked up the road. "How far do you think we've got to go?"

I looked back down in the direction from which we'd come. "What do you think? We've been on this road for what, maybe nine or ten miles?"

Lutz shrugged.

"Another half mile." I pointed up the narrow cut. "There's a crossroad. That's all Blue Bean property north of the road. I pointed at the trees to the left. "There's a creek in the woods a few hundred yards over there. That's the boundary for their property."

"Every time we come out here you act like you know where all the property lines are."

"I do," I told him. "When we have a job out here by one of these farms, I like to know where the lines are I can't cross. We're not allowed to kill on their property, and they like to shoot at trespassers like us."

"All these corporate farms are the same way." Lutz looked back up the road. "We turn left at the T-intersection?"

"Yeah."

"Then it's what, five or six miles, trespassing with the risk of being shot the whole way?"

"Ricardo said Sienna Galloway's house is up there in a residence compound by all the admin buildings."

"She must be pretty important," said Lutz. "Otherwise, she'd be out at one of the satellite compounds and not stuck in the middle of the whole goddamn place."

"It's not the middle. That would be another twenty miles in. The admin compound is pretty close to the eastern edge of the property." I thought I saw something move up in the sky, and I looked hard to try and see it again.

"What?" asked Lutz. "You see it?"

I pointed into the sky above the road, pretty high up. "There."

"Is that Ricardo's?"

I activated my phone again and stepped out in front of the truck as though the extra ten feet might help improve the signal.

"Is he coming this way?" asked Lutz.

I looked up again and then looked back down at my phone—it had to be Ricardo's drone. At least I hoped it was, real hard. If it were somebody else's, they'd likely be aware of the warrant out for me. And any spotter drone pilot who did his homework would know Lutz was my partner, and they'd know Lutz drove an old boxy black Mercedes.

Lutz stepped up beside me, eyes fixed on the drone. "You got a signal yet? Is it Ricardo?"

Chapter 26

Sienna turned the shower off and dried herself with a towel as she looked at the bruises and scrapes on her skin that had been hidden by the dirt. She'd been reckless running through that cornfield and the woods to get away from the rogue Regulators who killed the farm workers—the degenerates she'd been informally studying.

Sure they were all mentally diminished by the Brisbane virus and its prion surprise, but they'd still been capable of working productively on Blue Bean's farm and they had enough depth of thought to imagine a life outside of the present, even to speculate about what might wait for them beyond death. Those dead degenerates, like other groups she'd read about in scientific journals, had formed a rudimentary belief system complete with a crude temple and simple rituals.

Only a tiny, tiny percentage of d-gens did this, but just like fully functional humans, these relatively few degenerates gravitated toward religion.

And those bastard Regulators had killed them for it.

They'd almost killed her too, but for some reason, no bullet found her.

Now, what was she to do? Report the Regulators? Admit she'd been out in the woods, breaking company policy by observing farm workers doing things they were forbidden to do during a time when the rules mandated they be in their barracks?

Such an admission would mean she'd be fired at least. Given the depth of management's animosity toward her, she'd probably get the blame for the deaths. They'd say she'd led the degenerates out there, that she'd put them in danger. The company would hold her financially responsible for the loss.

And what could she do about it?

She could hardly claim she'd come upon the group by accident. She would have had to follow them miles to the site of their ceremonies out in the woods.

And even to do that, she'd had to win their confidence over the course of months, keeping company with them outside of the normal work routine. She'd befriended them. She had feelings for them.

Goddammit! Degenerates are people.

Maybe not all of them, but some were.

Sienna didn't understand how seemingly good people could flip some switch in their brains that turned off empathy when it came to degenerates.

The group she was studying in her free time didn't live in the same barracks. They were spread across seven buildings, males and females. They never all worked together on tasks. They didn't eat together. Yet they'd somehow recognized one another for what they were—not normal humans, but not regular degenerates either. They communicated in a language of simple syllables and gestures and formed a community that depended on their ability to share simple ideas and coordinate actions.

Sienna didn't understand the nuances of the language. It was speculated that it spread in the state schools, devolved from whatever human language skills they learned before Brisbane's prions did the worst of its damage to their brains. With the leftovers, these few were able to communicate effectively enough to sneak out of their barracks at the same time and meet at a remote location in the woods.

The group had been fascinating. Watching them was like looking through a time machine window to see prehistoric humans invent culture.

There was so much to be learned.

They'd been her only reason for remaining at Blue Bean Farms, the one thing still worth doing.

Now they were all dead.

Having toweled her body as dry as she was likely to get in the steamy bathroom, Sienna wrapped the towel around herself, tucked in the top edge to form something of a dress, and reached for a comb to run through her hair as she opened the bathroom door.

A guttural chuckle frightened her into stopping.

She screamed as she saw a hulking bruiser of a man, standing droop-shouldered by the wall, staring at her.

"Hush!" Goose Eckenhausen ordered.

Sienna stepped back into the bathroom and reached to shut the door.

Goose jumped over to stop the door with a foot as he grabbed her by the wrist. "You settle down, honey."

Sienna's eyes burned with fire as she spat, "If you and your friend don't leave right now I'll—"

"He ain't my friend," Goose laughed, letting go of Sienna's wrist. "That's Toby. He's my Bully Boy. Just got 'im a coupla weeks ago. Used to be in the Army. Did some fightin' down in Columbia or some such shit. He's a war hero."

Drool ran down Toby's chin as he leered at Sienna.

"You get your friend Toby and get out of my—"

"Nope." Goose stepped in close to Sienna. "Mr. Workman wants them papers signed."

"I told you—"

Goose put one of his dirty fingers on Sienna's lips. "Don't say nuthin'. You been refusin' to sign yer paperwork and Boss Man is tired of listenin'. We talked 'bout this on the porch." Goose looked over at his Bully Boy. "What do you think, Toby? You think maybe Dr. Galloway needs to stop protestin' and do what she gets paid to do?"

Sienna jerked her wrist out of Goose's hand. "Mr. Workman will hear about this."

"Why would ya think he don't already know?" Goose pointed at some papers spread out on Sienna's small dining table. "Sign 'em."

Sienna hated Goose so much she could taste it. She looked at the papers. Those papers, if she signed them, would put over a hundred debilitated farm workers in the queue for extermination. And it would happen today.

"Ya know," said Goose. "Toby's got needs if ya know what I mean. I don't think they let him, you know, get any satisfaction when he was in the Army. You see the way he's lookin' at you standin' there in that towel." Goose took a step back to make it clear he wasn't going to be in the way should Toby decide he couldn't control his urges. "Toby's a big boy. Not sure I could do nuthin' to stop him should he decide you were too purdy not to have a go."

"You're going to let your goon rape me if I don't sign those papers?" Sienna wished more than anything she had a gun to shoot them both. "Is that it?"

"I ain't doin' nothin' of the sort." Goose feigned innocence. "I'm just tellin' you we're stayin' 'til you sign them papers. If it takes a long time for you to git 'round to it, well, so be it. I'm just sayin' I can't be responsible for keeping a handle on old Toby boy with you struttin' your purdy stuff 'round in that towel. That's all."

"You're a pig."

"No, I'm a goose."

Frustrated and angry, Sienna wanted to scream her rage. But she was afraid of what Toby and Goose might do. Looking at Toby's dead eyes and drooling mouth, she feared a lot worse than rape.

She looked at the papers. She had no choice, at least not in the moment, but she had every intention of fighting this once she got to the meeting with Mr. Workman and the State Inspector. She cut a glance at Toby and then focused on Goose. "You tell him to wait outside, and I'll sign the papers."

"Sorry, can't."

"Why not?"

"Can't let him outa my sight," said Goose. "Rules."

"Bullshit. He wasn't with you when you were on the porch. How'd he get here?"

"He was on your neighbor's porch. Right behind you the whole time we was talkin'. You just didn't see 'im."

Was that true? Had the steroid giant really been there? A shiver ran up her spine.

She took one more glance at the oaf and pushed her way past Goose as she gripped the top edge of her towel to keep it in place.

She bent over and shuffled through the papers. "What's this?"

"What you askin?"

"There are at least a hundred more names here."

"More defects," Goose told her. "You want I should step outside while you and Toby talk about it?"

She hated Goose Eckenhausen more than ever.

She scrawled a fast, angry signature on each page, pushing so hard the paper tore beneath the pen. Once done, she scooped up the papers and shoved them at Goose. "There. May I get dressed now?"

Goose stepped back and looked her up and down.

Sienna suspected that was the same look all of his rape victims had seen.

"You sure are a purdy one."

"Get out of my house," she ordered. "Get out. I gave you what you came for. Leave."

Goose smiled and nodded as he let his eyes linger on her visible bare skin. "C'mon Toby. Let's go." To Sienna, he said, "We'll be outside waitin' for ya."

It was against the rules, but Sienna decided in that moment she was going to buy a gun. She'd never again be on Blue Bean property unarmed.

Chapter 27

"I got the signal." I looked up and scanned the sky that I was able to see between the tall pines on both sides of the road. I spotted the drone, nearly a hundred feet up, directly overhead. I pointed.

"How'd it get there?" Lutz asked.

The spotter drones were harder to see than it seemed like they should be. With the Wifi connection established between Ricardo's drone and my phone, messages started to pop up. I read and summarized as I went. "The road is clear. Two turns. We take the left turn twice. Should get us within a mile or so."

"Nobody out there?" Lutz asked. "Nobody to catch us?"

"I'm reading," I told him. "I don't know yet."

"So what's the plan, then? I drop you off. You do your shit, and I drive you back out again?"

"Yeah," I told him. "You stay with the car." I read more. "Shit."

"What?" Lutz asked, panic rising in his voice as he looked around. "Did Ricardo see something?"

"We're safe for the moment."

"What then?"

"Buzz bikes."

"Army?" Lutz asked. "What are they doing here?"

I shook my head.

"Police? Already?"

"Ricardo says maybe police. Maybe private. Too far away. He can't tell."

"Private?" Lutz scoffed. "Not likely."

"If the Army or the police are surplusing them out, Blue Bean would probably be able to buy them," I speculated. "They've got the money."

I'd seen plenty of cops riding the things, hovering over the streets, avoiding all the crap in the roads, zipping across the suburbs at eighty miles an hour. That's how fast I'd heard the cop versions flew. People said the military versions could carry up to five hundred pounds and hit a hundred and ten.

The buzz bikes, or hover bikes, were a natural evolution of drone technology. Four ducted fans—two in front, two in back—engines powerful enough to get a man off the ground and software built in to keep the things stable. I hated them because I'd heard about all their shortcomings, but now with the possibility of them being available in the private sector, my jealousy turned practical. I looked at Lutz. "Sell the Mercedes. We need to get our hands on a couple of those things."

Lutz shook his head. "No way."

"Think of it," I said. "No more roads. No more obstacles. No more having to reroute to get around a riot and missing our sanction. How many times has that happened? Once a month at least. Hell, forget that. We'd get to our sanctions quicker every time. I bet we'd get twice as many kills."

"No," said Lutz. "We can't afford them."

"You don't even know what they cost."

"We just spent five thousand on a goddamn spotter drone," Lutz spat as if it had been his money I'd laid on Ricardo's desk. "I'll bet you'd spend fifty or sixty on one of those, at least."

"It'd pay for itself in a few months," I argued.

"Not if we're in Mexico."

"Christ, Lutz. Are you back on the Mexico thing?"

Lutz pointed down the dirt road. "Buzz bikes. You said it yourself. There's no way they won't see us."

"They're not up there for security," I told him. "It's not like we're trying to sneak on to an Army base. Maybe they're private. Maybe Blue Bean uses them to wrangle stray d-gens. They're not going to be looking for a Mercedes on a dirt road minding its own business."

"They'll see us."

"What if they do?" I asked. "How big is this place? How many people work here? Normal people, I mean. Several hundred, you think? A thousand?"

"Don't know."

"How many does it take to manage all those d-gens?"

"The work camp prisoners manage the d-gens," said Lutz. "That's the way the work camps function."

"But there are employees too, right? Like Sienna Galloway. They've got their own cars. Everybody working this far out from town has to have a car."

"What's your point?" Lutz spat.

"Those guys riding the hover bikes can't know every car owned by every employee. That's all I'm saying. We just drive on in like we belong there, and it won't be a big deal. Like I said, this isn't exactly Fort Knox. It's a corporate farm spread over three counties. Hell, you could probably shoot Roman candles off from the top of your Mercedes and drive through in the middle of the night, and nobody would ever notice. That's how big this place is."

"I doubt that."

"That's because you have a cloudy disposition. Lighten up and smile for a change."

Lutz looked at me like I was screwing with him.

Black Rust   137

I was.

I walked to the passenger door and got in. Lutz followed my lead and got into the driver's side as he started the engine with an exaggerated sigh. "I don't like this."

"Drive," I told him, as I went back to reading the messages from Ricardo.

The Mercedes started to roll. Lutz said, "I'll keep it under twenty so Ricardo's drone can keep up."

"He's not coming."

"What?"

"The hover bikes," I told him. "Ricardo thinks those bikes can take out his drone?"

"Can they?"

I shrugged. Military bikes might be armed, but not the cop bikes. They didn't have the payload for that.

"So we're going in blind?" Lutz asked.

"We know what's ahead of us." A long, narrow country road. We were at least five miles from the nearest cultivated field.

"This is bullshit."

Chapter 28

In a country accent, Irene said, "Hey Goose, how're you this morning?"

With Toby breathing too close behind her, Sienna followed Goose through the building's glass doors, glaring at the receptionist, a plump hag with a syrupy voice and dull mind. She presided over the sterile lobby of Blue Bean's central administrative building.

"How you doin', Irene?" Goose stepped up to the receptionist counter and leaned his elbows on the polished granite. "Got some papers here for the Boss Man."

Irene glanced toward a door at the back of the lobby. "Mr. Workman is in the small conference room with the State Inspector." She reached out for the death orders Sienna had signed. "I can give these to him when he finishes."

"Sure," said Goose, passing the papers to Irene. "Before his eight-thirty meeting."

"Of course." Irene took the papers, took her flirty eyes off Goose, and turned them cold for Sienna. "Your meetin's in the executive conference room." She pointed at a door across the lobby as though Sienna didn't know where the room was.

Sienna stepped up to the counter. "I need to speak to Mr. Workman before the meeting."

Irene turned and made a show of looking at a big clock on the wall behind her. "I'll tell him, but I doubt he'll have time."

Sienna held firm. "It's important."

"You run along and take a seat in the conference room." Irene pointed again. "I'll let him know." She turned her doe eyes and coffee-stained smile back at Goose.

It was puke-worthy. Irene knew Goose was a lifer. She had to know what he was in for. Still, she seemed to want little more than to drag him beneath her cloying sheets to entertain him between her lumpy thighs.

"I need to run," Goose told Irene before exaggerating a wink. "You make sure Boss Man gets those." He gave Sienna a glance and a snort. "I gotta get all them defects to the Bloodmobile. Shoulda been done yesterday but somebody got lazy 'bout signin' their paperwork."

Sienna didn't rise to the taunt, satisfying herself instead to see Goose head for the door with his drooling Bully Boy in tow.

"The conference room," Irene reminded Sienna before turning her attention to some papers on her desk. "Coffee and pastries inside."

Chapter 29

"Did you see that?" Lutz asked, pointing into the sky above the road.

"No." I looked up from the map on my phone.

"Hover bike. I think it was a cop."

"Ricardo said they were Blue Bean's buzz bikes."

"Looked like a cop bike to me."

"By himself?" I asked as I stared at the narrow strip of sky I was able to see between the trees that bordered the road in front of us. "Just one?"

Lutz took his foot off the accelerator as he craned his neck to look above us through the windshield.

"Keep going," I told him. "We need to get to Sienna Galloway."

"If that was a cop up there, you're not going to be seeing anybody."

"Speed up," I told him. "If the guy on the hover bike saw you, going slower isn't going to help anything."

Lutz shook his head but pushed his foot on the accelerator anyway. "I can't get caught with you."

"You can say you didn't know there was a warrant," I told him, guessing the root of his worry. "It isn't even twelve hours old."

"How are we going to explain being on Blue Bean property?"

"Lie." I laughed. "Say we got lost. It's not hard. No road signs. All these dirt roads look alike. Besides, we're not on their property yet."

We were racing along over fifty, and the Mercedes was bouncing and rattling everything around in the back not strapped down. Thankfully, the dirt was moist in the shade of the trees, and we weren't throwing up a dust plume. That would be a hard thing to miss from above.

"What do I do at the turn coming up?" Lutz asked.

"Left," I told him.

"You sure?"

"Yeah."

A dark streak crossed over the road above the trees ahead of us.

"You see that?" Lutz shouted.

I did.

"Cop bike?" he asked, making no effort to hide his anxiety.

"Looked like a cop bike to me," I agreed. "But it was moving too fast to tell."

"It was a cop bike." Lutz looked around at the trees. "The kill site isn't far from here, I bet. Maybe ten miles that way."

Lutz was wrong about that. By my guess, we were three or four miles away. "What are you getting at? Why's that important?"

"Maybe they're investigating. Maybe they're out here looking for us."

That was possible.

Chapter 30

Sienna was tempted to lean across the wide table and slap the jelly-filled donut out of Mike Rafferty's mouth. "The Mobile Retirement Unit is here, on the property. Today."

"I know," Mike mumbled through the sugary mush filling his cheeks. "We brought it in with us."

"That's not the point." Sienna crossed her arms and clenched her jaw. She glanced at the closed conference room door and then turned back to the State Inspector's assistant. "You've been telling me for months that we can't do anything right now. *When* can we do something? Blue Bean is murdering degenerates the moment their productivity slips so they can get an allocation of fresh ones out of next month's class from the state school."

"Kill and fill." Mike swallowed the rest of what was in his mouth as he lifted the donut for another bite. "Everybody does it. Impossible to prove."

"It's illegal." Sienna didn't yell it, but she'd wanted to. "They all get away with it because they're all a bunch of inbred cousins running the corporate farms out here. They collude to make sure they put similar percentages on the kill list every month, so nobody looks like they're sending too many, so nobody looks like they're guilty."

"Or nobody is doing anything illegal, and the similar stats prove it." More donut into the mouth.

"That's bullshit, and you know it."

"I know what you keep telling me." Mike tried to stuff more on top of what he was already chewing.

"Don't," Sienna told him.

Mike looked at the donut. "Blue Bean makes a lot of money. You might be used to getting donuts. But me, on a state salary, you know how often I eat anything but grits for breakfast?"

"I don't care about the damn donuts and grits!" Sienna realized she was starting to yell, and she made an effort to bring her voice back down to a conversational level, or at least one that Irene out in the lobby wouldn't hear through the door. "You know how many you're going to run through the Bloodmobile today?"

"The Mobile Retirement Unit," Mike corrected. "The Inspector doesn't like it when people call it the Bloodmobile."

"It's better than Murder Wagon," Sienna spat. "That's what it is, isn't it?"

Mortified, Mike said, "Don't call it that in front of him or you'll never get his help."

"Why do I have to be nice to him to get him to do his job?" Sienna shook her head in disgust. "I should go to the media."

"You can't," said Mike. "I told you that. Not with what you have. At least not with what you've shown me. It's not proof."

"I'm the one who certifies degenerates for retirement." Sienna felt dirty just for using that word. *Retirement* was a euphemism for euthanasia. Hell, what they were doing wasn't even euthanasia. It was slaughter.

"The Mobile Retirement Unit only retires defective degenerates — the violent ones — on the list you've signed."

"I've told you before," said Sienna, "They've been lying to me about violence and cannibalism. Ninety percent of the retirees they ask me to sign for aren't guilty. They lose their training because of the progression of the encephalopathy. Ongoing training makes them more expensive to keep around. That's why Blue Bean and every other farm in the area lies and sends them to the Bloodmobile for you to slaughter."

Mike glared at Sienna, taunting her by stuffing half a cream-filled donut in his mouth and speaking through the mush. "Mobile Retirement Unit."

Sienna bit back her anger. She'd had hope when she'd first contacted Mike, but not because he had any love for the degenerates. Like her, she thought he recognized the degenerates had a right to life if they could still fill a productive roll. She thought Mike held the same view. "Last time we talked, you told me to get proof. Well, I did that. I sequestered every degenerate in the training compound and my staff scrupulously observed them for days. We didn't witness one single savage act. Not one."

"That doesn't prove anything," said Mike. "You can't know they weren't violent before they were put on your list."

"Exactly," said Sienna. "How am I supposed to prove something didn't happen? Goose Eckenhausen is Mr. Workman's gopher boy, and his trustees will say anything he tells them to say. They all lie."

Punctuating each slow word, Mike told her, "You have to have *proof* they lied."

"I'm going after the Inspector when he comes in here." Sienna was tired of having the same discussion over and over and over again with Mike. "I'm tired of asking you and nothing happens. I'm tired of him looking the other way. My proof might not hold up in court, but if I put this out on the Internet for the whole world to see, enough people will care, Mike. Because whether you like it or not, whether all of the inbred hillbillies running these farms believe it, mankind will perish from the face of this earth if we kill too many degenerates. Plenty of us still understand that. We need the degenerates to sustain the species. The Inspector better come around. I'm not making threats. He needs to do his job, or I'm calling him out in public along with Keith Workman and all the others."

"Don't," Mike warned.

"As soon as he comes in here," she said, "you'll see."

"You'll regret it if you do," said Mike. "You know he and Workman go back a long way. They were in the Army together back in the day. Inspector Doggett won't side with you." Mike put his donut on the table and leaned forward. He was serious. "He'll see you fry."

"What about an investigation?" Sienna pointedly asked. "You keep telling me you're going to tell the proper authorities to come here and do a real investigation."

"These things take time," said Mike. "You have to trust me on this. This isn't easy. I have to be careful who I talk to."

"No," Sienna nearly shouted. A long night, two dozen killed right in front of her, threats in her own house, had pushed her past her ability to control her frustrations. "Another two hundred degenerates are going to die today with my signature on the paper and all they need is to be retrained. I've got that on my conscience, Mike. I'm tired of the guilt. I'm tired of trying and getting nothing done to save them. If Inspector Doggett won't do something, I'm going to the media and telling them everything I know."

"Whatever you do, don't do that." Mike was nearly pleading when he said, "Blue Bean is a powerful company."

They both ran out of things to say and they sat in silence. Sienna stared at the table. Mike fidgeted with the remnants of a pastry until he said, "You know what the most popular show on TV is right now?"

Sienna didn't look up. "I don't watch TV."

"Bash."

Sienna shrugged. Despondently she asked, "What's Bash?"

"Reality crap. They show video from spotter drones and voyeur drones of the funniest sanctioned kills they can find each week."

"The funniest?" Sienna didn't believe it. "It's not funny when anything dies."

"They run it to music. They run it fast-forward and in reverse. They add graphics. The hosts of the show make snide comments."

"That's sick."

"Most people find it very funny."

Sienna shook her head and stared out the windows on the back wall of the conference room. She should have quit a long time ago, as soon as she'd suspected what was happening. But the money had been good. Mr. Workman's lies and promises were still believable when she tried hard enough. She'd thought he was a good man managing bad people.

And Goose Eckenhausen was Workman's right-hand man when it came to dealing with the trustees and other prisoners. As unthinkable as it was, he was Workman's foreman, Keith Workman's dog. If Workman could keep a predator like that on a leash and not recognize — or not care — what he was, then Keith Workman wasn't worth any faith she'd put in him.

Chapter 31

The conference room door opened, catching Sienna's attention, and freezing Mike Rafferty's jaws mid-bite. Sienna recovered quickly, just as a blob of purple jelly dripped off Rafferty's lip.

Sienna pushed her chair back and jumped to her feet.

Inspector Doggett stopped in the doorway, startled at Sienna's sudden animation.

Sienna saw the sheath of papers in Doggett's hand, the kill list Goose Eckenhausen had forced her to sign. She looked up at Doggett's wide eyes. She pointed through the door. "I need to speak with Mr. Workman."

Doggett made an indecipherable sound as he stepped aside, allowing Sienna to rush past him, out of the conference room and into the lobby.

Once past Doggett, Sienna spotted her boss—a tall, wide-shouldered man with a thick wave of silver hair on a melon-sized head, steering his big round gut toward Irene's desk. He wore cowboy boots made from the leathered hide of some animal so exotic and expensive its identity couldn't be guessed. His jeans were ironed with a crease and he wore a linen shirt starched stiffly enough that one couldn't help but guess he had the means to afford domestic help that tended his laundry. He wore a gaudy gold watch and ridiculously large gold rings. His appearance told anyone who saw him that he was a man who never lost at anything.

Irene stood up, leaned over the counter, and softly spoke to Workman while looking at Sienna.

Workman's face turned to a frown.

Trouble. Sienna turned back to Doggett, smiled sweetly—she hated having to kowtow with false niceties—and said, "We'll be there in a moment. Go on in." She turned back to her boss.

Workman looked Sienna up and down as he put his smile in politician mode. "Dr. Galloway, what's got you running outta there like a wet cat?"

Sienna ignored Workman's good-ole-boy bullshit as she marched up to him and pointed at the door to the small conference room. "May I have a moment of your time before our meeting with Inspector Doggett starts?"

Workman looked up at the clock on the wall over Irene's chair. Turning back to Sienna, he said, "We're already late, little lady."

Yeah, because you and Doggett were in the other room reminiscing about drunk girls you banged back in your Army days. "It'll just take a moment."

"If it's just a moment," said Workman, reinforcing his grin and nodding to encourage the answer he wanted, "just tell me right here." He glanced over at Irene. "We're all family. We've got no secrets."

Total crap.

Sienna chose her words carefully, "The retirement list, I need to get it back from Inspector Doggett. I'd like to make some revisions."

Workman's smile disappeared instantly. "I've been asking for that list all week long. You were supposed to have it to me on Monday."

"I know," said Sienna. "I was running tests on the defects. I wanted to confirm—"

"There's nothing to confirm. Goose's boys witnessed their behavior. That's why they're on the list."

"I—"

"If you had doubts about the degenerates on the list," he said, "you should have taken off the names you weren't sure of."

"I didn't," stuttered Sienna. "I couldn't."

"It's done." Workman took a step toward the conference room.

Sienna put a hand on his arm to stop him.

Workman scowled.

"Mr. Eckenhausen came into the residence compound this morning." Trustees were not allowed in the residence compound. It was an unbreakable rule—or so Workman had told her when she first started. Sienna wrestled with what more to say. Anything she said would get back to Goose through Irene, if not Workman himself. Then what would happen?

"I'm afraid that's *my* fault, Ms. Galloway. I needed that report for Inspector Doggett. I had Goose stop by your residence."

"But—"

"I take full responsibility for him, Dr. Galloway. I know why he's a permanent resident here. He's a little rough around the edges, but you have to admit he's a good man. He works hard for Blue Bean."

A good man?

That knocked Sienna's anger off track.

Goose had threatened to let his drooling Bully Boy rape her in her own kitchen. Mr. Workman needed to know. She only hoped Workman hadn't stooped so low as to order Goose to do what he'd done.

As she opened her mouth to lay her accusations out, the front door swung open, and Goose came hurrying through, his Bully Boy right on his heels.

Chapter 32

"How many are up there?" Lutz asked, frantic as he looked through the windshield.

Our first sighting of the hover bikes could have been coincidence, but they kept showing up in the sky above the road. They were looking for a good place to make an arrest or they were tracking us until reinforcements arrived in wheeled vehicles.

"Watch the road," I told him.

Lutz swerved past a tree that would have put a dead stop to our getaway.

"Three, I think." In the glimpses I'd gotten of hover bikes through the pine boughs overhanging the road, it was hard to tell how many exactly.

"Cops?" Lutz asked. "Can you tell for sure?"

I nodded. I was pretty sure.

The road straightened out in front of us, but it was rough. I said, "Go as fast as you can."

"Cop buzz bikes can do eighty," Lutz bawled. "We can't go that fast on this road."

Calmly, I told him, "Do it. As fast as you can."

"Dammit!" Lutz floored the accelerator and the Mercedes bounced over rocks, holes, and gravel. He wrestled to keep the wheels straight.

I angled the side mirror so I could get a jittery view of the sky above and behind us. After a lag, the hover bikes accelerated over the treetops to keep pace. Through the jostling, I managed to keep my focus on the bikes and got a count. Three. Definitely three. Definitely police. They'd apparently connected me to Lutz and Lutz to the black Mercedes.

Somebody in downtown Houston had a woody for Regulators. What other explanation was there for them to be so far out?

I asked, "How fast are we going?"

"Forty," Lutz answered.

"Give me another twenty if you can."

"On this road?" Lutz glanced at me, his eyes burning with fear. "We'll break an axle."

"Faster."

Lutz hollered something that had no meaning, and the Mercedes lurched to a higher speed.

We careened over a series of rocks, and I hung on tightly as I expected the Mercedes to bounce sideways and roll.

To Lutz's credit, he kept us moving forward.

"Shit," I grinned. "I thought you'd lose it."

Lutz laughed loudly in total-crazy mode. "Seventy. We're gonna die."

Spotting what I'd hoped to see, I pointed.   "See that cluster of old mailbox posts up there?"

"No."

"No worries."   I took another glance at the sky.   "When I tell you to, brake hard and take a sharp right. Don't roll us."

"Are you crazy?" Lutz shouted. "Turn into the trees?"

"There'll be the remains of an old driveway there."

"Just say the—"

"Brake!"

Tires skidded over the rough dirt road bouncing us even more than when they were rolling. I was thrown forward against the seatbelt. Lutz grunted at the deceleration as his seatbelt drove all the air from his lungs.

I pointed at the remains of the mailbox posts and shouted, "There! Turn!"

Lutz cut the wheels, and the Mercedes leaned way over before running down saplings and bushes to get into the trees.

Lutz hollered. "Where's the goddamn road?"

Pointing straight over the hood, I shouted, "Right in front of us. Slow down now. The road's overgrown, keep us moving between the old tree trunks on the sides. Look at the tree trunks—you'll see a corridor that marks the road below."

We moved into the bushes as branches snapped and limbs dragged along the sides and bottom of the SUV.

Lutz hollered, "I don't see shit!"

I kept pointing, "That way, keep it straight. Slower."

Lutz brought us down to twenty as the forest engulfed us. "What the hell are we doing? We can't run from them in this!"

"Cop buzz bikes aren't maneuverable," I told him. "At the speed they were going it'll take them a half mile to slow enough to make a turn to come back and find us."

"Shit!" Lutz grinned. "You're right."

"Keep going this way," I said. "The road angles to the left up here. See?"

"No."

"I'll tell you when to bear left."

"You better," he told me, "because I still don't see what you're talking about."

"We haven't hit a tree big enough to stop us yet."

Lutz looked in the rearview mirror. "Look behind us. Some of the saplings are popping back up straight."

Black Rust

I shrugged. The dense pine canopy overhead would keep us hidden from the hover bikes above. The trail we were leaving wouldn't matter until the cops got a wheeled vehicle after us. We needed to be on Blue Bean property before that. The cops wouldn't chase us there. Probably not. They'd likely let Blue Bean security handle us.

"You know where this leads?" Lutz asked.

My guess was probably nowhere, except deeper into the woods with no way out but the way we'd come. Back when people lived out here, the narrow road through the forest probably led to their houses and nowhere else. "Let's hope we come across another road. Maybe a field we can cut across."

"If we drive into a field they'll see us."

"Yeah," I answered. "But we bought some time with those cops back there. It'll be a while before they figure out where we went into the woods but that will only give them a general direction. They'll have to search randomly from above and hope they get lucky."

Lutz seemed awed. "You're good at this shit, aren't you?"

Of course, I was. "Veer right. Past that big tree."

Chapter 33

"Boss Man," Goose said, out of breath as he came to a stop beside Sienna.

"What is it?" Workman asked. "What's wrong?"

"The police," he went on, pointing through the glass wall on the front of the lobby, "they're out past the eastern edge of the property, investigating that dirty kill from last night."

Sienna took a step back. How did Goose already know about that?

"Yes?" Workman prompted.

Did Workman know as well?

Goose said, "They think the Regulators who did it are here."

"What do you mean?" Workman asked.

"Police called the Warden. Warden Smallwood called me and said the police came across 'em Regulators sneakin' down an old road, headin' for the cotton fields just north of here."

"Why would they go there?" Workman asked.

"Don't know. Police don't know either. They're chasin' 'em now."

Workman rubbed his chin. "Why do you suppose they're still around after what they did?"

Sienna couldn't help but notice the way Workman had asked Goose that question. Workman wasn't looking for speculation, he'd expected Goose to give him something concrete.

"Can't say."   Goose rubbed his chin, too, copying Workman's gesture. "You want I should round up the d-gens and put 'em back in the barracks?"

"Can't see why we'd need to do that," said Workman.

"Warden says the police is askin' whether they should come on the property to chase 'em down."

"Is the Warden going to handle it?" Workman asked.

"Warden and his boys is on one of them huntin' trips they go on or somthin' like that," said Goose. "My boys can handle it if you want. We keep a thousand inmates and thirty thousand d-gens from gittin' out with no help from the Warden and that lazy bunch of his. Ain't no reason we can't keep two dirty Regulators from gittin' in."

"Yes," Workman told Goose, decisively. "Do that. Make it a priority. Whatever it takes. I don't want them disrupting the harvest, you understand?"

"Yessir." Goose glanced over at Sienna, anger clear on his face. "Dependin' on how long this takes, I might not be able to git all them defects out of Dr. Galloway's trainin' compound and put 'em in the pens in the retirement stagin' area today."

Workman turned a pair of icy eyes on Sienna. "If you'd gotten your list approved on time, all the defects would be in their place already."

"But—"

"No buts." Workman leaned forward, towering over her, bumping her with his protruding trophy gut. "I'm clear with my expectations. I always am. I expect my employees to meet them." He looked over at Goose. "You go get your security boys and get this wrapped up. I don't want crooked Regulators on my farm killing the productive degenerates." Turning back to Sienna and drilling her with a hard stare, he said, "We're already at risk of not getting our allocation from the state school. If we don't get our kill done by the end of business tomorrow and present the executed defect list to the clerk, we won't be able to fill our allocation until next month. I don't want to run three hundred workers short for a whole month just because somebody can't stop themselves from hugging violent degenerates who aren't any use to anybody anymore."

Three hundred?

Sienna realized she should have taken a closer look at the list Goose had forced her to sign. He'd added a lot to it.

Chapter 34

I don't know how long we drove—fifteen minutes, thirty —all on overgrown roads under a canopy of pine boughs that blocked the sky. Along the way, I spotted a few houses, a barn, and some pickups, well off the road, abandoned and slowly deteriorating as the forest consumed them.

"You know where we are?" Lutz asked. "We gotta be on Blue Bean property by now."

"Probably not," I told him.

"How's that possible?" he argued. "You said it was right by the road, way back there before we turned left."

"It was. Back there. It's not like Blue Bean is one big square on the map. The property line is up and down, back and forth, all over the place. The road we turned on ran north of the property line for a while. Now I can't say for sure. I looked at the GPS-enabled map on my phone. The road didn't show. As far as the map knew, we were in a dense forest on a goat trail. The nearest marked road was miles away.

"Is there a way out?"

"I think we're near some cleared fields," I told him. "Can't tell if it's old cattle pasture or what. Maybe we can cross if the buzz bikes are gone."

The vegetation ahead of us suddenly seemed to grow thick with vines growing up the trees and hanging off branches, totally blocking the view of anything beyond.

Having caught the spirit of our adventure through the woods, Lutz gunned the engine and rammed the Mercedes through the vines.

We burst into bright sunshine. Lutz instinctively hit the brakes and brought the Mercedes to a skidding halt in a field of well-tended furrows with cotton in rows that ran to the horizon.

And d-gens.

Maybe a hundred. They'd been picking and hauling, but now they were all frozen, staring straight at the big black Mercedes that had burst from the trees.

Lutz muttered, "Oh, shit."

"Reverse," I told him as I took a quick scan of the sky. "Get us back in the trees."

Lutz fumbled with the shifter for a moment, stuck the Mercedes in park, and gunned the engine to no effect.

"C'mon," I told him, holding my voice calm to keep him from panicking.

Lutz found reverse. He looked over his shoulder and spun the wheels as he rolled the Mercedes back through the car-sized tunnel we'd just blown through the curtain of vines. "Where do I turn around?"

"Just keep going backwards." I took a hard look at the d-gens scattered across the field. They weren't the dangerous, feral ones, these were harmless farm workers, trained, sorted, and allocated by the state school. They might turn violent one day, but at the moment, they weren't a worry. Near the d-gens, I spotted a handful of men, all wearing hats, all standing up straight, armed and staring at Lutz and me. Those had to be the trustees. They likely had walkie-talkies or cell phones connected to the Blue Bean private network. They were the danger.

I refocused on the map, looking for an answer there that maybe I'd missed.

Lutz bounced the Mercedes back down the path in reverse. "Anything?"

I shook my head. Lutz was praying for another fortuitously hidden escape route.

I couldn't fault him for it. "Keep going."

Lutz kept racing backward as the road slowly curved into the woods.

When I guessed we'd gone maybe a half-mile, I ordered Lutz to stop.

Lutz mashed the brakes, looking at the trees on both sides of the road, looking for another road he just knew had to be there.

"Have you got a full charge on your phone?" I asked.

"What?" He looked at me like I was speaking nonsense.

"Check."

Lutz huffed and dug his phone out of his pocket. "There's no signal out here. Why the hell—"

"Do you have a charge?"

Lutz powered up his phone. "Yes. No signal."

"That's okay," I told him. "Does the GPS work on that phone? Can you open the map and see where you are?"

"I don't know."

"Check, Lutz. We don't have a lot of time."

"I—"

"Just check."

Lutz grumbled, fingered his phone screen, and after a moment turned it and showed it to me.

I reached over, pinched my fingers on the screen to get a larger view of the map and saw he had the same thing on his phone as me. "Okay. You're not going to like this, but this is what we have to do."

Lutz's mouth opened, but he was lost for words.

"You need to get out of the car. Take your rifle, pistol, some water, whatever you think you might need."

"It's my goddamn car! If anybody's getting out it's you."

"Dammit, Lutz! I'm trying to save your ass here." That wasn't my goal so much as it was a fringe benefit for Lutz. If I got busted, I needed someone on the outside who would take a bribe to do just about anything. And that was Lutz. But that was secondary to my primary reason for getting rid of him. With all the attention we were getting, Lutz would turn into a larger and larger liability. I had the ability to move fast and stay hidden when I needed to. Once out from behind the steering wheel, Lutz had no remarkable skills except in the way of making every situation worse. "I'm going to take the Mercedes."

Lutz put a hand on a pistol.

"Don't," I told him calmly. "I'm helping you here." I pointed northeast. "About three or four miles straight through the woods, you'll come to a farm-to-market road. If you follow it east for a bit, you'll come to a small town."

"I'm not hiking through the woods."

"Use your head here, Lutz. I've got a warrant on me. The cops are after us. Those guys we just saw in the field, they're alerting their higher-ups about trespassers in a black Mercedes running over the cotton crop. We're not going to get out of this in your car."

"I'm not losing my car."

"Go through the woods," I told him. "It might take you the rest of the afternoon. Use your phone to keep yourself headed in the right direction. When you get in range of a cell tower or Wifi signal, contact Ricardo. Tell him to have one of his gopher guys come out and pick you up."

Lutz slumped. "He'll charge me a thousand dollars."

"No, he won't, but he'll charge you something. I'll pay, whatever it is."

"What are you going to do?"

"I'm going to make a scene to draw them away from you. I need to get a lot closer to Blue Bean's admin complex. All three places Sienna Galloway might be are over there. I'll ditch your truck somewhere along the way. The cops will impound it. All you need to do is tell them I was driving it. Tell them you were back in Houston the whole time. I'll cover the impound fee and towing, and you'll have your truck back in a few days."

Lutz looked at the trees, gears turning inside his skull.

"You got a better idea?" I asked, "I'm open."

"I could dump you here and go back the way I came."

"Up to you." I shrugged. "If I have to hike, it might take me the rest of the day, maybe longer, to get to the admin compound and find Sienna. I think you'd agree with me, the sooner we make our deal with her the better off we'll both be. You make the call."

Lutz stared at the trees for several long moments. "You're an asshole."

"I know."

He opened his door. As he was stepping out, he said, "If I don't get my truck back—"

"I know."

Chapter 35

Inspector Doggett, a chinless man with sagging gray skin and thinning hair, was pedantic about sticking to the agenda, which consisted of topics that were no more than a list of forms Blue Bean was mandated by the state to provide. Being a corporate farm that serviced many state contracts and utilized degenerate labor as well as labor from a penal system work camp, Blue Bean Farms was required to submit a daunting list of forms, some monthly, many quarterly, and even more annually. And they submitted them to Inspector Doggett in a series of meetings with various department heads according to Inspector Doggett's agenda.

The meetings proceeded according to the same script each month, and the meeting with Sienna started going off the rails at about the same point every time they arrived at a particular agenda item—the review of reports on the methods spelled out in Blue Bean's operations manual for training and disciplining degenerates, and the curricula Sienna had developed for educating the staff on those methods. Sienna took to pointing out that having the materials in place and filling out the form—hence compliance, as defined by the law—was pointless. Documentation was worthless if none of the procedures listed in the documents were being put into practice.

The first time Sienna voiced her concerns, Keith Workman's face turned red under his generous coif of silver hair, and she thought he might be having a stroke. That fear vanished when he let loose a tirade that embarrassed her but was ignored by both Inspector Doggett and his assistant, Mike Rafferty, both of whom looked at the papers on the conference table in front of them and pretended like nothing had occurred.

That had happened months and months ago.

Now it all proceeded according to a memorized script: Sienna told them the documents asked the wrong questions. Keith Workman insisted Sienna's concerns were good-hearted but founded in idealism rather than practicalities. Blue Bean Farms did its utmost to meet all the aspirations listed in its official procedures. Doggett always followed Workman with an admonishment directed at Sienna for trying to create the illusion of impropriety where none existed. Blue Bean was in compliance with the law, and Sienna's signatures on the documents proved it.

Sienna's protests grew weaker with each passing item on the agenda, each form submitted, each pointless meeting, until they got to the kill list. That's where Sienna made her stand.

"That brings us to the last item on the agenda, The Defect Retirement List." Mike Rafferty said it as he flinched at the words.

"I have it," said Inspector Doggett, dragging his bored gaze up and down a few of the sheets lying on the table in front of him. "All seems to be—"

"No," Sienna told him. "It's not in order."

Mike Rafferty deflated. He knew what was coming.

Keith Workman glared silent threats at Sienna, and Inspector Doggett heaved a great sigh. "Oh, good God. Do we have to do this today?"

Into Doggett's disrespect, Sienna pointed at the papers and said, "That Defect Retirement List is not—"

"Every month it's something with you," Workman spat.

He said it with such vitriol that Sienna was surprised into silence. Her relationship with Workman had grown contentious, no doubt on that point existed, but the tension seemed suddenly to have escalated to a new level.

"If you hate your job so much, why don't you just quit?" asked Workman.

The question had been coming up between them with some regularity over the past few months. Each time Workman brought it up, she'd made the case that she was determined to fulfill the goal of making Blue Bean Farms a model of productivity under humanitarian guidelines— exactly what she'd been hired to do.

In the face of Workman's animosity that Sienna now realized must have been brewing under the surface all along, she gave up on trying to push him in the direction of the aspirations he'd said he had. "Why don't you fire me?"

"Fire you?" Workman's jaw clenched, and so did his big fists. "I wish I could."

"You're the CEO," Sienna told him, finding it easy to play it cool now that she'd decided she could live without Blue Bean's paycheck and all the crap that came with it.

"The only damn reason I hired you was to settle the state's civil suit against Blue Bean Farms. Now I can't fire you without having three million dollars in fines reinstated."

Sienna opened her mouth to retort as Workman's words sank in.

"Leaves you speechless, doesn't it?" His face did something that was supposed to look like a grin but looked more like he was baring his teeth. "You believed all that bullshit I told you about how you were perfect for the job, and you thought it was your qualifications and your passion I was interested in. I could have lived without your passion, but you were the only goddamn one who applied for the job —hell, I still can't find anybody else. Well, the state told me what Blue Bean had to do to comply, and by God, that's what we did, exactly what we did. So here you sit. All that documentation you wrote has been incorporated into our standard operating procedures manual, just like it's supposed to be." Workman reached and tapped his big fingers on the stack of papers in front of Doggett, "And you sign the necessary papers for the monthly meeting."

Sienna snapped her gaze over to Doggett. "I'm retracting my signature from those documents."

Doggett tisked and shook his head. "That's a new one, but you realize that's not possible, don't you?"

Mike Rafferty sat up straight and said, "The paper is signed. It's been submitted to Inspector Doggett. Now it's state property, Sienna, an official record, to do anything to alter or destroy it is a felony."

"That's right, little lady." Workman smirked. "Tear it up if you want. We can put you in the prisoner barracks up in the work camp. You'll get all the time you please in the company of d-gens. You'll love it."

Ignoring Workman, Sienna told Doggett, "I was coerced into signing the Defect Retirement List."

"How so?" Doggett asked.

"One of the trustees brought a Bully Boy to my cabin this morning and threatened to rape me if I didn't sign it."

Doggett didn't respond except to look over his glasses at Sienna as if she were lying.

"In your bungalow?" Workman mocked Sienna with a booming laugh. "In the residence compound, where only employees are allowed. Is that what you're saying?"

"That is what I'm saying," Sienna told Workman. "I just told you about it in the lobby. Goose Eckenhausen and an oaf named Toby came into my house."

"Wouldn't happen." Workman pushed out his lower lip and shook his head as though that would help his appearance of contemplation. "Couldn't happen."

Sienna was dumbfounded by how boldly Workman lied.

Doggett took on a tone of a disappointed father, and he planted his elbows on the table and leaned across. "Why do you put us through this, Ms. Galloway?" He spun one of the sheets of paper from the kill list and slid it across the table for her to see. "It's dated last week. Why did you wait a week to bring up this fantasy about coercion?"

"That date was already on the paper when I signed it," she told him.

Workman harrumphed and took Doggett's attention away from Sienna. "I told you, she's unstable. She needs to be on medication. Will you finally accept my request to have her removed without paying the fines? I'll find someone to fill her job eventually."

"Mr. Workman," Doggett said, sadly shaking his head, "If you were able to convince Ms. Galloway to bring in an assessment from a psychiatric professional that indicated she was incapable of handling the responsibilities of her job, then the state—"

Workman laughed again. "I can't even get her to quit? How do you think I could get her to see a shrink? Paranoid people don't know they're paranoid."

"I'm sorry, Mr. Workman," said Doggett. "Without a professional opinion from a psychiatrist, there's nothing the state will do."

Workman jumped to his feet, sending his rolling chair slamming into the wall behind. "I suppose this meeting's over, then." He turned and stormed out the door.

Chapter 36

As Lutz got himself situated to trek through the trees, I examined the map on my phone, finding the landmarks I would need to guide me once the chase was on, and finding the tracts of forest I could run the Mercedes into when it came time to ditch it and disappear.

I got out of the Mercedes and went around to the driver's side where Lutz was standing. "Use your map. It'll take a while to get there, but you won't have any trouble finding the road. You good?"

Lutz looked at me, not shaking his head, not nodding. I was pushing him down a path he didn't want to take, but he wasn't pushing back.

"Alright." I got into the driver's seat, belted myself in, and put the Mercedes in drive without giving Lutz another look.

I gunned the engine, gave the gas gauge a quick check, and sped forward.

I wondered how much time had passed since we burst through the trees and were spotted? Ten minutes? Something like that.

As the road curved through the trees, the break in the vine curtain came into view. No trucks were coming down the overgrown road to find me. That was one worry ticked off the list. No vehicles were parked in the field just at the end of the road. Another worry gone. No band of d-gens and their foremen were standing in the sunshine looking in. Tick.

I pushed the pedal to the floor to build speed.

Seconds passed.

I burst into the sunshine again, raging through the cotton at nearly forty miles an hour. Bushes and bolls flew in every direction as I bounced toward the d-gens spread across the far end of the field.

Many of them stopped what they were doing and stared. Others ran. I tried to pick out the foremen as I scanned. I knew they were ahead, probably raising their weapons.

I slid down in the seat, exposing only my eyes and the top of my head above the dashboard, just enough to see the general direction of where I was going.

A bullet hit the windshield, high up on the passenger side, sending a spider web of cracks across the glass.

Lutz wasn't going to like that.

Looking for the guilty asshole who'd shot, I spotted a man holding up a rifle, standing a dozen paces from a parked truck, looking defiant and brave.

I swerved toward him and accelerated.

It took him all of two seconds to understand what was happening. He'd missed his shot, and his prey was pissed. He turned and ran for his truck.

So much for bravery.

A moment later I zoomed by the truck in a cloud of dust, leaving the cotton field and the harvesting d-gens behind. I straightened the Mercedes onto a dirt road that ran in a straight line between two fields. I mashed the accelerator to the floor and pushed the Mercedes up past fifty as I sat up in my seat and scanned the sky.

No buzz bikes?

Maybe the police had backed off to let Blue Bean handle the problem of the black Mercedes.

Chapter 37

Sienna walked away from the admin building, fuming, not sure whether she was walking toward her cottage to sulk, to her office in the training compound, or to her car where she might start it up and drive away, putting Blue Bean Farms behind her forever. Her resignation, she finally understood, was exactly what Workman wanted. He'd evidently wanted it ever since it registered in his mind she wasn't a malleable stooge who'd rubber-stamp his forms for the chance to double her salary.

Now what he wanted was of no more concern to her, except as a target for her defiance.

For Keith Workman, Blue Bean Farms had only one purpose to its existence, to fatten his bank accounts. To that end, he treated degenerates, work camp prisoners, and employees like consumable resources—use one up and replace it with the next.

Employees came and went faster than the change in seasons. He hired more.

Work camp prisoners were the dregs of society who needed to be punished into submission. Workman had said on many occasions he wanted to grind them down with long, sweaty hours of work to fill the wormy holes in their souls with good character.

Degenerates were nothing to him. Actually, less than nothing, because they ate food he would otherwise have sold to fatten his profits. They slept in barracks built on ground he otherwise would have tilled. Left up to him, he'd work them all to death before their minds had a chance to deteriorate into uselessness. And why not? He seemed able to get any allocation of fresh d-gens filled from the state school and they didn't cost him a penny—not counting the bribes he likely paid for Blue Bean's spot on the state school's priority list. All Workman had to do was provide an executed kill list to the state school's clerk to get a refill on the first of the month.

That's why the kill list was such an easy thing for him to fill. It provided him a convenient avenue to cull any degenerate whose productivity waned. Workman hated Sienna because he wanted to turn that avenue into an eight-lane highway and she stood in his way with her loudmouth complaints and high ideals.

A subversive thought caught Sienna mid-stride and stopped her cold.

She blinked at the idea as though the shimmering genius of it might hurt her eyes. It was elegant. It was perfect.

She glanced back at the admin building, as though the idea had been so brilliant, Workman behind his tall windows might have seen it from his desk chair.

The kill list was turned in. Before lunch today, Goose Eckenhausen and his trustee thugs would herd the degenerates out of the training compound and into the pens for the Bloodmobile.

But what if the degenerates weren't in the training compound when Goose came for them?

Sienna couldn't take the degenerates off the list, but she could still give them a chance to live.

She headed for the training compound, urgency in her steps.

Chapter 38

Knowing Warden Smallwood wasn't in his residence, knowing the guard barracks were empty, and knowing the armory wasn't, Goose drove the pickup toward the gate of Warden Smallwood's compound. The double row of barbed-wire-topped fences stood tall and intimidating. The sign that warned of a deadly electric jolt for anyone who dared touch the fence was even more frightening. But Goose knew the wiring on the fence had fried nearly eight months prior, and the Warden hadn't been able to get a work order pushed through the State Comptroller's office.

With Deke, his right-hand man in the truck beside him, Goose pulled the pickup to a stop just outside the gate. A second pickup containing four other trustees—Rusty Jim, along with Bart and the two former cops, Taylor and Flores, now prisoners like the rest of them—came to a stop on the road behind.

"You still think this is a good idea?" Deke asked.

Goose swung the pickup door open as he looked at Deke. "Boss Man said, and I quote, 'do whatever it takes'."

"He didn't mean this." Deke looked worried.

"This is what it's gonna take," Goose told him, looking like a kid who'd just stolen a handful of candy.

Goose hopped out of the truck, took out his phone, and dialed.

On the fifth ring, Goose decided if Warden Smallwood didn't answer, he'd call it tacit approval. He waited two more rings and as he was lowering the phone from his ear to hang up, the ringer cut. A voice came on the line. "Smallwood."

"Warden, Goose Eckenhausen, I'm just outside the guard compound gettin' ready to come in and see you." Keith Workman had given Goose free run of Blue Bean, but the guard compound was not technically Blue Bean property. It belonged to the state prison system. If Goose went in without permission, any one of the guards would be within his rights to put a bullet or two into Goose's head.

Warden Smallwood said, "I'm not at the compound." Goose knew that.

"Any of yer guards 'round?"

"We're out at a…" the Warden took a long time to find the right words, "a training event."

Goose knew that wasn't true. He knew, too, when he drove up, how unlikely it was any guard on the state's payroll would be within twenty miles of Blue Bean Farms. It was a Thursday. Most of them were in the habit of starting their weekends early—very early—probably off hunting whatever animal was in season at the moment or sleeping off hangovers after spending Wednesday night in Houston's bar district, plying promiscuous ladies with alcohol. "We got a problem here on the farm."

"You handle the escapes most of the time without any help from us," Smallwood replied. "The weekend's almost here. Can you get this one yourself?"

"It's not an escape, Warden."

"What then?" Smallwood sounded mad.

Goose didn't care. "It's about them crooked Regulators you called me 'bout earlier. The ones the police called you about. Now they're rampagin' 'round, tearin' ass through the fields, runnin' down workers and disappearin' into the woods."

"I thought you said you were going to handle that problem. Besides, me and my men don't handle people trying to break *into* prison." Smallwood laughed. It was the closest he could come to actual humor.

Goose persisted, "I need to git into the guard compound and—"

"Why would you need to enter my compound?" Smallwood asked testily. "Are your crooked Regulators in there?"

"No," answered Goose. "The Regulators are in an SUV. We're having trouble findin' them so we can catch 'em. Boss Man is pissed 'cause all the damage they causin' not to mention throwin' off the work schedule. They're gonna put us behind on the harvest, and you know how Boss Man likes to stay on his schedule."

"Oh yeah," Smallwood mocked. "I've heard it all before about losing money on contracts and the commodity markets, and not meeting city contracts and empty troughs and rioting d-gens in the streets in Houston. God damn, if I never hear one of Workman's speeches again about how the whole goddamn world depends on this one stinking-ass farm, it'll be too soon. Reminds me of my old man. I wish he'd just whip me instead of blabbering on like he does."

Goose knew none of that stopped Smallwood from taking the envelope of money Workman gave him every quarter to keep his nose out of Workman's management of the prisoners in the service of Blue Bean's profits.

"What is it exactly Mr. Workman wants me to do?" Smallwood finally asked.

Time for the lie. But that was okay because lying came easy to Goose. "I need them new hover bikes Workman bought for your boys."

Smallwood laughed heartily. "You have got to be kidding? Give hover bikes to trustees? You must think I smoke as much of that wacky weed as you do, boy."

"I'm serious, Warden. We got to find those crooked Regulators before they shut the whole damn farm down. You know how serious Boss Man gits about that. You just said so yerself."

"Goddamn." Smallwood was getting frustrated.

"I ain't pleased about it neither," Goose lied, and then lied again. "I don't wanna ride one of them thangs. I'm afraid of heights." Total bullshit.

"Well, you know as well as I do, these hover bikes belong to Blue Bean Farms. They're on loan to the guard unit. They ain't mine to lend out. I got to have direct permission from Mr. Workman himself."

"You go ahead and call 'im," Goose bluffed, knowing and having it just reinforced that the Warden hated more than anything having to sit through Mr. Workman's lectures.

Goose waited on the Warden, letting him stew with the decision.

The guards didn't need the damn hover bikes anyway. Even when they were around, they never did anything for Blue Bean Farms except horse around or try to scare up the local deer for target practice. They didn't need the hover bikes for that. Goose could put them to good use. Mostly, he liked the idea of riding one around the farm and looking down at everybody like a flying-carpet genie.

"I'll tell you what," said Goose after he figured he'd given the Warden long enough, "I'm gonna go on in and git them bikes out. You might be on the phone with Boss Man for an hour or more gittin' an earful 'bout how yer slowin' shit down."

Warden Smallwood groaned.

"You know I'm right," said Goose. "You go ahead and do it, though."

Smallwood sighed. "Not the two military bikes."

"Say what?" Goose asked, deciding to play a little bit dumb. He knew there were six bikes in the armory—four police models, bought from a department upgrading to newer ones, and two expensive military grade bikes, brand new. If the rumors were to be believed, the new military models were as fast as all git-out and could turn on a dime. Those cop buzz bikes took damn near half a mile to make it all the way 'round if they were moving at top speed. That is unless you came to a dead stop. But slowing to a stop and accelerating to any decent speed took five minutes.

"You take them four old cop bikes out, but you leave the military bikes there."

"Probably just take one or two anyway," Goose told him. "Just need to spot them dirty Regulators so my boys can round 'em up in their trucks."

"If any of your boys runs off," threatened Smallwood, "it's on you. Not me. You be sure Mr. Workman understands that, you hear?"

"Yessir, Warden."

Goose wrapped up the conversation. He had what he'd come for, permission to take out the bikes.

Using the keypad, Goose opened the gate—Workman had provided Goose with the master code for all the keypads on the farm and he'd given him the secure code to Smallwood's compound, too. It was good to be the Boss Man's favorite.

Goose strode across the guard compound, heading straight for the armory's garage. He didn't have any intention of taking one of the cop bikes. He was going to fly one of the military bikes over the fence, and by the time the day was done all six bikes would have a new home at the trustee barracks.

Sure, arguments would follow, but in the end, Warden Smallwood would give in because he didn't give a beagle's butthole for Blue Bean or the handful of work camps he oversaw. He was happy to draw a dependable state salary and take his envelopes full of money. He wasn't about to make a big stink about stray buzz bikes that his higher-ups at the state didn't even know about.

Chapter 39

If not for the certainty that the work camp's trustees would eventually figure out where I was, I could have been on a lazy Sunday drive through the country. Once I got some distance between me and the pissant who took a shot at me just because I ran over a bunch of his little cotton bushes and scattered his d-gens across a couple of acres, I took a turn onto a red dirt road and slowed down to what I guessed might be an inconspicuous speed for driving around Blue Bean Farms.

I drove by the remains of a country house, one of many family homes back when all this land belonged to small farmers working plots measured in a few hundred or even a few thousand acres. Most of those houses were in ruin. The people who'd lived in them had died or turned d-gen twenty years back. That's why the land was available for Blue Bean Farms to squat.

In the distance I saw barracks, some in pairs, some in groups of four or five, all identical, all surrounded by tall fences. In truth, they looked like barns more than barracks, a place to store the d-gens when they weren't working the fields. From the satellite photos Ricardo had provided, I knew small complexes of barracks were spread all over Blue Bean's property—better to keep the livestock close to the land, I guessed.

I passed stands of trees and fields, some tilled under and ready for autumn planting, others with crops waiting to be harvested by d-gens. I saw crews here and there, toiling in the sunshine. I knew every group of d-gens was supervised by work camp prisoners—normal humans serving a sentence—but I figured none of them carried weapons. The trustees who oversaw the other prisoners were armed, and as I'd found out, eager to shoot.

I came to an intersection with a signpost on one corner providing directions: cannery, go straight; grain silo number seventeen, go left; administrative complex, turn right.

Right I went.

According to the information Ricardo's hacker—Blix—had gathered for me, the places Sienna Galloway might be were in or near the administrative complex. All I needed was to get close, ditch the Mercedes in a stand of trees, and find a stealthy way to get myself to each of the three places I might find her.

One way or the other, the solution to my legal problem would materialize.

Bobby Adair

Chapter 40

"You ridden one of these things before?" Goose asked.

Deke looked up and down the length of the camo green hover bike. He glanced at the matching bike Goose was inspecting. "Yup."

"You sure?" Goose asked.

Deke looked down the row at the other four bikes, all painted in Blue Bean colors with logos on the sides. "Something wrong with these two? They didn't paint 'em yet."

"These two came in yesterday," said Goose. "Come in from the Army. They ain't had time to paint 'em."

"Do they work?" Deke didn't look comfortable with the idea of getting on the bike.

Goose was getting a bad feeling about his choice to put Deke on one of the Army bikes even though Deke was his number two. Goose looked over the other trustees he'd brought along. The two former policemen had spent plenty of time on hover bikes before their bad behavior had gotten them thrown into the work camp. Bart was former Army. He'd ridden the Army model some years ago for sure, at least several models older. Rusty Jim was a braggart who fancied himself a daredevil who claimed to have ridden or driven everything with a motor, most of them stolen. They all had more experience than Deke.

"I can put Bart on one of these fast ones," said Goose. He pointed at the daredevil. "Or Rusty Jim."

Deke looked down the row at his fellow prisoners.

Goose came around his bike and put a hand on Deke's shoulder. "Yer my right-hand man, Deke. But if you don't wanna ride one ah these thangs, well, that ain't nuthin' but a thang. I just figured you an me, on these two here buzz bikes…you know."

Deke shook his head.

"We run this camp," said Goose. "We borrowin' these from the Warden but we ain't givin' 'em back. What you ride outta here, is gonna be yours long as yer here."

"Which is forever," muttered Deke.

"Everybody's gonna look up to us whether they like us or not," said Goose. "These bikes, they're power. Matter of fact, bein' in the work camp won't mean nuthin' no more fer you an me. We can skip into town, any town 'round here and git right back. All we got here is free food and a free place to sleep, long as we keep the rest of these fart suckers doin' their jobs."

Deke nodded. "I like the sound of that. But we can already drive into town now and again. I don't think we need these buzz bikes."

"It'll be easier." Goose was getting frustrated. Why did he have to sell Deke on the idea of freedom? He was going to be stuck on this goddamn farm for the rest of his life. "You wanna git on or not? I can git somebody else."

"No, no," Deke rubbed his face. "I'll do it. I just ain't never been on one — one like this before."

The other trustees were dragging their bikes out into the yard and mounting up.

Goose told Deke, "I'll show you."

He straddled Deke's hover bike and sat down, placing his feet on the rails that served both as foot rests and supports for the bike when it was sitting on the ground. "See, just like a motorcycle." He reached forward, rested his elbows on the padded supports, and put his hands on the controls. "Looky here, see?"

Deke leaned in for a close look at the controls.

"Easy as fuckin' a chicken."

Deke chuckled.

Goose fingered a button. "Turn it on and off there. Use this joystick over here to move right, left, up, down. This one here is the accelerator."

"Where are the brakes?" Deke asked.

"Ain't no brakes, you inbred peckerwood. You're flyin' in the air. What you gonna brake against?"

"How do I stop?"

"Pull back on the joystick, and pull back on the throttle."

"What if I do it too far, and I fall out of the sky?" Deke asked.

"Software inside keeps you from killing yourself," Goose told him. "Don't you know nuthin' 'bout how these things work?"

Deke shook his head.

"It's simple. Just do like I said. Take it easy at first. Don't go racin' or nothin'. Don't go tryin' to keep up with me. Just scoot along slow 'til you get the hang of it."

Deke took a headset out of a small compartment on the side of the bike. He put it on with headphones over his ears and mic in front of his mouth. "We can all talk to each other on this. I'll walk you through it if you got questions. You got me?"

Deke nodded and pointed at the large, horizontal fans on both the front and the back. "Why's all them other bikes only got two big ones on the front and two on the back? These two got these other small fans?"

"Acceleration and steering," answered Goose. "Them other bikes with just the big fans are more stable, but these two are fast as hell and can run little circles 'round them others. So be careful with the accelerator. If you pull back too far, without expectin' how fast this thing will take off, you'll fly right off the back."

Deke grimaced.

"Take yer time, like I said. It ain't that hard."

The other trustees, all except Rusty Jim, had their bikes running, and two of them were hovering — one a few feet off the ground, one about ten feet up.

"Kinda sound a bit like bumble bees," said Deke.

"Makes you wonder why they call 'em buzz bikes." Goose shook his head. Maybe Deke wasn't as smart as Goose thought. Maybe he was just a liar and hadn't ever ridden a hover bike. "Now you wanna git on this thing or not?"

Deke took a big breath to reassure himself and said, "I'll do it."

Goose got off Deke's bike and showed Deke where to grab it to drag it out into the courtyard. He stayed close while Deke positioned himself correctly on the hover bike and got the engine started. Over the sound of the motor and spinning fan blades, Goose hollered, "Now keep that joystick straight up and down, and ease forward on the throttle."

The hover bike's fan blades spun loudly, and Deke rose into the air. His worry turned into a grin.

"Told you." Goose gave the other riders a quick glance. Rusty Jim still wasn't in the air. He seemed to be confused about the controls. Maybe Rusty Jim was a liar, too.

Goose jogged over to where his bike was sitting, still in the shed. He dragged it out, mounted it, and put on his headset. "You boys hear me alright?"

All acknowledged.

"Good. Y'all listen to me once we git up there, ya hear? Any man don't do what I say, and I'll put yer ass on the ground and git somebody else to fly that thing. You got me?"

More acknowledgments.

Goose started his engine. Feeling the machine vibrating and humming beneath him, he couldn't help but smile.

During the eighteen months he'd been in the Army back before he turned twenty, he'd spent a lot of time on military model hover bikes. He'd never ridden one on any kind of military mission. He was assigned to a maintenance squad as a flunky in charge of changing the oil and handling the most routine of maintenance tasks. It was in the evenings after the sergeants and the officers went off duty that Goose and his buddies took the bikes out and raced them around the training courses. That's when Goose earned his nickname. It was also when his buddy—a guy they called Mach 5—crashed his bike while racing drunk on a Saturday night. Mach 5 died. Goose earned two years in the stockade and a dishonorable discharge.

That was the last time Goose flew.

At nearly twenty feet up and hovering, Goose looked down on his men. All were in the air around the yard in front of the armory except for Rusty Jim. Goose called into his headset, "You comin' Jim?"

"Yeah," he answered, as his bike lifted off the ground and started to spin. "Just takin' a minute."

"We'll all stick together at first…"

Rusty Jim was drifting close to Deke.

"Jim!" Goose snapped. "You give Deke some space. Deke, come this way."

Deke looked up, eyes wide, shaking his head. "What do I do?"

Goose yelled, "Left hand, Deke!"

Rusty Jim spun faster, getting dangerously close to Deke.

"Down, Jim!" Goose hollered, "Go down."

Deke shouted something into his headset that Goose didn't understand, and he started to jerk his controls too quickly for his machine to respond. The hover bike leaned left and right.

"Sorry, Goose," said Rusty Jim, agitated. "I got this. I just—"

Rusty Jim's bike pitched up just as Deke's bike rolled in his direction and accelerated. The two collided. The men yelled, and Deke panicked as he gave his bike full throttle instead of backing off. His bike got hung up on Rusty Jim's, and the two careened across the courtyard.

"Let go of the throttle!" yelled Goose.

Deke didn't. His bike pushed faster until it violently rammed Rusty Jim's into the chain-link fence.

Chapter 41

I passed a big, white, official-looking sign covered with rows and rows of blocky black letters and a State of Texas seal. The sign held way too many words to be read by anybody driving by but I did catch the gist of it, and that was the fenced compound a quarter-mile down a driveway was part of the state prison system.

Buzz bikes were in the air down there, hovering over an interior yard, not organized, not ready to come after me. A section of the fence was down. Something, maybe one of the bikes, had crashed. Dust and smoke were in the air around it.

So much for my lazy Sunday drive.

I punched the gas pedal. It was time to see just how fast Lutz's boxy beast would get me up the road to Blue Bean's admin complex.

Chapter 42

The training compound covered an area the size of three football fields laid side-by-side. It was completely encircled in an eight-foot, barbed-wire-topped fence. Nearly half the ground was dedicated to cultivated rows of the crops grown on various parts of Blue Bean Farms. Those crops were used for training and retraining. There were also several large pavilions where Sienna's staff of five employees and two-dozen work camp prisoners provided instruction to degenerates, either one-on-one or in groups.

Along one side fence were the barracks where the degenerates each had a place to sleep while they were in her care. She didn't, however, have enough sleeping space for all the degenerates Goose had dumped on her.

Also in the compound was the training admin office where Sienna's desk sat in the back corner of a tight room with the desks of her five direct reports. Three prisoners also had desks in the office, so there were nine in all. None of the rest of the prisoners needed a desk.

Over the past week, Goose had stuffed over three hundred degenerates into the compound, probably hoping the crowding would incite the short tempers and violent acts he said the degenerates had all demonstrated. One more thing to hate him for.

Sienna sent her paid staff home as soon as she arrived at the training compound. It didn't help any with their attitudes toward her.   Not one had a kind word for her as they were leaving, even though she assured them they'd still get paid for the day.   The consensus among them seemed to be that she'd been wasting time with a bunch of degenerates headed for the Bloodmobile and forcing the staff to waste its time on unnecessary work.   After that, she told the prisoners to go back to their barracks.   They had the day off as well.   She didn't intend to have any of her people helping Goose organize the d-gens for transport to the Bloodmobile's slaughter pens.

Once everyone was gone, Sienna unlocked the training compound's main gate and propped it wide open.

The degenerates in the yard didn't catch on right away to the fact they were free.   She moved quickly among them and herded them through the gate, but once she got some of them moving, the rest followed.

She stepped out of the flow of bodies and watched as they left, some headed for the woods.   Those might get lucky and evade Goose's trustees.   They'd have a chance at living.   Most of them headed straight for the white admin buildings scattered in the distance.   Why?   Who knew with degenerates?   Those would probably be rounded up by day's end and find themselves in a pen near the Bloodmobile, unwittingly awaiting their turn for humane extermination.

Setting the degenerates free wasn't a solution to anything, but it was defiance, and deviance felt good.   It felt like poking a finger into the eye of a bully and recapturing all that he'd tried to steal away from her.   It was empowering.

Bobby Adair

Chapter 43

Bart said, "They're both dead."

From atop his hover bike, twenty feet above the tangled bodies of Deke and Rusty Jim, Goose watched the black Mercedes pass by on the main road, heading toward the admin complex. He heard the SUV's engine rev across the distance. The Mercedes was running away. That had to be them, the guys the cops said were coming onto the property, the Regulators who'd killed the d-gens last night without even doing everybody the favor of shooting that blue-eyed bitch, Galloway.

"I said, they're both dead," Bart repeated from where he stood on the ground beside the wreckage. "What're we gonna do, Goose?"

Flores, one of the two corrupt cops, was descending and steering his bike toward the hangar he'd dragged it from minutes before. "I don't want none of this shit."

Taylor, the other ex-cop, looked at Goose, looked at the bodies of Deke and Rusty Jim, and turned to Flores. "Wait for me."

"Wait!" Goose commanded.

The three remaining trustees stopped talking and looked up at Goose.

"Way I see it," said Goose, "we're all fucked here."

"Not if we stay quiet and get the hell outta here," said Flores. "Then it's just you."

"No, it ain't," Goose told him.

"You gonna roll over on me?" Flores asked, a deadly threat lurking between his words.

"Don't matter," said Goose.

"Yeah?" Flores asked, sounding ready to pull his rifle up and shoot Goose right off his buzz bike. "Why's that?"

"Don't matter which one of us Warden Smallwood and his boys drags into an interrogation cell, we'll talk." Goose cackled and then went on to explain, "We're criminals. We ain't saints. And if we don't talk, them hicks the Warden hires will beat the hell outa us 'til we do. It don't take no mastermind to know what's gonna happen. Just a matter of who spills a story first. Then the rest gonna take the blame."

"Speak for yourself," spat Flores. "I ain't rollin' over on nobody."

"Shut up you self-righteous prick." Taylor laughed mockingly. "I know why you got life. I've still got friends on the Force. You would have gotten the needle if it weren't for everybody you turned on."

Flores stood up on the foot rails of his bike and stabbed a finger at Taylor. "You better—"

"Shut up!" Goose shouted. "Both you fart suckers! You listen. Way I see it, we tell a story—the same story—and none of us takes a lick a shit over this. We still run this work camp the way we like it. We still eat steak. We still get all the pretty little cooter we want."

"D-gens," Flores grimaced.

"Never stopped you, that I saw," said Bart.

Taylor laughed.

Goose took a hand off the joystick on his buzz bike and pointed at the dust cloud drifting over the road. "Any ah you boys see that black Mercedes pass by a minute ago?"

"What?" Taylor asked. "The one we got these bikes to search for?"

"One in the same," Goose told him.

"You're lyin'." Flores was always the contrary one.

Bart said, "Shut up, Flores."

"Way I remember it," said Goose, "them Regulators was drivin' by just as we was gettin' into the air. Didn't see 'em 'til the last minute. They crashed that SUV through the fence, took out Deke and Rusty Jim before they took off again." Goose pointed down at the bodies of his two friends. "Them Regulators murdered two trustees."

"That's what I remember." Bart looked at Taylor.

"Yeah," said Taylor. "Took us by surprise. Only it couldn't have happened that way. That's why you're in jail, Goose. You're a bad liar."

"You're in jail, too," Goose snapped. "So you ain't that good yerself."

Taylor pointed at the fence, then quickly put his hand back on the throttle. "The fence is knocked down from the inside. If that Mercedes would have come through, it would be laying in the other direction. The story won't hold up."

Goose looked at the fence, looked impatiently at the road. "The way I recall, they came in through the gate and tried to run us down as we were liftin' off. Some of us got high enough to escape. Deke and Rusty Jim didn't. They got smashed into the fence, and the Mercedes made a getaway." Goose glared at Taylor, daring him to voice another objection.

"Sounds right," said Taylor. "That's the way I remember." He looked over at Flores.

Letting his bike float and using only one hand on the controls, Goose put a hand on the butt of his pistol. "What do you say, Flores? Did one of them Regulators shoot you in the head before they drove off, or you remember it that the same way as the rest of us?"

Flores glared up at Goose for a moment. He looked at the bodies one more time, took a resigned breath and said, "I don't remember nobody getting shot. Just that black SUV ramming through the fence and you telling us all that if we tracked that Regulator down and put a few extra holes in him, then you were going to owe all of us a big favor."

"What big favor?" Goose asked, suspicious.

"Maybe teabag your mother," said Flores. "Don't know yet."

"You'd like my mother," said Goose, grinning. "She ain't got no teeth." He turned toward the road and saw the dust cloud left by the Mercedes starting to settle back onto the road. "Let's go get them dirty Regulators."

Chapter 44

I crested a rolling hill and spotted the admin complex—seven white stone buildings with lots of glass, spread over nine or ten acres of flat ground, people milling everywhere.

My view of the building slipped away as I flew down the road into a shallow valley between hills. The Mercedes rumbled through a rugged low-water crossing, and I gassed it to keep my speed up the next hill.

I leaned forward to get a good angle to view the sky behind me through my mirrors. That's when I spotted the black dots against the blue. Buzz bikes. I'd almost started to hope they'd missed me when I'd driven by.

Oh, well.

If things were easy, they wouldn't be interesting.

I hit the top of the next hill, and it opened up to a grassy plateau sprinkled with the widely spaced admin buildings of various shapes and sizes, all single-story structures except one, the main building. Century-old live oaks dotted the ground between the buildings, spreading their boughs over a quarter-acre each.

The loiterers I'd spotted from down the road were d-gens, Blue Bean agricultural workers wearing collars, matching baggy shorts, and dirty t-shirts. Most of them seemed to be going nowhere, just wandering.

The main admin building, the sole two-story structure, was unapproachable without being seen. According to the information I'd gotten from Ricardo, that was one of the places Sienna Galloway might be.

I turned onto a curved driveway I knew from Ricardo's photos ran a circuit around most of the admin complex, the only grouping of buildings on the farm that had no fence. On the far side of the complex, nearly three-quarters of a mile away, out of my view, sat the residence compound, a second of the three places she might be.

Taking a quick glance at the sky, I noticed one of the buzz bikes had crossed most of the distance from where I'd spotted it just moments before. Three were far behind. Three cop bikes and one military bike?

Bastard!

I was envious.

It was time to get my reconnoitering into high gear.

Don't get in my way d-gens. I'll run you down.

I zipped along the curved road around the complex, looking for anything that might give me an advantage when I came back through on foot. I wasn't planning on stopping the Mercedes and getting out while everybody on Blue Bean Farms could see me do it.

As I came around the driveway on the far side from where I'd entered, I spotted a compound containing three rows of small cottages, well kept, shaded by dozens of big trees, all behind a fence topped — of course — with barbed wire.

The residence compound sat on the top edge and down one side of the plateau, a topographical feature that hadn't shown up at all on Ricardo's map and exactly the kind of thing I was hoping to find. I caught a glimpse of forest stretching down at the bottom of the slope, and I instantly knew I had my access path. If I couldn't find a way to get to Sienna Galloway before the end of her shift, then I'd catch her in her cottage when she came home for dinner.

Bobby Adair

It was time to hurry and get away from the hover bikes. I sped so fast the wheels started to slip on the gravel as I rounded the expansive curve.

Heading back toward the main road, I spotted another fenced compound on my left and well away from the admin complex. Its front gates were wide open. It was immediately obvious I'd found the source of the wandering d-gens. Some were still coming out. That's when I realized it was the training compound—the one run by Dr. Galloway—the most likely place I might find her during work hours.

Best of all, the forest started just on the other side of the training compound.

However, the open gate was a concern. Something was going on I might need to get an understanding of. Or, Galloway might be in her compound, sitting in her office, possibly with a little less company than might normally be around. Her staff might be out wrangling d-gens. Hopefully she wasn't with them.

Opportunity?

Possibly.

I needed to find a suitable place to ditch the Mercedes and lose the hover bikes.

Easy.

I was nearly back at the road when I spotted several trucks racing up the dirt road, coming from the direction I'd driven to get to the admin complex.

Up in the sky in that direction, the trio of slow buzz bikes was getting near. That meant the fast one—the military one—had to be close.

I stuck my head out the window for a glimpse above.

Fucker!

He was above me.

Chapter 45

In a rush of words and wind, Flores called Goose over the headset wirelessly connected to his bike, "D-gens are all over the place down there."

Goose had already seen them, but he was too busy to pay them much attention. The d-gens were a problem for later. Later would likely come as soon as Mr. Workman noticed them. Once that happened, the yelling would start. The threats would follow. Workman wasn't a bad guy for a Boss Man, but when he got pissed, he could holler for an hour before he wound down.

Now with the screw-ups starting to stack up on Goose's head, he knew a hollerin' was a comin'. He just needed to get something in the win column before Workman called him in.

At least he was close to taking care of the Regulators in the black Mercedes. Once the Mercedes got back out to the road that ran in front of the admin complex, he'd have to turn right or left. Only two choices. And Goose had trustees in trucks coming from both directions. Lots of men. Lots of rifles.

"Hey Goose," Bart called over the headset.

"What?" Goose asked.

"Look over there at the training compound," Bart told him. "These d-gens are coming from there. The gate's open."

Goose glanced and immediately saw Bart was correct. "Dammit. Who the hell did that?"

"I got one guess," Bart answered, "but you don't need my guess to know who done it."

Bart was right. No guesses were necessary. It was Sienna Galloway's doing. Goose was certain. "Bart?"

"Yeah," he answered.

"You peel off, gather up a coupla fellas and get to work roundin' up them d-gens before Boss Man has a fit."

"You want I should put 'em back in the training compound?" Bart asked.

"No," said Goose. "Bloodmobile is here. Get 'em to the staging pens. Boss Man wants 'em all taken care of before tomorrow so he can get a new allotment from the state. Otherwise, we gonna hafta wait 'til next month. Flores and Taylor, you git over here with me. Let's git these assholes in the Mercedes taken care of and be done with it. Head for the intersection up there. He's gonna figure out in a second he can't escape in either direction."

With the Mercedes moving at a quick, but steady speed, Goose took his left hand away from the throttle, drew his old revolver, and took aim. With the motion of his buzz bike through the air, swaying and bucking over invisible currents, and with the Mercedes drifting back and forth on the dirt road, Goose realized it would be difficult to hit anything. Still, he had nothing to lose by trying. He fired, and couldn't tell where the bullet hit. He fired again to no effect. "Damn."

He couldn't reload while flying. He didn't shoot again.

With the intersection coming up fast, Goose holstered his pistol and throttled back. The nimble bike slowed. He prepared to make a turn in whichever direction the Mercedes chose.

Goose glanced right to see Flores and Taylor finally closing in. They were heading for the intersection and slowing. They expected the shootout to occur there.

"Git ready," Goose told them.

The Mercedes waited until the last moment before braking. Tires skidded on the dirt, throwing up a cloud of dust. The SUV drifted and started to spin. Goose thought for a few fleeting seconds the Mercedes was going to flip onto its side, maybe roll.

It was leaning.

Leaning.

Dammit!

The Mercedes' wheels spun, and it started to accelerate around the turn to head down the road to the left.

"He's runnin' south!" Goose hollered into his headset as he looked down the wide dirt road. Three trucks and eight or nine trustees were coming up that way, and he couldn't figure why the guys in the Mercedes hadn't seen them. Well, they were in for a surprise in a couple of seconds.

Goose grinned. He leaned hard, sacrificing altitude to sharpen his turn to the left to follow the Mercedes.

At just that moment, the trucks carrying his men from the south crested a small rise. There was no way the Mercedes driver didn't see them. Goose let off on his throttle, expecting the SUV to brake.

It didn't. It accelerated.

"Damn!" Goose shouted.

The first of his guards' trucks swerved off the road. The second and third veered off to the other side, sending them bouncing across tilled ground. One of the men riding in the back of a truck got bounced out of the bed and landed in the dirt.

The Mercedes raced by.

"He got past 'em!" Goose yelled into his headset.

Flores and Taylor both cursed, and Goose heard their engines whine as they throttled up.

Goose pushed his throttle all the way forward to close the growing gap between him and the Mercedes. "Mover yer asses!" he yelled into the headset. "We can't let him get away." The road the Mercedes was on only had one ninety-degree turn and a few bends, but in eight or nine miles, it would leave Blue Bean property. Ten minutes, max. Once the Mercedes got off the farm, Goose and his men would have to break some pretty serious rules to follow.

Sneaking off the farm to visit a bar and look for some cooter on a Friday night was one thing, but going off the property with thirty or forty armed trustees was a whole 'nother thing.

The trucks that had swerved off the road were getting turned around to give chase, but Goose saw immediately they'd have no chance of catching up. The Mercedes was driving too fast.

Goose was going to have to do something himself. And that was okay.

He descended further, down into the danger zone where trees and road signs would be collision dangers.

He jockeyed with his throttle to come up slowly on the Mercedes.

The Mercedes crested a hill and started down a long piece of flat road with a slight decline. Goose knew it ran for a couple of miles. He took a hard look ahead to make sure the right side of the road was clear of anything taller than a cornstalk.

He bumped the throttle to close the gap with the Mercedes while he dropped down a little more.

Twenty feet off the ground, fifteen.

He wanted to bring the Mercedes up on his left side. He had to keep his right hand on the steering joystick which meant he had to fire with his left. He didn't want to have to shoot across his body, so he had to be on the right side of the Mercedes.

He was gaining quickly, knowing the driver had no chance of seeing him, coming down into the blind spot on the passenger side.

With any luck, both Regulators would be surprised when the bullets exploded their skulls.

Nine feet. Eight feet.

Warnings were blaring through the headset telling him he was too close to the ground to be going so fast.

And it felt fast as hell with the ground rushing by just below him.

Nevertheless, he kept his hand on the accelerator.

He flew right beside the Mercedes, just a dozen feet right of the passenger window.

He looked into the SUV and saw only one occupant, the driver. He let go of the throttle and reached across to his right hip to pull his revolver.

Just as the gun came out of its holster, the driver of the Mercedes glanced over at him, and in what seemed like an impossibly short instant—not even enough time to give it a thought—the Mercedes swerved off the road and into a fallow field, leaving Goose to zip away up the road.

"Shit!"

Goose stuffed his gun back into its holster, and he nosed the bike skyward and pulled left to trade speed for a turn. That's the way it was with these bikes, you trade altitude or speed for a tight turn.

As he came around, Goose saw the Mercedes racing for the cover of a patch of forest that spread out south and back north. He knew the woods covered thousands—maybe tens of thousands—of acres.

If he gets there—

Goose only got half that thought process through his brain before the Mercedes careened through the underbrush and disappeared under the pine canopy.

"God dammit! God dammit!"

Chapter 46

I hadn't seen a buzz bike since I rammed the Mercedes through the undergrowth to get back among the concealing trees. They were still up there, zipping this way and that, their riders hoping to get a glimpse of me to guide the growing posse of noisy trustees to my position.

They'd found the Mercedes—there was no way they could have missed it. They knew I was on foot, and the trustees had spread out in groups of three or four, across a wide front, driving me, trying to encircle me.

I wasn't running like a panicked animal, I was moving stealthily, dashing from one hiding spot to the next, stopping, trying to gauge the distance and direction of my unseen pursuers, trying to move toward my goal, the training compound which was well north of my position.

A bike buzzed directly over the tree I was crouching beside, blowing a burst of rushed air through the branches and knocking off loose pinecones and needles that rained down around me.

He was down too close to the trees for safety, thinking that might enhance his chance of seeing me. It didn't, but it did show me his path as needles fell to the forest floor as he rode away.

He wasn't a worry. He was an idiot.

Or not.

What if he was trying to make as much noise as possible? What if he wanted me to know exactly where he was?

If so, then he was hoping to put a scare into me, trying to herd me in a direction.

I looked around. I couldn't guess which direction that was.

Another buzz bike came riding just over the treetops, not following the same path as the one that had just left, but following a parallel arc, dropping pinecones, needles, and bark as it flew.

I had a guess on the direction—unfortunately, the direction I wanted to go. Crap. They were herding me off to my left. It was probably a tactic that worked perfectly when the Blue Bean goobers were trying to corral stray d-gens who'd wandered into the forest.

It wasn't going to work on me.

It was time for a sprint. I got up and ran at full speed along the wide arc the bikes were tracing.

After covering several hundred yards, I stopped.

The bikes were moving much faster than I could run. Their sounds mixed as they flew around in the distance and I couldn't pick out the individuals to follow.

I knelt by a tree, looked, and listened.

Nothing of any size was moving that I could see.

I heard another truck racing out on the road. They were calling in the reinforcements to catch me.

Doubts started to tell me I may have put too much confidence in my woodsman skills. Perhaps I'd silently disparaged too deeply the capabilities of Blue Bean's work camp trustees. Or maybe I'd pushed my luck a little too far.

No.

That's how I am when I get in these situations. Sure, I have doubts like anybody else, but they don't tend to hang around long.

How many trustees were out there?   I slowly turned, focusing for a moment in each sector surrounding me.   If I had to shoot my way out, could I kill enough of them to make a getaway?

Probably.

No, who was I kidding?   I knew I could kill enough to make my escape. The question was whether I should kill all of them. They were inexperienced. They were spread out in the woods in small groups.   They were noisy.   It was tempting to make a statement, to teach these overconfident butt-scratchers a lesson about chasing strangers into the woods.

But that choice would seal my fugitive status.

I was starting to wonder whether all the trouble of trying to stay on the right side of the law was worth it. Would it be easier just to go down to Mexico and kill the Camacho brothers and their henchmen?

That would be one solution.

It wouldn't be nearly as easy to do in reality as it seemed in my imagination. But then, what ever was?

I decided to try stealth a little longer. But at some point, I'd have to make a decision. I couldn't let the trustees box me in and get an insurmountable numerical advantage.   I had no intention of being killed by a bunch of goobers who weren't even smart enough to keep themselves out of jail.

Chapter 47

Keith Workman said his goodbyes, passed his best wishes to the other three people on the call, and watched the animated face in each video window on his computer screen wink to black. He smiled and exhaled a relaxed breath. The contracts would be emailed over by the end of the day on a deal he'd just negotiated with the City of Dallas. Blue Bean was locked in to supply its surplus corn yield to them for the next three years. All at a profitable price.

Now to find out what had Irene so irritated that she kept trying to break into his videoconference with messages, calls, and emails. He opened one of her messages, and it took only a few seconds to understand her urgency—degenerates were apparently running wild through the admin complex.

Workman grabbed the remote control for the blinds that kept his office in shade during the part of the day when the sun beat down on his side of the building. He pushed the button to raise the blinds on all the windows. Motors whirred, and the blinds over the floor-to-ceiling windows raised.

Workman spun in his chair, stood up, and looked out, waiting the thirty seconds for the blinds to slide from bottom to top. The office slowly flooded with a glare from the Texas sun that was harsh even through the tint on the windows.

Outside, around the other buildings on the grass under the trees, in the fallow fields across the road, wandering in an out of the trees in the distance, degenerates loitered, strolled, and ran.

That was money out there. Man-hours—hundreds of them—going to waste right before his eyes.

Workman grabbed his phone, dialed Goose Eckenhausen's number, and waited.

Rings.

Voicemail.

"Goddammit!" Workman hung up and dialed again.

Rings.

Voicemail.

"Goddammit!" Workman waited for the beep to tell him when to speak. "Goose, I got d-gens all over the goddamn place up here. You better get your ass up here and get this mess straightened up, or you'll be picking cotton with the d-gens come this time tomorrow. You better call me, goddammit!"

Chapter 48

Putting my ass into high gear, I ran, I squatted for a moment, I listened, and I sprinted again. The noose was closing around me—the trustees were easy to hear. If I could slip past them before they got too close, I'd get away. If not, bullets would have to be my answer.

With a handful of men making a little too much noise a hundred yards behind and at least a few trying to be quiet as they stalked in my direction from somewhere off to my right, I stepped out of the tall pines and saw a river of ruddy water with steep, red clay banks.

It was wide for a Texas river, swollen by heavy rains somewhere far north and west. A current rippled the surface, warning me away from attempting a swim across.

That warning was for regular folks.

The current didn't worry me.

My worry was that being exposed in the water with hunting guards coming at me from two directions and buzz bikes zipping around above, I'd be spotted and earn a few bullet holes for the mistake.

Looking up and down the river, I couldn't help but notice huge mounds of broken trees, washed against the banks in spots. There'd been a flood, earlier this season or last, a big one.

The trees would make a good hiding place. But I couldn't get there, not without leaving footprints or a big skid down the steep bank to show my pursuers I'd gone into the water.

Dilemma.

Run balls out along the top edge of the bank, only to get to the first clump of trees and still have the same problem, no way to get down to the water's edge without leaving a sign?

Jump from the bank to one of the downed tree trunks and hope I could land without spraining an ankle or worse? Doable, but algae on the tree trunk, loose bark, rotten wood, any of a dozen possibilities could skew that bet out of my favor. With my life as the stake in that bet, it wasn't one I was willing to take.

The noise of one of the buzz bikes suddenly grew out of the background as it passed overhead.

While it was zipping across the river and starting a wide, slow turn, inspiration showed me the path to my next step.

I leaped off the bank, pushing as far from the shore as I was able.

I splashed into chest deep water. The noise of my splash was partially drowned out by the sound of the bike still close enough to mask it.

I submerged, let the weight of my guns pull me down to the bottom, and opened my eyes to mere inches of visibility.

I grabbed hold of roots and rocks and dragged myself downstream with the current.

With forty or fifty yards to go to get to the first large clump of washed-out trees, I wanted to make the whole distance underwater while I prayed that I didn't stick my fingers near the mouth of a snapping turtle the size of the one that lived in my swimming pool.

My other problem—one I'd created for myself when I jumped in—was that the two phones I'd overpaid Ricardo for and kept for myself were ruined.

Bobby Adair

I held my breath and swam.

Time seems to drag slowly when there's no air in front of your face to breathe.

When I bumped into a mess of branches under the surface I knew I'd come to my goal. I reached forward, grabbing wood, and pulled myself further into the jumble, feeling thicker branches as I went, knowing I was getting closer to a tree trunk.

When I came up for air, I breathed deeply, filling my nose and lungs with the smell of a dead armadillo's ass. A lot of crap was caught in the tree limbs and was rotting. Looking up, I saw spots of sky through a dense mess of broken limbs and twigs.

I'd made it.

I glanced around, got an idea of how deeply I'd worked my way into the pile, submerged, and crawled further before coming up between two logs.

Another buzz bike made its noisy way over the river before starting a long turn.

No worry of mine. I was invisible from above. In fact, no one would know I was there except the catfish in the water and the crickets in the branches. Nobody would have a chance of finding me unless they jumped in the river and came up inside the jumble of logs like I did.

I was safe.

All I needed to do was wait out the searchers, and I'd be golden. That, and I needed to find a comfortable position to lie in the water. A branch was poking me in my back, and being between the logs, I couldn't move to either side.

My solution? Pull myself along between the half-submerged logs to find a spot—

Holy shit!

What's that?

Black Rust

I jerked my hand back, convinced I'd just grabbed a huge, slimy water moccasin. I lost all sense of my situation and scrambled away as fast as my confined space and poking branches let me.

When my heart settled to a normal rate, and I realized I hadn't been bitten, I struggled to turn myself over on my belly so I could look up the gap between the logs and see where that giant fucking snake was.

Relief was quickly followed by surprise.

There was no snake.

An arm of a corpse was wrapped over a trunk. That's what I'd grabbed. A head lay face down in the water. Around the corpse's neck was a leather collar—a Blue Bean collar. I didn't need to see the rest of the submerged body to know it was wearing a d-gen's shirt, shorts, and work boots.

I stared at the body, not because it made me feel one thing or another. It didn't. The dead are the dead. What I saw in the body was an idea.

Chapter 49

Grousing for no one but the polecats and the opossums to hear, Lutz scratched at his arms and rubbed his eyes. Somewhere along his hike through the woods, he'd put a hand on poison ivy or poison oak, or something. He had welts on his arms now, and they itched like mad. Mosquitoes were buzzing his ears, and those big-ass black horseflies kept biting his neck.

Lutz hated the woods, and he hated Christian for convincing him to give up the Mercedes.

He took out his phone to see if he had a signal. "Damn."

Lutz screamed at the forest. Nothing reacted.

He looked at the map to guess how far he still needed to go. He couldn't tell.

He started trudging again but stopped. He heard something. He turned his head, held his breath, and listened.

An engine.

A car.

Thank the heavens!

The car was far away. It was hard to pick the direction with the sound bouncing off the tree trunks.

Off to the left somewhere.

Getting louder. Maybe. It wasn't the sound of a car on pavement. It was a truck on a rough road, taking it slow.

There had to be a dirt road close by, one not on the map. He'd had it with the woods. He needed to get a ride. Lutz picked a direction he hoped was right, and he ran.

Chapter 50

Groups of men passed by on the bank so many times I stopped counting. The first group tried to be quiet and sneaky. They were hunting for me, believing I might be hiding behind the next tree. I overheard them talk about the riverbank and how it would be a dead giveaway if I'd gotten into the water. The bank was too muddy not to have some sign of me passing by. I guess not one of them considered I might have made the jump to the water.

Good for me.

A little later, the squad that passed talked about a splash someone had heard and they were eyeing the water and paying particular attention to the mounds of trees and brush deposited by the floods. But they only looked in from the bank. Not close enough.

As time passed, my pursuers gave up any pretense of staying quiet. Some of them believed I'd given them the slip. Others believed I'd gone into the river and drowned. There was talk of a big gator that had been spotted several times downriver. They even joked about it eating a couple of the d-gens who'd been stupid enough to get into the water to cool off.

I couldn't tell if they were serious or ribbing a new guy. Mostly they were tired of marching through the woods and one-upping one another on how pissed they were about it.

After I first hid in the clump of washed-out trees, I heard hover bikes pass overhead with some regularity. A few were the cop models that had chased Lutz and me earlier in the day. One made a different sound when it zipped across the sky. It made tight turns. It was the military model, the one ridden by the goober who'd aimed that big cowboy revolver at me when I was driving the Mercedes before racing into the woods.

But I hadn't heard a buzz bike in a while, maybe an hour. It had been at least thirty minutes since I last heard a handful of trustees pass by.

It was time to execute my plan and get on the move.

In the mess of branches, it took me a good half-hour to strip the rotting d-gen of his clothes, boots, and collar. Once finished, I wriggled my way carefully out through the maze of branches and maneuvered myself into obstacle-free water. I swam around to the downstream side of the pile of wood, spotted the place I wanted to get to, and started climbing.

The branches at water level were slimy with algae, but that didn't prove a major obstacle. After a few careful minutes, I made my way to the end of a broken log that jutted above the rest of the pile.

I was totally exposed. Had a buzz bike flown over, or had another patrol come out of the woods, there's no doubt they would have seen me.

Still, I paused.

When I'd spotted the jutting tree trunk from down below, it looked like the perfect place to stand prior to a jump across the steep part of the bank to the flat, top edge.

Standing up there, though, looking down at a jumble of broken limbs, many of them looking like sharpened stakes laid there to skewer me if I misjudged the distance, I had second thoughts.

The gap looked too long, the fall too far.

But time to fret the situation or time to find a better way to get to the top of the bank without leaving evidence of my passing wasn't a luxury I had. In fact, time was distinctly against me. Every minute that ticked by brought me closer to a work camp sentence that would last into my fifties.

In that light, the spikes below didn't seem so bad.

I drew a deep breath, crouched, and leaped across the gap.

Chapter 51

Goose had been up and down the river a dozen times, flying high on some passes, skimming over the water on others. The Regulator had to be in the river. It couldn't have gone any other way. Goose's men had searched the woods until they were all frustrated and cussing him.

That Regulator just wasn't in there.

It didn't make any sense.

And now he'd put off Workman too long. It was time to accept his medicine.

Goose told Taylor to send the men back to their duties around the farm. He flew over the training compound and saw d-gens still scattered among the admin buildings. He cursed Bart's name. Those d-gens had been Bart's responsibility, and it looked like Bart had done nothing.

As Goose's hover bike floated down in front of the admin building, he saw a scowling Keith Workman standing behind the windows in his office on the second floor. Goose had given half a thought to parking the bike elsewhere and driving up, but with everything on the farm seeming to be running down the crapper all at once, what was one more thing?

Workman was going to yell however long he was going to yell, whether it was about that bitch, Galloway, and the damn d-gens she'd let loose; the slippery Regulator who'd parked his Mercedes SUV in the trees; dead Deke and Rusty Jim — if he even knew about them yet—or the buzz bike Goose had commandeered.

It was a long list of screw-ups, the longest Workman had ever had to deal with in one sitting.

Sure, there'd been things in the past, an abused d-gen girl from time to time, maybe dead, maybe not. There were some failed inspections from Doggett, some bullshit about d-gens with too many bruises and scabs in places their work couldn't have put them. But those weren't Goose's fault. Goose knew if Workman had paid his bribes at the right time in the right sums, there'd have been no trouble with the state, but Workman was always looking for a way to cheap-ass his way out of everything.

And that's why he'd wound up with those civil fines he'd only been able to have commuted by hiring that damned woman.

Every goddamn thing that was going to shit on the farm at the moment, every bit that Goose was going to get the blame for, was rooted in Workman's choice to weasel out of paying his bribes. And there wasn't a damn thing Goose could say about it. Mention one word and Workman would have him transferred to one of those starvation camps out in West Texas.

That was Workman's favorite threat.

On slow feet, Goose reached the lobby doors, and he let himself inside.

Irene peered over the top of the reception counter in front of her desk. "I hope it's not you he's pissed at. He's been stomping around up there like a bull wearing a flank strap."

"'Fraid it is," Goose drawled. "'Fraid so."

"Well, you better get up there and settle him down," said Irene. "He's likely to stomp a hole right through the floor."

Goose stopped by the counter to lean across it with a grin for Irene. "Don't you worry, honey. I'll straighten thangs out." He glanced out the window at d-gens on the lawn. "Galloway let 'em out."

"On purpose?" Irene's mouth hung open as she shook her head.

Goose nodded. "She's a bitch."

"I can think of dirtier words than that," said Irene, "but I'm too much of a lady to say them."

"You are," Goose confirmed.

"I'm not the kind of person to wish ill on other people, but sometimes, I just wish she'd get hit by a truck."

Goose cackled and headed for the elevator. "You and me both, honey."

Chapter 52

A little bit surprised I made the jump to the bank without an injury, I scooted quickly into a stand of shrubs. The ground I'd come down on, at least where it was bare dirt, was tracked in the boot prints of the men who had passed by looking for me. With all that, the marks I'd left on the dirt would not give me away.

Not that it mattered. I wasn't staying.

It was time to execute my new and improved plan, which was sub-optimal in every way, except it gave me the only path I could come up with to get near Sienna before too much of the day disappeared.

I stripped myself bare, wrapped my weapons in my clothes, and stuffed them under a thick bush. I put on the pair of pants I took off the dead d-gen I'd found in the river. I slipped into his torn t-shirt, wrapped his grungy collar around my neck, and buckled it. I sat down and put his work boots on. They were a few sizes too big for my feet, but I pulled the Velcro straps tight. They'd do. I completed my disguise by rolling on the ground to get a good layer of dirt on my skin, taking care to put some smudges on my face. And there I was, no longer a Regulator on the run from an ad-hoc posse, I was one of thirty thousand d-gens on Blue Bean Farms, indistinguishable from the rest except for the randomly assigned name and numbered tag on my collar.

I put my cash and a knife in my pocket, not worried I was leaving my rifle and pistols. They were tools that made it easy to kill a lot of people quickly. I had plenty of skill at making people die without a gun in my hands.

I jogged in the direction of the admin buildings.

Chapter 53

"You better do some talking, and do it quick," Workman told Goose without turning away from the windows.

Goose walked across the Persian rug, past the couch—it wasn't going to be a couch conversation—and dropped his butt into one of the high-backed leather chairs in front of Workman's desk. That's where Workman liked to put him when he did his yelling. "Where you want me to start?"

"Yeah," Workman laughed meanly, "you got a list, don't you?"

Goose didn't answer. He knew how these things went. Workman was finding his excuse to start the yelling. Talking would come after.

Workman snapped around, took one long, hard look at Goose, seated himself across the desk, and leaned forward. He picked up an old horseshoe he used as a paperweight and gripped it in his hands, pulling hard at it, turning his knuckles white as his forearms trembled from the effort. It looked to Goose like Workman might be trying to bend the steel into a straight rod.

This was a deviation from the norm.

Goose got worried.

Goose pulled a bandana out of his pocket and rubbed it over his face. He took off his straw hat and laid it on the chair next to him. He looked at Mr. Workman and stretched his face into pained sincerity before he said, "I been workin' hard, long hours, doin' everything you asked and more you didn't."

Workman clenched his jaw as he tried to twist the horseshoe.

"You know that's true," said Goose. "Ain't nothin' I wouldn't do to make this farm work out for ya, Boss Man. You know it."

Workman looked at Goose like he was trying to burn a hole through him.

No yelling?

Goose leaned forward, and he laid a dirty hand on Workman's desk. "You know all I done, Boss Man. I done some things. Sure I screwed up here an there, but you gotta admit, I get shit done you want done. Ain't nobody gonna work fer you like me."

"If your work's so damn good," Workman spat, "why'd you screw everything so far to Hell today, yesterday — dammit, all week for all I know. Goddammit, Goose, I'm trying to remember the last thing you did right."

Goose shrunk back into his chair as he mumbled, "Most of what I do you don't see 'less it breaks. I keep the trustees in line. You know that. I keep the prisoners on them d-gen lazy asses, and we get our production numbers every month, you know that's true. You know it."

Workman worked at that horseshoe like he might squeeze some resolution out of it. When none came, he spoke in words, slow and simple, the kind an angry man might speak to simple-minded children. "This fiasco started with you telling me you could fix my problem with Dr. Galloway. Now I've got degenerates running all over the farm. I've got fugitive Regulators up to who knows what. The inspector can't work through the kill list 'cause all the defects are running loose. I won't be able to get my replacement requisitions put in because I'll miss the deadline this month.

You've stolen the hover bikes Blue Bean bought for the Warden's men, and I've got two dead trustees I don't have any explanation for."

"'bout Deke and Rusty Jim," said Goose, "them Regulators killt 'em. Ran 'em down with that black SUV. Well, one of 'em anyway. Might only be one Regulator we're trying to catch."

"But they wouldn't be dead if they weren't there trying to steal those hover bikes," Workman accused.

Shaking his head—it was time to spin another lie—Goose said, "Wasn't like that. I noticed the direction them Regulators was headin' and I figured they was goin' for them buzz bikes. I figured they'd want to steal 'em and fly 'em off to Mexico or whatnot."

"And why not just drive there?" Workman asked.

"Can't speak for 'em," said Goose. "They was on the farm. Police chased 'em onto the property. I was just trying to catch 'em 'fore they caused any harm."

"Well you didn't do that," spat Workman.

Goose didn't agree. No real damage had been done except that of letting the d-gens run free, and that blame fell squarely on Dr. Galloway. "They was plannin' to steal them buzz bikes. We stopped 'em. They killed Deke and Rusty Jim fer it. After that, I figured we'd better fly the bikes that was left to keep 'em from goin' back and tryin' to steal 'em again."

"The ones that are left?" Workman asked.

"Them Regulators wrecked two of the buzz bikes when they killed Deke and Rusty Jim."

"Sounds like bullshit to me," said Workman. "Here's what you're going to do about those hover bikes. You're going to park them out front of the building here where I can look out and see them, and you're going to get it done the minute you leave my office. You got me?"

Goose nodded.

"Now," Workman went on, "why don't you tell me how you screwed the pooch in the first place? That's what I want to know. You told me this Galloway plan of yours was a sure thing."

Goose rubbed a hand over his chin, suddenly wondering if Workman was trying to get him to admit his crimes on a recording. When he spoke, he chose his words carefully. "I do exactly what you tell me, but when you tell me you don't want to know the details of what I'm gonna do, I don't give 'em."

"What the hell are you talking about?" Workman yelled.

Goose flinched back in his chair.

"I asked you a simple goddamned question. Answer me."

It's just yelling. He'll burn through it pretty quick.

Goose answered, "You said it couldn't look like nobody here at Blue Bean Farms or the work camp could have anythin' to do with it. That's what you told me."

In a voice coming back down in volume, Workman said, "And you told me she was sneaking away from her cottage at night and that you followed her, and you had an idea to scare her off without getting our hands dirty."

"I did." Goose nodded.

"How many times to do I have to ask you for the goddamn details?" Workman raised his voice again. "You want me to ship you out to Lubbock? Is that what you want? You want to see what the rest of your life in a real hellhole looks like?"

"She was followin' a handful of d-gens," Goose blurted, "off the property where they was meetin' up with other d-gens. Out there in the woods about a mile east of the fence, they had themselves some kind of temple made of rings of old broken-down appliances and such. They built a big fire and danced around it a coupla times a week, cookin' raccoons, and possums and such."

"And Galloway was participating in this?" Workman asked, disgust on his face.

"Just watchin' at first," said Goose. "Mostly, I guess. Eventually, she did strip down, get all covered in blood and dance 'round the fire with them."

"Human sacrifice?" Workman asked.

"None that I saw, but I figured they'd either done it before or would do it soon."

"And?"

It was time for a lie to get some credit he hadn't earned. "I called it in. Told the police I saw the bodies of the kids they was killin'."

"And there weren't any kids?" Workman asked.

Goose shook his head.

"And the phone you used?"

"I ain't completely stupid," said Goose. "Can't be traced back to me."

"But the call had to go out from Blue Bean's network. There's no public cellular network out this far."

Goose shrugged, hoping Workman wouldn't berate him on that implication of his lie. "Can't avoid some things."

"So you called it in. Then what?" asked Workman.

"I figured some Regulators would show up, see all the dancin' and the blood, and just shoot everybody."

"Which they did," said Workman. "Would have been nice if one of them would have accidentally shot her."

Goose shook his head. "I figured it'd be enough to run her off, if not permanent, then maybe fer a week or two."

"No," said Workman, "because you screwed up. Once the shooting started, you should have taken a shot, winged her, or maybe one in the leg." Workman rubbed his hands over his weathered old face and exhaled as he thought about how the weight of his responsibilities was wearing him down. "Maybe you should have just shot her in the head. Maybe we need to stop pussyfooting around this and do what needs to be done."

Goose gulped. In the past, Workman had implied dozens of times that Goose should break the law, but Workman had never explicitly told Goose to do something illegal, especially not when a drone might get a video recording of the whole thing. "Yessir. You're right about that."

"From here on out," said Workman, "I'm in on every detail of everything you do to fix this mess. You need some help with that. It's obvious to me. Is it obvious to you, Goose?"

"Yessir."

Workman tilted his head in a curt nod. "Now, what about these Regulators on the farm? Why are they here?"

"I can't say it's both of them," said Goose. "So far we've only seen one in the SUV. Maybe the other one skedaddled down to Mexico. Anyways, we got one of 'em. Sure of that.

"How can you be *sure* of that?" Workman drawled. His accent always went back to natural country boy when he got riled up. "You either got 'em or you don't."

"The woods that starts up over there on the other side of the trainin' compound," Goose started, "we trapped 'im over there."

"Trapped?"

"We run him off the road," said Goose. "He drove that Mercedes right into the trees." Goose figured he'd embellish. "Prolly got hurt in the crash. He hit them trees awful hard."

"He ran into a tree?" Workman asked.

"Mostly branches and such." Goose rushed to the next part so as not to get caught in an exaggeration that Workman would call a lie. "You know them woods is bordered on the east with the Brazos River. Down south, we got nothing but acre an' acre of soybean fields. There ain't that far to go in them woods."

"Across the river?" Workman asked. "He didn't go that way? Plenty of places to wade it."

"Not now." Goose shook his head emphatically. "When was the last time you was down to the river? All that floodin' up by Waco washed this way. The river ain't much to look at most times but right now, it'll drown you and wash you right down to Freeport 'fore you know what hit ya."

"What are you saying?" Workman asked. "He drowned in the river?"

"Exactly," said Goose. "We cornered him in them woods. Had near fifty men in there lookin' fer 'im. If he'd a been in there, we'd a caught 'im. Only way out was in the water, and we was onto that right off the bat, the buzz bikes running up and down the river, men patrollin' the banks the whole time. A coupla guys heard a big splash." Time for more embellishment. "One saw him jump off the bank. Never come up for air." Time for certainty. "Got caught in that current and drown. Sure as Christmas."

"Did you find the body?"

"Lookin' for it." A new lie.

"No idea, then?" Workman asked.

None. But Goose wasn't about to admit that, now that Workman seemed to be past yelling for the moment.

Workman sat back, intertwined his fingers and scratched his lips up and down with his thumbnails. He was thinking.

Goose didn't interrupt. He waited.

Finally, Workman asked, "Did you see the video on the Internet and on the news about those Regulators killin' our degenerates?"

"You know we ain't allowed to have none of that kinda—"

Workman stopped Goose with a raised hand. "Don't lie about something that's so easy to check. I know you boys have TVs in the trustee dorm."

Embarrassed, Goose admitted, "I seen it."

"You notice anything odd about it?"

Goose shook his head. "I ain't no expert in that kinda stuff, but no."

"You notice how fast it happened?"

"Yeah," said Goose. "Now that you mention it."

"You were there," said Workman. "Did it seem fast to you?"

"I was a couple hundred yards away across a cornfield," said Goose, "watchin' through some binoculars. It was foggy, so I couldn't always see, but once the shootin' started, it was like somebody set off a string of firecrackers and just like that, it was done. The fat one took some shots to clean up the wounded, but that skinny one, he just killed 'em like roaches. Damndest thing."

"Looked like a goddamn science fiction movie robot to me," said Workman. "First time I saw it I figured it was sped up like they do on that show, Bash—you know, making the kills look funny?"

Goose chuckled a little. It was his favorite show.

"It bothered me, though, because it didn't look right," said Workman, "so I had one of my IT boys do some research. That video wasn't sped up."

Goose nodded. "I 'spose not."

"You know why that was?" Workman asked.

"I don't know what you're gettin' at."

"My IT guy did some more research," said Workman. "That video was spot on. My IT boy did some measurements and made himself up a number he called the kill rate."

"Kill rate?" Goose asked.

"You ain't got to look too far to find video of Regulators killing degenerates," said Workman. "Most of them do it slow and methodical, but lots of degenerates run off when the Regulators go slow. The flip side is if they go fast, they miss, maybe wound some."

Goose nodded but didn't interrupt.

"How fast the Regulators kill the degenerates, how accurate they are when they shoot," said Workman, "that's what my IT boy called the kill rate. The higher the number the better, for the Regulator anyways."

"That skinny Regulator did most of the shootin'," said Goose. "How does he compare?"

"Ain't nobody close to that skinny one," answered Workman. "That boy's a killer. My IT guy can't find anything about his past, thinks he might be an assassin out of Mexico, maybe some kind of spy or something."

Goose's voice squeaked up an octave before he could catch it. "What's he want with us, comin' back here to the farm?"

"Can't say." Workman shook his head. "But one thing I do want, is you to get seven or eight of your trustees—your best shots—and put them on guard around me until we find his body in the river."

"You think he's here to kill you?" Goose asked. "Why?"

"I don't know, and I don't want to find out," said Workman. "I'm out of ideas on this one. I'm just not taking chances."

Chapter 54

"The last thing we've got to take care of," said Workman.

"Yessir. What's that?"

"Dr. Galloway."

"I got no problem with it," said Goose, seeing a chance to redeem himself in Workman's eyes. "I'll do it myself."

"It can't be you," said Workman. "Not now. There'll be state scrutiny of this mess with that bastard Doggett onsite. He knows what opportunity looks like. He'll call in the Texas Rangers to investigate, and they won't leave until he squeezes enough money out of me to buy himself another mansion in Dallas with a new whore to keep the bed warm." Workman's anger came to a quick head and he pounded a fist on the desk. After snorting a few times, his voice returned to sinister calm. "I need to make sure Galloway's...." Workman took a moment to firm his resolve, "...death doesn't have anybody's fingerprints on it."

Goose was disappointed, he wanted very badly to take Sienna Galloway out in the woods, find an abandoned house to keep her in, and put her to good use. The thought of those defiant blue eyes turning to tears, getting his hands on those perky tits, squeezing that ass was just too much. Goose could smell her sweaty fear. He could taste her on his lips. He could —

"Goose! Goose!" Workman snapped his fingers to get Goose's attention. "Stay with me. Sometimes you drift off. You make me worry."

"Sorry, Boss Man. Just tired. You know."

"You've got a criminal mind, Goose. Have you got any ideas on how to solve our Galloway problem?"

Goose sprawled in the chair, scratched his neck, and put on a show of dredging his imagination but he already had an idea. He just didn't want to make it look easy. "This morning, when I was getting them signatures you asked for…" Goose paused, fishing for some gratitude along the way.

Workman nodded slightly and said, "Good job with that."

"I took that big Bully Boy, Toby. Told her I was gonna let him do things if she didn't sign."

Workman nodded as if he hadn't heard this story.

"Thing is," said Goose, "I think if I left Toby in that cottage alone with her, I think he'd take care of her all on his own. He ain't right in the head, not by a long shot. I think he might tear her up."

Workman grimaced.

"He's sweet on her in 'is way, if ya know what I mean," said Goose, "but I think we won't find nuthin' but pieces when he's done."

"I didn't realize he was that bad."

Goose showed Workman the Taser he kept on his belt. "I got to urge 'im a lot, to keep 'im in line, you know." Goose patted the pistol in its holster. "I figure he won't be 'round more than another month or two anyway before the Brisbane eats what's left of his brain. I'll have to put 'im down."

Workman understood and moved back to the question at hand. "What if she gets away?"

"All I got to do is get 'em in the same room, same house, don't matter," said Goose. "Toby's awful fast for a big boy and ever' bit as strong as he looks. She won't be goin' nowhere."

Workman gave it some thought. "Get it done, as soon as you can."

"I'll git Toby over there right away."

Chapter 55

After she'd loosed the degenerates, the satisfaction she'd felt from her rebellion had lasted about fifteen minutes. Now she felt disheartened over the futility of it as she sat in a chair staring at the door on the far end of the occupational therapy room. Through that door sat her desk in the office she shared with her staff.

Despite the apparent unassailability of her employment status, she didn't want to go back there. She didn't want to have to face what was probably waiting for her—a summons from Keith Workman, an email or a message on her phone.

In whatever form that message came, it would formalize the escalation in the war between them.

She'd be required to go to his office for a meeting. He'd yell and stomp like a gorilla defending its territory, all the while making sure she knew just what a physically powerful man he was. He'd make sure she understood how close he teetered on the verge of losing control.

The threat of violence would be perfectly clear but completely unprovable.

The worst of it was that she didn't know if the tantrums were an act. If not, then she knew a day would come when he'd cross a line in his mind, and he'd harm somebody, likely her.

Do I want to risk my life for this job?

She knew she was sacrificing her health already. She wasn't sleeping well at night. She hated getting out of bed to face her days. When she looked at herself in the mirror in the morning, she saw a woman who was aging past her years.

Her eyes wandered over the brightly colored walls painted in murals of simple, happy people working the fields, tending farm animals, hauling the harvest. It was Soviet-era propaganda art with degenerates in the place of proletarians.

In her hands, she fidgeted with a simple puzzle toy, one of hundreds in the room used for assessing and training degenerates with rudimentary skills.

When was the right time to admit defeat and quit?

Maybe in releasing the doomed degenerates, she'd already decided, but hadn't admitted it to herself.

She looked again at the door on the back wall of the occupational therapy room. Her computer waited for her back there.

Maybe her best path forward was to go to her desk and put together the exposé she'd been fantasizing about for months. She could write a compelling piece—complete with supporting documents, pictures, and video she'd surreptitiously collected—that would show everyone the truth about the abuses in the corporate farm system, Blue Bean in particular.

Chapter 56

From where Goose stood under the tree facing Toby, he was able to see the training compound nearly a half-mile away. The gate was still open, and from what he'd been told by Workman—whose IT guy had triangulated the position of her cell phone—Sienna Galloway was in there, probably sitting at her desk. Goose had one of his trustees sneak around the training compound to confirm. Except for a few d-gens too stupid to leave the compound, not a single trustee or employee was anywhere near.

It was like she was begging for it.

Hell, maybe she knew Workman's revenge was coming and she'd given up.

It was possible.

Goose had seen women break before, seen them stop fighting, seen the last speck of hope drain from their eyes. You could do most anything to a woman once she ran out of hope.

But that moment when the hope faded…Goose savored it.

He sighed. Big, stupid Toby was going to have all the fun with Galloway. He'd be there the moment the hope blipped away from those bitchy blue eyes, and he was too stupid to appreciate it. The worst part—Goose would only get to see the mess afterward.

"Ya see them buildin's over there?" Goose pointed at the training compound.

Toby looked in that direction, drool dribbling down his chin.

"Close yer mouth," Goose ordered.

Toby turned back to Goose and did as told.

"You see that open gate?" Goose pointed again.

Toby looked.

"Nod if you understand."

Toby nodded.

"See that buildin' right there by the gate, the white one?"

Toby nodded.

"You know how to open a door?" Goose wasn't sure. A door handle, sure, you pull or push and the door opens. With a knob, it needs to be turned, and *then* pulled or pushed. Connecting an action that seems to produce no result with the action you want takes a small degree of abstract thought. Most d-gens couldn't make the leap. But Toby was a few grades up from your standard dumbass degenerate.

Toby didn't give Goose any indication he understood.

Goose reached up and slapped Toby on the cheek. "Listen boy! A door." Goose pantomimed turning a knob and opening a door. "You understand? Can you open one?"

Toby looked at Goose for a few long moments with nothing but confusion on his face until a sudden spark flickered somewhere behind his eyes. He nodded.

"Good, good." Goose laughed. He pointed again. "There's a door on that white building inside the fence. You walk down there and go through it. You understand?"

Toby nodded.

"You go inside and go to the back of the room. There's another door back there. You gittin' what I'm sayin'?"

No response.

"You understand what I'm tellin' you, boy?"

Toby nodded, and when his head pitched forward a gob of drool spilled over his lip and ran down his chin.

"You think you're droolin' now, boy? Looky here. You remember that pretty lady you and me saw this mornin' in her towel, all that nekkid skin hangin' out?"

Toby nodded enthusiastically.

"I knew you wasn't too dumb to forget that. Prolly the nakedest woman you seen that didn't stink like a hobo's ass." Goose grinned again as he thought about all that smooth skin.

Toby was still nodding.

"She's in there. She's waitin' fer you." Goose reached out and grabbed Toby's crotch. "You take this here little pecker, and you stick it in her. You hear me?"

Toby made some garbled noises that didn't mean anything in an educated sense, but Goose understood.

"Now if she tells you no, don't you listen. If she tries to stop you, you go right ahead anyways. She ain't got no sense. She's crazy. You just do whatever you want. Now git." Goose slapped Toby on the shoulder. "Run on down there and do it."

Toby took off at a jog.

Goose watched for a bit, making sure Toby was heading to the right place.

Satisfied, Goose turned and hurried toward the administration building. If any question ever came up as to how Sienna Galloway had come to be raped and murdered by Toby, Goose needed to be sure he was free and clear with an alibi.

Chapter 57

Goose swung the lobby's glass door open and displayed his snaggled teeth in a lascivious grin at Irene. "Anybody call you 'bout that big dumb Bully Boy wanderin' 'round?"

"What's that you're talking about, Goose?" Irene sat up straight in her chair and scooted away from her computer monitor.

"With everything else goin' on," said Goose as he reached the reception counter, "seems that boy wandered off too. Been tryin' to get him put back in his cage." Goose stopped and corrected himself. "I mean, room."

Irene shuddered and looked through the glass walls on the front of the lobby. "That boy scares me."

Goose shrugged. "That's what they supposed to do. Scare regular folks, I guess. He was an Army d-gen, you knew that, right?"

"I knew." Irene glanced at her computer. "Saw the requisition before it got sent out."

Goose made a show of looking around. "Some of the boys said he come this way."

"Well, I haven't seen him."

Goose looked back out through the glass. "Hell, prolly went on back to his bed anyway. I'll prolly find him there later." He looked down at the phone on Irene's desk. "You mind?"

Irene shook her head and scooted the phone closer to Goose.

Goose picked up the receiver, "Dial the Boss Man for me, honey, please?"

Irene did so.

The phone rang once before a familiar voice came on the line. "Workman."

"Boss Man," Goose glanced at Irene and gave her a wink to make sure her attention stayed on him. "I'm down here waitin' just like you asked."

"Good," said Workman. "Is that thing we talked about taken care of?"

"In the works."

"Good. You stay in the lobby with Irene. Sit in one of the chairs and wait. Tell her I'm delayed. How long do you think this might take?"

"Not long, I should think," said Goose. "How long you wanna give it?"

"I'd feel comfortable with a couple of hours."

Goose had too much to do to waste two hours sitting in the lobby working on his alibi. "Oh yeah, somethin' you should know."

"What's that?"

"We picked up one of them Regulators."

Workman's tone changed instantly, from baseline annoyed to something near happy. "That's good news."

"A couple of the boys got him up north of the property, wanderin' in the woods like he was lost."

"Off the property?" Workman asked, slipping back to annoyed again.

"Don't nobody know that, 'specially him."

"Did he say what they were doing coming back here today?" asked Workman.

"Didn't say nothin' about any of that, far as I know. You want me to have the boys ask him some questions?"

"No," Workman answered quickly. "Nothing like that. Not yet. I'll tell you what. Have your boys bring him over. Make sure he's not armed, and then you bring him on up here. We'll have a talk and get some answers."

"Yessir."

Chapter 58

Sienna Galloway heard the outer door open, but with the door separating her office from the occupational therapy room standing only slightly ajar, she didn't have a line of sight to the outer door. Irritated to have her privacy intruded upon, she immediately guessed it was one of her direct reports, coming back to fetch something forgotten from a desk while rushing out the door after being sent home earlier.

Making good progress on her exclusive for the media and not wanting to be distracted by having to pretend that the civility between her and her subordinates was anything more than a veil, she opened a drawer, took out a pair of headphones and plugged them into her computer.

With her ears safely muffled, she turned her music on and concentrated on the last thing she'd ever do as an employee of Blue Bean Farms.

As she searched for a video file she knew she'd saved, she started to wonder if she was engaged in something illegal, exposing what might be considered corporate secrets. But if Blue Bean Farms was acting illegally, could that behavior still be a corporate secret?

It's bullshit that I even have to worry about this!

Sometimes Sienna wondered if humanity had become too clever for its own good. Would the world be a better place when Brisbane finally sank its prion-generating mutation into every last human? Would a world ruled by halfwits be a better place?

Different halfwits?

Sienna laughed at the private joke.

The door flung open and banged against the inner wall.

Sienna looked up.

In the doorway stood a familiar, hulking silhouette.

She screamed for help.

Chortling, with slobber running down his chin, Toby grasped the doorjamb and leaned into the office.

Frozen in her seat, Sienna looked right and left for a weapon as her mind ran through an inventory of what items lay in her desk drawers that might serve to protect her. Nothing. In desperation, she shouted, "Goose, you better come in here and get your pet!"

The purse! The pepper spray!

Sienna looked to the floor. Where was her purse?

Kicked under the desk while she was working?

It wouldn't be the first time.

Toby locked Sienna in a feral stare and stepped into the room. He crouched and spread his arms wide as he moved forward, ready to pounce left or right.

Sienna scooted her chair out and stood. "Stay where you are."

Toby ignored the command.

"Do as you're told. I order you!"

Toby raised one of his meaty hands and dragged it across his mouth, leaving a glisten of the drool he'd smeared.

Sienna glanced at the desk sitting against the wall opposite hers. It belonged to her second-in-charge, a backwoods nephew of Workman named Caleb. Sienna had reprimanded him on three occasions for using a cattle prod on the degenerates in the training compound, and after each incident, she'd caught him using the cattle prod again. She knew he kept it at his desk.

Keeping her eyes on Toby, she started across the floor toward Caleb's desk. She pointed a finger at the door. "You, go!"

Toby kept coming, slow and careful. He was a hunter. She was the prey.

"Goose!" she called. For the first time since she'd laid eyes on Goose nearly a year ago, she wished the creep would answer. She hoped this was just another of his intimidation tactics. "I'm quitting. I'm leaving. You and Workman can have this whole goddamn place. Call off your dog!"

If Goose was out there, he didn't let on.

"You win. I quit." Sienna heard fear in her voice as she yelled.

She stepped behind Caleb's desk and took her eyes off Toby in quick glances as she pulled each drawer out.

Toby was close. His breathing grew rapid, he smiled, giving a frightening hint of what he was planning to do to her.

Sienna glanced at the other desks. Could she jump up on top, leap from desk to desk along the wall to stay out of his reach and get to the door?

Maybe.

She was lithe. She was fast.

He was a brute. Slow. Stupid.

Then she saw it—three feet long, dull prongs at one end, tape-wrapped handle leaning between the wall and the desk —the cattle prod.

Yes!

Sienna grabbed the cattle prod and pointed the business end at Toby. She didn't see recognition of the device on his face, but he paused. She said, "You know what this is? You want some?" She poked it toward him. He didn't flinch.

She put a foot on Caleb's chair, poked the prod at Toby once more and stepped up onto the desk. "Back. Back!"

Toby waved a hand at the prod, but Sienna jerked it back before Toby could get hold.

He scooted closer, holding up his hands.

"Have it your way." She pushed the button on the handle, jammed it at Toby's grasping hand, and touched skin.

Toby yelped and jerked his arm away.

She poked toward his face and Toby stepped back. "Yeah. That hurts, right? You don't want any more of that." She gauged the distance to the next desk. Poked the prod at Toby one more time to get him moving back, and she made her leap.

Toby rushed in while she was in the air between the desks. He thrust a powerful arm across her waist and flung her.

Sienna felt helpless, like a child's doll.

She'd never have guessed Toby could be so strong.

Her heels knocked Caleb's computer off his desk as she flew over and hit the wall behind.

She crumpled to the floor, dazed and trying to catch her breath.

A big fist hit her in the face, blinding her to anything but flashing stars and pain.

Toby hit her again.

Big hands lifted her and threw her over a desk. A chair flew across the room. Computer equipment crashed. Sienna struggled to get away, to move, but a hand pressed on the middle of her back, holding her bent over the desk. She pushed. She elbowed. No matter how much she tried, she couldn't get out of Toby's god-awful, strong grip.

He jerked at her blouse from the back. Plastic buttons popped off and tinkled across the floor. He jerked again, pulling her arms back as he yanked the shirt all the way off.

She screamed.

He grasped her bra and pulled, snapping it into pieces.

"Don't!" She was regaining her senses. She knew what was happening. "Don't! No!" She kicked. She flung her elbows back and hit arms, legs, torso—nothing seemed to phase the ape.

Toby's fat fingers slid under her waistband inside her pants at the small of her back.

"No!"

He jerked and her jeans dug into her stomach.

He jerked again. The button on the waistband popped off and the zipper separated. She screamed as the jeans went down and the zipper's metal teeth dragged down her thighs.

One of his hands mashed her face onto the cold metal of the desk as he pushed himself against her, his other hand groping, his mouth making animal noises.

She turned her head to pull free and he grabbed a handful of her hair. He jerked her head back and then banged it against the desk. Everything went hazy again.

Chapter 59

Lutz hadn't been hurt. He hadn't even been threatened, not since he'd first been ordered to stand still after seeing the Blue Bean logo on the door of the truck. He'd made a feeble attempt to run back into the woods, but with each step he took, he was silently pleading to be ordered to halt.

No warrant for Lutz had yet been issued. Blue Bean could inconvenience him at worst. What they most certainly would do was haul him out of this hellish forest where the plants and insects were intent on killing him, one micro-bite at a time.

Since the moment of his capture—rescue—he'd done as told with the exception that he hadn't answered any questions aside from providing his name. He complained when they took his rifle, pistol, billfold, and phone. He'd demanded his freedom at least a half-dozen times and each time was ignored. That was the extent of their conversations.

They'd driven him onto Blue Bean property and eventually unloaded him in front of a remote building that might have been a ranch house a hundred years ago. It was built of weathered limestone with rusty iron grates bolted into the stone over the windows. An old wooden barn was slowly collapsing from rot nearby. A windmill with half the blades missing stood beside the remains of a water tank. No other houses or buildings were visible across the fields in any direction.

After they stowed him in a holding cell in the country-house-turned-jailhouse, he was subsequently ignored. He had plenty of time to wonder whether they'd torture or beat him for information they might think he had—he was certainly in the right kind of place for that. He wasn't sure what he'd tell them, but he had an ace up his sleeve he'd show if he had to.

His only other worry was that a rattlesnake might crawl up through a crack in the old wooden floor and try to snuggle with him.

When they finally came back to his cell, they led him out, and loaded him into the pickup. None of the guards would say where they were taking him or what his fate might be. He figured—hoped—they were going to set him free, maybe by taking him to the property line and telling him to get lost, hopefully on a road frequently traveled.

That wasn't to be.

The pickup drove up in front of Blue Bean's admin building, a structure Lutz recognized from the images sent over earlier by Ricardo. What Ricardo's images didn't show were the armed men strolling around outside the building, keeping an eye on anything or anybody trying to approach.

The guards were an irrelevancy now. Lutz figured he was scot-free. He'd come to the attention of the people in charge. Unlike the dipshit trustees, the people running Blue Bean must have realized they couldn't hold him. In fact, they had probably come to understand that by holding him against his will they were breaking the law in a felonious fashion.

The trustees hauling Lutz opened the back door of the pickup and told him to get out.

Just as Lutz planted his feet on the ground and started to ask questions, one of the admin building's glass doors swung open and out strode a country boy who looked like he'd lived forty hard, hard years. He wore cut-off sleeves, a beat-up straw hat, and a smile that would frighten a dentist.

262

"Howdy," the man said. He extended a hand to shake as he stepped up in front of Lutz. "Goose Eckenhausen."

Lutz walked over to shake Goose's hand, and Goose immediately took his hand back and put his hands up in front of him. "Whoa. Looks like you got yerself in a mess of poison ivy." The ragged smile stayed on his face.

Lutz ignored the comment. "Are you in charge here?"

"You have no right to hold me."

"Hell," said Goose. "We ain't holdin' ya. We're lookin' after ya."

Lutz looked at a plastic bag being held by one of the trustees guarding him. It contained his possessions. "I need to use my phone to make a call." He motioned toward the bag as he looked at the guard on the other side. "I need my rifle and pistol back, too."

Goose waved a hand, gesturing at everything that could be seen from horizon to horizon. "This here's a work camp on Blue Bean property. It's part of the Texas penal system. Unless you're a Texas Ranger or State Trooper, you can't be totin' no guns 'round here. It ain't lawful."

Lutz nodded at the gun on Goose's hip. "You're armed." Lutz glanced at the other men. "They are, too."

"We work here."

"Give me a ride off the property." Lutz told Goose.

Goose slapped Lutz on the shoulder. "Yer gittin' all worked up 'bout nuthin', son. Why don't you come on in? Boss Man wants to have a word with you." Goose turned to go.

Lutz didn't move. "I thought you were in charge."

Goose spun around, giggling. "In charge ah these boys, that's all. Mr. Workman runs the farm. He wants to talk to you."

Lutz looked at the bag containing his phone.

"Don't worry 'bout that stuff," said Goose. He took the plastic bag containing Lutz's effects and told the trustee to leave Lutz's weapons at Irene's desk. He then led Lutz inside.

Chapter 60

Getting through the woods had been easy. The search for me had moved on. When I came out of the forest on the backside of the training compound, I saw d-gens loitering still. Whatever effort Blue Bean was putting into getting them corralled wasn't enough.

With no trustees around I could see in the immediate vicinity, and with the gate still wide open on the other side of the compound, I walked the perimeter, keeping a pace to match the d-gens I saw. I'd sacrificed my weapons for the d-gen disguise I was wearing, it made sense to act the part as well.

Once I arrived at the front side of the compound, I noticed in the distance a group of men herding a small group of d-gens into a fifth wheel livestock trailer hooked onto the bed of a pickup. They were far enough away that none of them noticed me. I was just another stray.

I passed through the gate and went toward the first building on the left. Sienna Galloway's office was supposed to be inside. With luck, I'd find her there. Unfortunately, the door didn't face the gate. I figured it faced the expansive open area in the center of the compound, so I walked along the wall to get to the front of the building.

Something inside bumped the wall.

A woman inside screamed, but the sound stopped abruptly.

I hurried around to the front of the building.

Following the sound of the scream, I opened the door with caution and saw down the length of a room with propaganda art on the walls and children's toys scattered across gaudy carpet. At the other end of the room, a door opened to reveal an array of desks in a back office.

Down toward the end, I saw the source of the noises I'd heard, a steroid-juiced Bully Boy was struggling to get his pants open with one hand while he held a blonde woman bent over a desk in front of him. I saw a familiar tattoo on her arm. I'd found Sienna Galloway.

I've heard it said that it's those choices you make when you don't have time to think that tell you who you are—behind the façade you show other people, behind the lies you tell yourself.

I don't know if it's true.

I think maybe it's a rationalization to help people feel good about mistakes they've made that happened to turn out well.

Either way, that's how I made my decision, in an instant, when I saw that bald-headed gorilla trying to rape the blonde woman I'd almost shot the night before.

I let go of the door and ran on feet practiced at silent sprints, like a jungle cat coming in for a kill.

The Bully Boy could have seen me running at him had he glanced up just once. He didn't. His libido had hypnotized him with naked skin and the possibility that his waggly little Johnson was going to do something naughty.

I was running at full speed when I passed through the doorway into the office, when something—a sound maybe, or a peripheral blur in his vision—caused Bully Boy's head to tilt up for a look.

I'd made my leap by then, and if his mind had time to understand what he was seeing, he'd have seen an angry looking d-gen flying at his face.

He had no time to react. In fact, his fate was sealed the moment I passed through the inner door at a run. After that, nothing he could have done would have made a difference in the outcome. No time.

My shoulder hit Bully Boy square in the face as I wrapped my arms around his giant head. I gripped tight and let my body swing around over his left shoulder—I wasn't trying to tackle him. My momentum carried me, torquing all my weight on his massive neck.

Through my hands pressed tight against his slick head, I felt the vibrations of bone snapping and grinding. My feet, and then my knees, hit the wall behind the desk, and I let go of him so I could catch my balance.

My back hit the wall, and I landed on my feet, looking at Bully Boy, who was looking at me with wide eyes, an opened mouth, and a body facing 180 degrees in the other direction.

His neck was broken. His spine severed. He collapsed between me and the desk.

I stepped on his genitals out of spite as I made my way quickly around to the side of the desk. Sienna Galloway was breathing, but she wasn't moving much. I laid a hand on her back. "Hey. You okay?"

She jerked.

"It's okay."

She looked at me, confused. She pulled away.

I stepped back to let her know I wasn't a threat.

She pushed herself off the table, covering her breasts with one hand as she looked down and spotted the dead Bully Boy at her feet. She stumbled and fell against the wall beside the desk.

"You okay?" I asked.

She had blood dribbling out of her mouth and flowing out of her nose.

"I'm not going to hurt you."

She looked down at the Bully Boy, tried to get away, but tripped on the jeans pushed down around her knees.

I pointed. "He's dead." I spotted what I guessed was the remains of her blouse laying on the floor on my side of the desk. I squatted down and picked it up. I reached it out to her. "Why don't you put this on?"

She was struggling to get her pants pulled up and giving me fearful looks.

I laid the blouse in front of her, turned my back, and took a few steps down the aisle between the desks. "Take your time. You've got a bloody nose and mouth. Are you dizzy? Can you keep your balance?" I was concerned she might have a concussion. "Anything broken?"

"I…" She was fighting with tears. "I'm fine." That sounded angry.

I decided that was probably good.

I heard the thud of a foot kicking dead Bully Boy meat. Maybe she was stomping his dead dick, too. Also good.

I gave her a moment and then glanced over my shoulder. She had her pants pulled up but was having no luck getting them fastened with shaky hands. I turned away.

"Who are you?" she asked.

"Christian Black."

"Why are you dressed like a degenerate? Why do you have a Blue Bean collar on?"

I glanced back again. She had her blouse on, open at the front except for a hand holding it together. Her other hand was keeping her jeans from falling down.

"Do you have something else to wear?" I asked, not knowing what she could possibly have. I was planning the next step, which I figured had to include leaving the building

—that meant clothing. I was guessing she wouldn't want to remain.

She glared at me. "You didn't answer my question."

"I did," I offered as an argument. "I told you my name."

"That doesn't tell me anything." She was already getting her fight back. "What are you doing here?"

I saw her face turn suddenly to hate, and she looked around for something.

I took a quick glance and saw a cattle prod on the floor between the desks near my feet. I leaned down, picked up the prod, and held it out to her, handle first. "You looking for this?"

She snatched it away. "Did Goose send you? Did you bring Toby in here? Because you can tell Goose—"

"I don't know any Goose."

"Goose Eckenhausen?" She clarified. "Your boss. Redneck with bad teeth. You don't know him?" She pointed at the corpse. "The moron who holds his leash?"

I shook my head.

"Who sent you?" she demanded.

I glanced down at the body. "I don't have anything to do with this. I heard the noise. I came in."

"You don't make any sense. You better stop lying."

Stop lying? "Or what?" Probably not the best thing to say. I looked down at myself. "This is a long story. I can tell you the whole thing if you want to hear it but it's not interesting. I'm here to see you. You are Sienna Galloway, aren't you?"

Sienna didn't answer.

"Doesn't matter. I know you are. I've seen your Blue Bean ID. Dr. Sienna Galloway. Five-Six. Green eyes. Behavioral Conditioning Specialist at Blue Bean Agriculture, LLC."

"You work for Blue Bean?"

"No," I told her. "I reached into the pocket of my pants and pulled out a damp wad of money and threw it on the table. Maybe it wasn't the most opportune moment to offer a bribe but I was on a tight schedule, and she seemed to be bouncing right back from her trauma. Perhaps she'd have nightmares later. That wasn't my concern, though.

She looked at the cash, more confused. "What the hell?"

"That's ten thousand dollars." I looked back down at the dead Bully Boy and in the face of what she'd just gone through, the money suddenly seemed like a paltry token. "I can get more if I need to."

"For what? So I won't talk? You don't want me to tell anybody that he tried to rape me?" She pointed at the corpse. "Goose did send you."

"I don't know what you're talking about with this 'Goose' you keep bringing up," I told her. "I was there last night. I saw you in the clearing."

The girl's brow furrowed. She tried to place me. "You… you got away. You were there?"

Shit. She thought I was one of the d-gens. "I wasn't dancing."

"But…" then her eyes showed me she understood. "You're a Regulator. You killed all those degenerates."

"It was an accident."

"An accident?" she yelled. "How do you accidentally shoot two dozen innocent people? How the hell does that happen?"

"We had a pending sanction, but the ID never got assigned." An unformed question in her eyes told me she didn't have any knowledge of the details of my business. For clarification, I added, "The sanction didn't get approved. It was a dirty kill." Everybody knew what a dirty kill was.

"How do you get a sanction for something that never happened? Nobody was hurt. No violence. They were roasting raccoons and dancing."

"Somebody called in a tip," I told her, "said they were sacrificing kids. With the fog, things got confused."

"Somebody called from the middle of the woods," Sienna mocked. "Am I supposed to believe that?"

"Look," I told her, as I gestured at the dead Bully Boy. "You're worked up. I understand that. I'm just saying that somebody phoned the police. Somebody called from the network here on Blue Bean Farms. That's why I was out there with my partner. This wasn't our fault."

"Why would anybody call from Blue Bean, that doesn't —" She stopped, mouth agape, like an epiphany was blazing bright in angel fire on the wall behind me.

"You know something. Tell me."

She shook her head, looked down at Toby, and dropped into a chair that had been pushed into the corner during the struggle. "It couldn't be."

"What?" I asked. "Tell me."

"I think they're trying to kill me."

Bobby Adair

Chapter 61

Lutz looked at Keith Workman in his starched shirt and primped hair sitting across the desk with a wall of windows at his back, rubbing his wealth in Lutz's face without stooping to the vulgarity of saying it out loud. Workman had shoulders that had maybe worked for a hard living many years ago, but now they were sagging. The callouses on his hands had gone soft, and he wore a gut bigger than Lutz's.

Bumpkin-done-good country boy masking a slimy business behind a megawatt smile.

Lutz hated him.

He hated the type.

In truth, Lutz hated most types of most people.

Who was he kidding? He hated them all.

Lutz glanced over his left shoulder. The Goose dipshit was lingering there. At the moment, Lutz hated him most of all.

It made Lutz nervous to have that lifer back there. And he had to be a lifer. Lutz knew how the corporate farms integrated with the work camps: d-gens did the grunt work, prisoners supervised them, trustees policed the prisoners — not a one getting paid — and some smiling palm-greaser like Workman sitting astride the golden goose and thinking himself a business genius.

"You're Lutz, right?" Workman asked. "Franco Lutz."

Lutz nodded at the plastic bag containing his things sitting on Workman's desk. "It's not a secret."

Workman smiled and leaned back in his chair, as if he and Lutz were sitting on the back porch sharing a beer and talking about a favorite hunting dog. "No, it's not a secret. I didn't have to look at your billfold to know who you are. I've got people."

Lutz's lip twitched. It was a nervous response that fired whenever his background was mentioned unexpectedly. "You smile like you want to pretend we're friends," said Lutz. "I'll play." He looked over his shoulder again at Goose. "No friend of mine would leave that guy standing there."

Workman waved a hand and Goose walked over to the window behind Workman's desk.

"Here, Boss Man?" Goose asked.

Workman looked at Lutz and asked, "Good?"

Lutz nodded.

Goose turned his back to the conversation. He leaned on a wall and looked out the window.

"What do you want with me?" Lutz asked.

"The question is," responded Workman, "what do you want with *me*?"

"Nothing," Lutz told him automatically. He deliberately reached out for the plastic bag containing his things and took it off Workman's desk. He opened it up and fished around for his phone. "I need to make a call."

Workman sat forward in his chair, reached out, and scooted a desk phone across to Lutz. "Your cell phone won't be able to access our network. Use mine if you want."

Lutz eyed the desk phone warily.

"Call whoever you like."

Lutz stopped rummaging in his bag, trying to guess what game Workman was playing.

"I know what you and your partner, Christian Black, did last night," said Workman. "You boys are guilty as hell. I suspect you and I might be seeing a lot of one another pretty soon."

Goose giggled behind Lutz.

Lutz shook his head.

"Disagree if you want." Workman shrugged. "Makes no difference to me. What I don't understand is why you and your partner came here instead of running off to Mexico. Hell, it ain't that far. You could have been across the border in time for breakfast tacos."

"Got other plans," said Lutz.

"And that's what I need to know," said Workman, leaning on his desk and turning serious. "What plans brought you back here, because it concerns me. It concerns Blue Bean Farms. It concerns our work camp. So why don't you tell me, Mr. Lutz, what are these other plans?"

Lutz kept his mouth shut as he stared at Workman, still trying to figure what was up. He was in a conversation he shouldn't have been having. There was no reason for it, at least not regarding what Lutz understood about the situation. And that made Lutz curious. "Why do *you* think I'm here?"

"Oh?" Workman rubbed his chin. "It's a game you want to play."

Lutz shook his head. "I'm a business man. I'm looking for an opportunity."

"By trespassing?"

"No," said Lutz. "By talking to you."

"Okay," said Workman. "Let me tell you what I think. My people tell me you're a ne'er-do-well Regulator with a spotty past—so spotty, in fact, I'm surprised you haven't been a guest at the work camp here before. Questions abound about the deaths of your former partners. And now you're hooked up with this Christian Black, some kind of hitman out of Mexico."

Goose giggled again. "He's drowned now."

Drowned?

It wasn't possible, not with Christian Black.

Lutz didn't want his disappointment to show, so he masked it with a question. "What about my car?"

Goose pointed toward a line of trees in the south. "He drove it into the forest a mile or two down the road, a little piece from the river. We looked for him a good while. One of the boys heard him go into the water. Damn stupid if you ask me with that current right now. He drowned tryin' to cross. Maybe a gator got 'em. Don't know."

"My Mercedes?" Lutz persisted.

"Damn thing's fine," said Goose. "Still sittin' over there in them trees, though."

"Forget about the car," Workman told Lutz. "What I want to know is why you brought a hitman here from Mexico?"

Lutz saw Workman's mask of confidence turn transparent for a second and Lutz understood—Workman was afraid of Christian. Lutz couldn't help but laugh. "You think I brought him here to kill you."

Chapter 62

She explained her list of clues to me: the brush with death down the sight of my rifle, the deteriorating relationship with Workman and his staff, culminating in the revelation in the meeting with Doggett that he was stuck with her, couldn't fire her without getting buried in fines from the state, the threats from Goose that morning, and now the dead Bully Boy.

To her, it all added up to concrete proof.

Through the string of stories she grew calm. She had an analytical mind and as it engaged she'd disconnected her emotions from what had just happened. That said something about her. She was strong.

Or she was on the sociopathic side of normalcy.

Sometimes it's hard to guess which.

"Why'd you come here?" she finally asked, turning her attention to the wad of damp cash I'd tossed on Caleb's desk. "Why that?"

"A bribe," I answered simply.

"For what?"

"For you."

"Why?"

"There's a warrant out for me. For last night."

"Because you murdered those degenerates?" She said it with no emotion at all. That seemed odd to me. She was disconnecting.

I shrugged. With no valid sanction to cover my ass, technically, she was right.

"That was quick."

I nodded.

"Why?"

"Don't know," I answered. "Sometimes things don't go your way." I pointed at the money. "I need you to lie for me."

"Lie for you? I don't even know you."

I cast a deliberate look down at the Bully Boy. "We're not friends, but I think I did you a favor with that one."

Sienna looked at her feet. "What do you want me to say?"

"Say there was a toddler on that fire before we arrived last night."

Shaking her head, Sienna said, "That won't do any good. I'll just go to jail for perjury or something. You guys have videos from spotter drones, right?" She was analyzing my problem now. "I don't watch TV much, but I've seen the kill videos. It's hard to miss them. Weren't there any drones up there last night?"

"There were," I told her, keeping my voice steady. "That part's being taken care of. Mostly. I need an eyewitness to seal the deal. I need you." I pointed at the money. "Ten thousand. I'll get you another ten if that'll make this go any smoother."

"Twenty thousand to lie."

I nodded.

"Or twenty thousand plus the obligation you want me to feel for saving me from him." She pointed at the body.

The obligation should have been enough by itself, but I didn't say that. "Whatever works."

Muttering, she said, "Everybody wants me to turn a blind eye so they can kill degenerates with the rubber stamp of the state. Everybody wants my integrity."

"It's not that." I told her the story of how the sanction appeared to me and Lutz, how Lutz thought he saw dead children and more to be slaughtered, how he'd started shooting and I had to shoot to keep him from getting killed. It was just an unfortunate incident made worse by the fog. It was a mistake, not a crime. I finally said, "It's just one lie."

"And it's *never* just one lie," she shot back.

That ended the conversation. She pulled her buttonless shirt together, and her eyes fell to the body on the floor as she retreated into herself, maybe thinking about my offer, maybe settling in with the emotions that were just now catching up.

That's how it was with most people. In-person violence is frightening in a sticky way that doesn't flit away with the next scene like scares in the movies.

To most, death is a sanitized, repackaged, repurposed product wrapped in Hollywood-generated emotions. Fictional movie heroes slaughtering d-gens to save virgins from monsters' lecherous grasps doesn't bother anybody. That's entertainment. Reality shows turning the killing into a joke, that's just a laugh.

TV turned death into something it wasn't. It peeled away the suffering. Flat-screen entertainment might show a pair of pleading eyes, but it can never convey the fright a thing feels when it knows death has come. The smell of the panic-piss never leaches through. Nobody every shits their pants before they die on TV. Nobody's skull explodes warm blood on your face. You never taste what gets in your mouth. You never have to spit out niblets of brain and gritty bone.

So when real death drops at someone's feet, with its overwhelming sensations, they're seldom prepared. They scream. They cry. They run. And sometimes, like Sienna, they withdraw.

I don't do any of those things.   I feel no empathy, no remorse.

That's not to say I don't understand the pain of others, especially the dying, but I understand it in a clinical way. None of it ever touches my emotions.

And it had always been that way. The state psychologist said I'd disconnected emotionally after shooting both my parents—back in those days it wasn't illegal to kill those whose brains were being rotted by the prions.   I let the psychologist think what she wanted. I knew I'd always been the way I was.

I'm not claiming to be a monster.   I don't get off on watching things die. In fact, seeing the dying brings me no pleasure at all.   For me, it's business.   I kill for money. Looking down at the dead Bully Boy, I supposed I killed for a few other reasons, too.

Some fuckers just deserve an untimely death.

Chapter 63

Lutz watched Workman's face flush as he sat back in his chair, harrumphed, and adjusted himself behind the desk.

"That's why you have those men outside with rifles?" Lutz asked.

Workman glanced toward the window.

Goose turned away from the glass and silently nodded at Lutz.

Still laughing, Lutz said, "If you did your research, then you should know if Christian *were* here to kill you, those men wouldn't do you any good."

"Why not?" Workman asked. "Is he that sneaky?"

"I don't know how much of what I read was true," answered Lutz. "But if it's half-true, then he'd just kill 'em."

"Kill them?" Workman asked, trying to force a smile onto his face. "You hear that Goose, the guy who drowned in the river was going to kill all those men downstairs just to get to me."

Seeing Workman's vulnerability, Lutz said, "You don't have anything to worry about. Christian isn't here to kill *you*."

"Wait." Workman froze. "Are you saying he *is* here to kill someone?"

Lutz realized he'd said too much. "No. I didn't say that."

"You did," Workman told him. He was back to being a superior prick again.

"Don't matter anyway," Goose said without turning away from whatever had his attention out the window. "He's drowned."

"I'm not going to threaten you, Mr. Lutz." Workman let that obvious lie sink in before he proceeded. "But if a man thinks he might be in danger, if his beloved employees might be threatened, well, there ain't no law all the way out here to protect him." Workman sat back in his chair again. He slowly opened a desk drawer, reached in, and took out a knife with an antler handle and a long, wide silver blade. Workman set to awkwardly scraping the tip of the blade under his fingernails. "A man's got to take matters into his own hands. You understand me, Mr. Lutz?"

Lutz looked at the blade. He understood the threat.

Goose took a glance at Workman and emphasized for Lutz's benefit, "That's a big knife."

Lutz rubbed his face as he thought about the best tack for fishing information out of Workman. Something about the guy wasn't right. And if Lutz's instincts were correct—and they usually were in these matters—then Workman was up to no good. He decided to put a few of his cards on the table. "If you did any research at all, you'd know Christian and me got into a little mishap last night just off your property."

"We know," said Workman. "Half the damn country's seen that video by now."

"That video might not be exactly accurate," said Lutz.

"How's that?" asked Workman.

"A clearer version might show up later that shows there were dead children there, so Christian and I were justified in the kill."

"The version I saw was pretty clear," said Workman. "Bits and pieces, but it was just as clear as can be."

"That was altered," said Lutz. "We have the original video, but we came here to convince one of your employees to back our version of the video when the police come to ask which version is fake."

"Convince?" Workman asked.

Lutz looked at his hands in his lap. "Bribe, maybe."

"With a hit man from Mexico?" Workman made his disbelief clear with his tone.

"I think maybe you're reading too much into this situation," Lutz told him. "Our business here has nothing to do with you personally."

Workman put his elbows on the table. He interlocked his fingers as he stared at Lutz with eyes that seemed to be trying to read his thoughts.

Lutz held Workman's eyes for a moment before he looked away, letting Workman think he was the biggest monkey in the tree.

"You know what I think?" Workman asked.

Lutz shook his head.

"I think you figured you'd kill her instead of bribing her. That way the only witnesses to tell the police which version of this video is real are you and your partner."

Lutz said nothing. He didn't move. He didn't blink.

Workman smiled. He got out of his seat, walked around the desk, and parked himself in the chair beside Lutz. "I think Ms. Galloway, the woman you're here to convince, isn't going to be with Blue Bean much longer."

Lutz kept his silence but showed a question clearly on his face.

"She's been unhappy here," said Workman. "I doubt she'll be around to be any kind of witness to anything so I don't think that will be a problem for you. You should just go on back where you came from."

Goose stiffened and slapped a palm against the glass. "Oh shit."

Workman jumped to his feet.

"Over there." Goose pointed out the window. "Way over there by the trainin' compound. Is that Galloway with that d-gen?"

Workman ran around the desk and looked out through the glass.

Lutz got to his feet and hurried over to the window as well.

"Goddammit!" Workman shouted, letting his anger slip out. "That *is* Galloway."

"And that's no d-gen," Lutz told them. "That's Christian Black."

Workman spun on Lutz and stepped close, jabbing his finger into Lutz's chest. "I don't know what your game is but I know you're a liar."

"I'm not." Of course, he was. Lutz backpedaled to get out of finger-stabbing range.

Workman stayed after him until Lutz made it around the desk and half-ran to the center of the office. Lutz stopped, turned, and raised his hands.

Workman was glowering.

Goose had a hand on the butt of his pistol.

Lutz saw the situation racing to a bad end with men who were motivated to get it there. He blurted, "You want her dead, don't you?"

Workman stopped. Goose glanced at Workman.

Workman cautiously said, "I want her gone."

Lutz knew then that his view into the hearts of black-hearted men was as sharp as ever. "Maybe we have some common ground here."

"If that's so," Workman shot back, "then why is your assassin running into the woods with her?"

"Christian is a clever bastard," said Lutz. "He doesn't always share his plans with me, but you can bet he's working an angle. There's an advantage in it for him and me."

"Like blackmailin' Mr. Workman," Goose snarled.

"Blackmail is for bitches," spat Lutz, "like you."

Goose pulled his gun. Workman cowed Goose with a sharp look, and Goose holstered the weapon.

Lutz, watching Workman's eyes, said, "I think we do want the same thing—me, Christian, and you. You know why we want it. I don't care why you do. Doesn't matter to me. I guarantee it doesn't matter to Christian. He doesn't have a conscience when it comes to this kind of stuff."

"What are you getting at?" Workman asked.

"Maybe we work together on this," answered Lutz.

Chapter 64

Why did I take Sienna into the woods with me? I couldn't answer that. I'd killed the brute who'd tried to have his way with her and the choice to save her seemed to carry an irrevocability that didn't make sense to me, especially given that she refused to accept my bribe.

Was I buying time to convince her, or delaying a decision to solve the problem? I wasn't sure.

I'd never hesitated in pulling the trigger before, though something about the whole situation had me feeling like a marionette. It occurred to me then, I needed to take a closer look around for puppet strings.

Listening to the modulated buzz of cicadas that seemed to get louder as the day wore on, I retrieved my clothes and weapons from where I'd hidden them in the forest and got myself dressed.

Sienna was wearing a d-gen shirt she'd had a supply of in the building. With the button popped off her jeans, she had them belted up with a piece of rope she'd found lying on the floor of the occupational therapy room outside her office. Now she stood on the bank watching the reddish-brown water flow. "The river cuts through the southern soybean fields south of here."

I nodded.

"Those fields are part of the farm." She pointed downstream. "We'll run out of forest before we get off the property."

"If we can't find a shallow place to wade across, we may have to swim it." The forest across the river ran twenty miles east. Blue Bean property ended in five or six. "Can you swim?"

"Yes," she answered.

"This is more dangerous than it looks," I told her. "The water runs swiftly in places."

"Why didn't we take my car?" she asked.

I looked up, listening for the sound that had been chasing me for a good part of the day. "Buzz bikes were all over me—cop bikes before I got onto the property, Blue Bean-owned bikes later. I'm not sure we can lose them in a car."

"Maybe we can wait until dark." Sienna looked up to get an idea of the time. "It'll be easier than running through the forest at night."

She was right about that.

"Christian," a voice sounded out of the trees.

I raised a weapon.

Sienna crouched into some bushes.

I stepped behind a tree, peeking around the trunk to see what I could see.

"Christian," the voice repeated. "I know you're close."

Sienna looked over at me with a silent question on her face. "Who's that?"

"Talk to me, Christian." The voice belonged to Lutz. He wasn't making any effort to be quiet.

I took a quick glance up the trail we'd followed along the river. It looked clear. I stepped over and squatted near Sienna and pointed back upriver. "That big cypress tree back there, the one growing right on the bank. You commented on it when we passed." It was maybe forty or fifty yards up the trail.

"What about it?"

"Go back there," I told her. "Hide nearby. I'll come get you in a little bit."

"And if you don't come?"

"I'll be there." I had the strong suspicion bullets were soon going to be in the air. Lutz was in the woods, miles from where he should have been, inexplicably aware of my location. He was either bait in a trap, or he was a duplicitous backstabber in need of retribution.

Other possibilities?

I'd know soon enough.

Sienna ran up the trail.

I silently worked my way into the thickest undergrowth.

"Don't run away," Lutz hollered. "Talk to me."

He was drawing closer.

I waited, ready to ambush.

"Christian?" Lutz called, louder this time.

He was on the trail, just downriver, following it up.

Moments ticked slowly by.

Leaves crackled as he brushed past bushes. Twigs snapped under his heels. It was the noisy way he always moved through the woods. The noise never bothered him because he was stupid enough to believe he was always the deadliest predator in the forest. He'd only hunted d-gens, prey too stupid to associate Lutz's racket with danger.

"Christian, you've stopped. Good. I'll be right there."

Odd thing to say.

A moment later, Lutz came into view. Behind him nothing moved that wasn't a natural part of the forest. To my flanks, nothing made a sound. He may not have been alone, but if so, he wasn't with the dullards who'd hunted me earlier.

I stayed out of view as he closed in.

"Christian," he called. "Come meet me halfway."

He was on the trail just a few feet from me, and then he passed by.

I gave the trail behind him one more quick glance. If a man was back that way, he was better at this game than me.

I silently stepped up behind Lutz, put the cold metal of a pistol barrel at the back of his neck, and grabbed his shirt collar to bring him to a stop and hold him in place. I hissed, "Not a word."

Lutz froze. He knew my voice, and he believed every bit of the threat.

I tugged on the collar and steered him off the trail until we were twenty feet into the trees. With an additional threat to keep him silent, I laid him down on his belly and took his belt to bind his feet. Over his mumbled protests, I used his shoestrings to tie his hands. I removed his boots, slipped off his socks, and knotted them into a gag.

When I was done, I leaned in close and whispered in his ear, "You be here when I get back. If I hear any noise from you—a grunt, a shuffle, even a fart—I'll kill you."

I didn't wait for an acknowledgment. If he screwed up that simple set of rules, then he'd have to deal with the consequences.

I crept into the trees to search for his new friends I was sure had to be out there.

Chapter 65

Maybe I was too jaded by the lies of men like Lutz to accept that I was wrong in my assumptions, but after running through a fast search of the forest nearby I was frustrated—I'd found no ambush forming up to capture me. Blue Bean's security forces were off doing whatever they normally did to fill their days.

I jogged up the trail to make sure Sienna was okay and told her to stay put. She had questions—a lot of them—but I had too few answers. I needed to get some information out of Lutz and I wasn't sure how hard I was going to have to push. I didn't want a witness infatuated with her integrity there watching me if I did go too far.

I returned to the spot where I'd left Lutz. I untied his hands and slipped the sock gag off his head. I asked, "What's going on?"

Lutz sat up, shaking his hands while opening and closing his fingers. "You asshole. I can't feel my hands."

"You probably can't feel your feet either."

He spit on the ground. "My mouth tastes like ass."

"They're your socks," I told him. "Now you know the importance of good hygiene."

"You've had your boots on since yesterday, just like me," said Lutz. "You wanna tell me what *your* socks taste like?"

"Like your mother's kisses."

Lutz ignored me and looked around. "Where's Sienna?"

"Close by," I told him. "How did you find us out here?"

"They triangulated on her phone. She's on the company network."

Dammit!

I'd not thought once about her phone. I apparently had a blind spot there. When I'd left Mexico, I'd been a finely honed weapon that didn't blunder the details. Too many months going soft while hunting d-gens in Texas was starting to look like a burdensome mistake that grew heavier at every turn.

I wasn't going to let the next screw-up slip by. Triangulation on Sienna's phone location was being done by a Blue Bean employee. That meant Lutz was working with Blue Bean.

"You need to tell me a story," I told him. "And I'm going to run out of patience quickly, so you better make it captivating."

Lutz ran through a quick version of how he'd been picked up by Blue Bean's trustees and taken to meet with Keith Workman, the CEO of Blue Bean Farms. "What you won't believe," said Lutz, to put an interesting climax on his little yarn, "is they want her dead, too."

Trying to discern the lies, I stared at Lutz. But it all sounded like lies to me. Maybe I'd been in Lutz's company too long. Maybe my preconceptions were tainting my judgment.

"It's true," he affirmed. "She's causing Blue Bean all kinds of regulatory problems with the state." Lutz looked around. "Is she close enough to hear us talk?"

I shook my head.

"Workman wants to do away with her. That's how all this shit started."

"Are you telling me it wasn't some random employee who called in the tip last night, it was this Workman asshole, the guy who runs Blue Bean?" It sounded like a stretch. It sounded like lies. "They wanted us to kill her accidentally. Was that the setup? They were going to sacrifice us to make their problem go away."

"No, no," said Lutz. "We've got it all worked out. You see, you just kill her and burn the body over there in the clearing. When it cools, we haul it to the kill site, and we say she was already dead when we got there. That's the evidence we need. That justifies the kill."

"And what, we make another version of the video that shows her carcass on the fire?" I asked.

"Yeah," Lutz agreed enthusiastically.

"And what about the police at the scene?" I asked. "Won't they wonder how a body magically appeared after they already checked out the site?"

"Details." Lutz threw his hands up as if all those little bits of fact could disappear in the breeze. "We'll figure something out. We'll have Ricardo make a video to match. Easy."

"And how do we pay Ricardo for whatever scenario you're dreaming up?"

"We don't," said Lutz. "Workman pays him. And Workman puts his lawyers on our defense, makes sure we walk away free and clear."

"Not believable, Lutz." The story was getting too farfetched. "Why go to all that trouble? Makes no sense."

"That's because I haven't told you everything."

"I'm out of patience, and I'm out of sarcasm." I drew an exasperated breath and scanned the bits of blue sky still visible through the trees looking for buzz bikes and drones. I looked at the forest around me, looking for assholes with guns. "Make it quick."

"Workman knows about *Oscuridad*.   He knows about *Oxido Negro*."

I said nothing for a moment and then told him, "Get off that shit, Lutz."

"He needs somebody from time to time to do things for him," said Lutz.   "Off-the-farm kinds of things.   Down-in-Mexico kinds of things. Blue Bean is going to expand."

"Expand into a failed state?" I asked. "That's insane."

"You're *The Darkness*," he told me.   "You can make it happen.   There's nothing you won't do.   I've told you, I researched you before I took you on as a partner. He wants to hire us. You get rid of the girl. He pays to clean the mess up. Then we work for him."

I wasn't biting.

"We'll make a lot more money than we do now," Lutz told me. "But that's not the best part."

"What's the best part?" Apparently I hadn't run out of sarcasm.

"He's going to pay your debt to the Camachos."

How the hell did that story spread all the way up here? "Nobody's going to pay that much money." I snorted. "It's not like you can just send them a check.   Workman's an idiot."

"He'll give you the cash. You just take it to them."

"Drive through lawless Mexico with a couple big bags of money?" I laughed.   "You're an idiot.   And what happens when I get there? I just knock on the door? Drop it off? Eat some menudo and talk about old times? You think they're just going to forgive and forget?"

"Wasn't that your plan all along?" Lutz asked.

It was.   It's just that its lunacy was much more obvious when spoken aloud than when swirling vaguely in my imagination. "How the hell would you know what my plans are?"

"Things you said."

"I never said those things to you."

"Yes, you did."

I glared at Lutz. Did I forget that?

"Pay them extra," said Lutz. "Pay them double. It's Workman's money. What the hell do you care? The Camachos are businessmen. They'll take the profit and tell you to piss off back to Texas. Let's go get the Mercedes. We can have the cash by morning. We can head out tomorrow. By this time next week, we'll have it made."

"The money isn't the solution to my problem with the Camachos," I told him. "The money is the prerequisite."

"What does that mean?" asked Lutz.

"My relationship with them is complicated." It was more complicated than my patience with Lutz allowed for discussion.

And why the hell am I even admitting to Lutz I know the goddamned Camachos?

"Doesn't matter," said Lutz. "Not one bit. We get the money from Workman. I'll go down with you. We do it together. This is a great deal for us. All you need to do is put a bullet in Sienna Galloway's head, and we're good as gold."

"A bullet in her head?" I asked. "Workman said that? He wants me to do it that way?" I was laying traps for lies I could pin to somebody in particular, Lutz or Workman.

Lutz was thrown off by the question. "Yeah, sure. I mean, who cares, you know? Like I said, you kill her. Ricardo fixes the video however you like. Workman pays the bills and his lawyers clean up the mess."

I was thinking it was probably time to put a bullet in *Lutz's* head. Either he was a liar or Workman was. I couldn't figure which.

Lutz caught me looking at the river. "Take the deal, Christian. There are more than a hundred guys at the edge of the forest on this side of the river. They'll come in and get you if you don't agree."

That sounded like bullshit, too.

"They're over there, across the river," said Lutz. "Maybe another hundred. I don't know for sure. That's just what Goose told me."

More lies?

Hooking up with Lutz had been a mistake, one of those mistakes that takes a long time to bear its fruit. The question in my mind was whether the fruit was poison or just thorny.

And now, standing here, listening to all his bullshit had my head spinning with trying to figure out which parts were true and which lies came from him and which came from Workman.

And a couple hundred halfwits with hunting rifles and shotguns were in the woods.

The count didn't worry me because I knew I'd not be facing them all, I'd only have to deal with a handful, the ones in my way as I made my escape. But if I killed them, my life in the States would end. No, it was already over.

That was the aching point of clarity trying to find its way to the surface of my messy thoughts.

My life in the States ended the moment this Keith Workman asshole and his Goose Eckenhausen dipshit decided they were going to set up a couple of gullible Regulators to do their dirty work.

I was the dumbass because I didn't see the truth of it until now.

There's got to be a way out!

Unfortunately, as I sat there looking at stupid, lie-spinning Lutz, trying to find my way out of the trap I'd stepped in, I couldn't come up with an escape that didn't involve me putting bullets in somebody's head.

Maybe a much older choice—one I'd made down in Mexico nearly two years ago—was the mistake I was still paying for.

And there I was thinking I'd already paid for that mistake with blood that was too precious to spend.

I felt cold metal press against the back of my skull.

So caught up had I gotten in Lutz's stupid yammering and my rotten thoughts, I'd let myself slip into another mistake, maybe my last.

I'd stopped paying attention.

The barrel of the gun pressed harder against my head and a nervous man's voice trying to feign bravery bellowed, "Don't move, asshole."

Chapter 66

When a man says, 'Don't move, asshole,' it sounds like he's giving orders, but what he's mostly doing is trying to convince his buddies and the guy he's talking to that he's a harder man than he is. He's silently praying the situation doesn't escalate. He's on ground he hasn't tread before. He doesn't know what to do next, doesn't know if he can pull that trigger, doesn't know if he can kill, doesn't know if his friends will support him or rat him out, doesn't know if he can do hard time, doesn't know if he'll muck it up somehow and get killed.

When the reaper stalks, amateurs quake. Their fear fills the air around them.

That was the nervous guy's problem.

Not mine. I wasn't afraid.

I never am when these things go down.

Death doesn't rattle me—not the possibility of my own, not the act of gifting it to someone too afraid of life to ask for it.

"You got me, asshole?" Mr. Nervous with the gun asked, because I didn't react to his previous imperative.

If he'd been a logical man, he wouldn't have asked that second question, because he'd have known I was following his previous instruction already.

If he'd been a smart man, he'd have taken three or four steps back, or never put the gun against my skull in the first place.

If he'd been a hard man, he'd have killed me already.

For my part, I'd already counted his buddies. They were trading irrelevant macho boasts and congratulations. They'd nabbed the cartel hitman. They were proud.

Too soon for hugs and hand jobs, boys.

The sounds of their voices told me which of them was cool, and which was nervous, which needed to die first, which could wait at the end of the queue. They were all too noisy, footsteps crunching leaves, denim on pants legs rasping with each step, breathing loud or slow. They freely gave me all I needed to know.

There were four of them—a pitiful number.

Mr. Nervous, the one behind me with a gun didn't have a reserved spot on my kill list. His spot wasn't for my choosing, though if I did everything right, he'd be last.

The guy off my right shoulder, eight paces back, would die first. He wasn't nervous. If anything, he was impatient. I'd heard him huff softly just after his amateur buddy, Mr. Nervous, made the mistake of talking instead of pulling the trigger. He was the most lethal of the bunch.

The one off my left shoulder, a little farther away—Mr. Anxious—would die second. He was eager to do something. He had something to prove to somebody. He'd act too hastily to fire an accurate shot.

The guy on the trail, a little behind and off to my left side, maybe twenty paces out, would go third, though that depended on how much of himself he had hidden behind Sienna. That was the part that bothered me the most—I'd been so distracted by Lutz's bullshit I hadn't heard him bringing her up the trail. I'd have to beat myself up about that later, though. By the sound of it, he maybe had an arm around her throat and was shuffling her forward, ahead of him. Holding her, he'd not be able to get an accurate shot off.

In the span of a few seconds, I had my plan. All I needed to do was wait for the prompt.

Human reaction time is about a quarter-second, depending.

People tend to have one-track minds. If you catch someone while their brain is busy doing something, then reaction time is a little slower because they have to get off the track they're on before they switch to reacting to the new stimulus.

I wasn't going to need the extra time, but I do like my insurance when I can get it.

"Hey, asshole," Mr. Nervous started on his new track, "you hear—"

I snapped my head in a turn to the right to move it quickly from in front of the gun barrel—safe.

I spun to my right as I moved my head, swinging up my right arm to get control of Mr. Nervous's gun hand.

I drew one of my pistols with my left hand, and as I came around, Mr. Lethal was in the first syllable of his "Oh, shit" thought, which came right before he would have decided to target me and pull his trigger. He never got past the word, "shit." My first bullet punched a hole through his face.

Still spinning with my momentum, keeping Mr. Nervous off balance and between me and Mr. Anxious, I fired my second shot through Mr. Anxious's throat.

Hostage Boy came into my pistol sight next, and I saw him standing mostly behind Sienna—left arm around throat, old-timey long-barrel revolver in his right hand, not pointing at Sienna, not pointing at me. His aim was way off because he was pressed against someone who was just starting to duck, and it threw him off balance.

The bullet I fired tore through his forearm, shattered his elbow, and blew a red haze out the back of his tricep.

Off balance from the spin I put him into by torquing his outstretched arm, facing away from me with feet twisted, Mr. Nervous fell, and my pistol followed him down, sending a round through the back of his head before he hit the ground.

I planted my feet, put both hands on my pistol and scanned in an arc across the trees and the targets I'd just downed.

No movement.

"Holy shit!" It was Lutz. His reaction time was slow.

Sienna finished dropping to the ground.

The big cowboy pistol dropped from Hostage Boy's hand at the end of the destroyed arm and hit the dirt. Hostage Boy was still spinning from the momentum of the bullet that had hit his arm and the last instruction his brain had sent to his body — get behind the girl.

He finally fell.

I rushed over to him, careful to step around Sienna.

The guy was on his back, his crumbled straw cowboy hat on the trail a few feet past his head. He was looking up at me.

I dropped down and put a knee in the center of his chest. "You must be Goose."

He spat something unintelligible.

"It's him," Sienna said. "That's Goose."

"Where's your boss?" I asked.

"Where do ya think?" Goose snarled, through what had to be a flaming shitload of pain.

Wasted bravado.

I smashed the barrel of my gun through Goose's teeth and jammed it into his mouth.

Goose howled. Blood, spit, and bits of teeth spewed out.

I pulled the barrel back out of his mouth. "Where's Workman, your boss?"

Goose put a hand over his mouth as he coughed and spit. He said something I didn't understand.

"Try again, Goose." I pressed the barrel of my gun against his cheek, just below his eye.

"Admin," Goose managed. "Office."

"He's in his upstairs office," Sienna interpreted.

Good enough. I stood up, pointed my pistol at Goose's head and pulled the trigger.

I holstered the pistol and raised my rifle, scanning again. I stopped on Lutz, who was wearing a perverse smile and eyeing Mr. Nervous's pistol, still gripped in the dead man's hand.

"Every time I see you shoot," said Lutz, "damn!"

"Sienna," I asked, "are you okay?"

"Yes," she told me in a distant voice.

"Go over there," I told her, "Frisk Lutz."

"Not necessary," said Lutz.

Probably true. I'd already frisked him. He'd had little time to pick up a gun. But I was tired of paying for mistakes. I told him, "Necessary."

Sienna hurried past me.

"Hands in the air, Lutz," I ordered. "All the way up."

"Don't worry about me," said Lutz.

Sienna quickly ran her hands over Lutz's clothes. She gave me a nod. "Nothing."

"Lutz, how'd you get here?" I asked.

He vaguely pointed at the corpses. "They drove."

"How many guys are in the woods?" I asked. "Let's be honest now. You've already passed your bullshit limit with me."

"You'll get no more lies from me," said Lutz, smiling as though seeing Goose and his buddies dead was the best thing that had happened to him all day. Hell, maybe it was. "There aren't any trustees in the woods. I lied about that. It's just us. Goose said something about them having a farm to run and needing to get back to work."

"Okay, Lutz, let's go see this Workman prick." I glanced at Sienna. "We can drop you at your car. You might want to get off the farm. Illegal things are going to happen."

Sienna looked pointedly at the bodies on the ground.

I shrugged. "Premeditated, illegal things."

"You should go," Lutz told her.

"What?" I looked at Lutz, surprised. All day long, he'd been doing nothing but encouraging me to kill her and now he wanted her to go. Fucking Lutz.

Sienna ignored him. "Let's go see Workman."

My kind of girl.

Chapter 67

The Mercedes was closer to us than the truck Goose and his knuckleheads had driven to find Sienna and me. Once we found it, still parked between a couple of tall pines, I realized it had been ransacked. Everything it held could be replaced, but the one thing I hoped to get—now the killing had started—was a good load of magazines. I always like to have more than I think I'll need. Unfortunately, the prison's trustees had taken my spare ammunition as well.

I instructed Sienna to get in the back seat and buckle up. Over Lutz's protests, I told him to get in the passenger seat in front where I could keep an eye on him.

"If you think I'm going to pull something," said Lutz, "do you think you can stop me if you're driving?"

"Roll the dice, buddy." I patted the butt of one of my pistols. I wasn't sure what to do with Lutz. Idiot or liar, I just didn't know, but I was going to get to the bottom of it when I finally got him and Workman together in the same room. Then I'd kill one or both of them. "Now get in the fuckin' passenger seat."

Lutz did. Sienna seated herself in the back.

I took the driver's seat, buckled my belt, started up the Mercedes, and gunned the engine before tearing backward out of the trees, skidding across red dirt and pine needles. I glanced back toward Sienna. "Buckle up back there.

Lutz decided that was good advice, too.

Moments later, I was speeding up the dirt road toward the admin complex. "We've only got a few minutes." I glanced at Sienna in the rearview mirror. "You said Workman will be in that two-story admin building, right?"

"Yes." She wrapped her fingers tightly around a handgrip over her passenger side window and stretched the other hand out to hold onto the seat in front. She didn't complain about the speed.

I gave Lutz a hard look. "You're quiet. Shouldn't you be bitching about your precious Mercedes?"

"Just don't kill us." Lutz slouched down in his seat, and he stuffed his hands in his pockets.

"What do you got in there?" I asked him.

"My dick," he spat.

"Sienna, are you sure he wasn't armed?"

"Sure," she told me.

I drew a pistol with my left hand and laid it in my lap, gripped it, and pointed the barrel at Lutz. I drove with the right hand only. "Tell me more about this place." I glanced at Sienna in the rearview mirror. "Where will I find Workman in there? What does he look like?"

"He's tall," she said. "Wide-shouldered. Old guy. Big gut. Looks like a politician."

"Anybody else look like him who works there?" I asked.

"No." She thought about it for another moment before shaking her head emphatically. "No."

"Where will he be?"

"He'll probably be in his office on the second floor."

"How do I get there?" I asked.

"Elevator at the back of the lobby. Stairs in the corner."

"If I ram this thing through the glass wall on the front of the building, will I hit anything? Concrete support poles, that kind of shit?"

"No," she told me. "Nothing in the lobby but furniture and Irene's desk."

"You like Irene?" I asked. "She might get hurt."

"It won't break my heart." Sienna almost smiled.

I laughed.

"You should know," said Lutz, "there are guys outside with rifles. Six or seven."

"Really?" I glanced over at him. "Is that where you and Workman made your bullshit plans? In his office?"

Lutz nodded.

"Any gunmen inside?" I asked.

Lutz shook his head.

I jiggled the gun in my lap. "Let's be honest, now."

"None were inside when I was there."

I glanced back at Sienna. "When we get there, you get down." I grinned. "Behind Lutz's seat might be your safest place."

Bobby Adair

Chapter 68

I pulled off the main road and followed a narrow driveway that curved gently among the oaks before spreading into a small parking lot in front of the admin building's glass face. Across the front of the building a giant sign proclaimed, 'BLUE BEAN FARMS, HAPPY PEOPLE, HAPPY FOOD.' Several cars were parked in the lot, off to one side, not in my way. Four hover bikes were parked on the asphalt, not really in my way, but not out of it either.

One of the riflemen Lutz mentioned was leaning on a hover bike, smoking a cigarette, looking into the distance, rifle in his lazy hands. Another rifleman stood in front of him, talking and gesturing. I spotted two more at the front door and another walking around the corner to the side of the building.

Not one of them had noticed the black Mercedes speeding up the driveway.

That would change.

No matter how lazy a man, it's hard not to notice a three-ton box of black steel bearing down on him.

I figured I'd screw with Lutz. Sometimes I get bored when I'm keyed-up to fight but things aren't yet happening. "What do you think, forty?"

"For what?" he asked, pressing his feet against the floorboard as if an extra set of brakes were on his side.

"For parking inside."

"Shit." Lutz braced himself against the dashboard.

Sienna shuffled in the back, getting ready for the impact.

"Fifty?" I asked. "Sixty?" I wasn't going to go in that fast but it was fun seeing Lutz squirm.

We were maybe a hundred yards out when I saw a muzzle flash. A bullet pierced the windshield dead-center and broke the back window as it passed through the SUV.

Gunmen ahead started to scramble.

The one who'd been leaning on the hover bike was too cool to jump and run when his buddies started to panic. He took an unconcerned look over his shoulder as he flicked the ash off his cigarette. His mistake. His hand-waving buddy dove to the left.

The Mercedes smashed into the pair of buzz bikes on the right, sending pieces flying in all directions. The guy with the cigarette went under the wheels, and the Mercedes bounced but didn't lose much speed. The carbon-fiber bodies of the bikes were light.

More guns fired, but the shots were wild. Nothing hit us.

We smashed the lobby's glass wall, and it turned instantly opaque with cracks before shattering.

I mashed the brakes.

Tires squealed.

The support framework for the glass wall shrieked as it bent.

The Mercedes skidded sideways into the lobby through an explosion of glass shards and came to a stop with the passenger side butted against the back wall.

I unbuckled my safety belt, flung my door open, and stepped out, scanning for targets.

The furniture that had been on the floor was broken and scattered. The reception desk, built against a side wall, came through unscathed except for a layer of broken glass. Lucky Irene.

I holstered my pistol and raised my rifle, pointing it at the SUV-sized hole we'd just made in the front of the lobby. Four targets were still out there, possibly more behind the building.

Out on the asphalt, near the two remaining buzz bikes, a man with a rifle was getting off the ground. He seemed dazed.

I fired three rounds. He dropped.

No confusion now, buddy.

Nothing else moved that I could see except d-gens, some wandering over the lawns in the distance, most of them staring at the shattered glass on the front of the admin building.

I didn't see the two armed men who'd been by the front door, but I knew they couldn't be far out of my view. I rushed to the hole I'd made where the door had been to get a glimpse from side to side. I needed to get a bead on the two door guards before they recovered from the shock of what had just happened.

Scanning right to left, I spotted one hollering at his buddy across the parking lot. Misplaced priorities with that one. He should have had his weapon pointed at me. I fired. He died.

The buddy getting yelled at had apparently bumped his head while avoiding the Mercedes' front bumper. He died with three bullets in his chest.

I looked to my left. A guy had been walking around to that side of the building. He'd had the most time to put the pieces together. He'd know he was in danger. He'd be more careful.

I heard a man yell from that side of the building. I heard another voice from over there. Two guys, at least.

I pointed my rifle, saw the barrel of a weapon come around the corner, a hand on a stock, an arm, a shoulder, and then a head. I fired, turning the head into a spray of blood, brain, and bone.

The next guy on that side would be a lot more careful before peeking out. The sight of his dead buddy would keep him neutralized for a few moments.

I ran to my right, staying close to the cube-shaped building. It wasn't large. I had a plan that would work if I executed it quickly.

I took the first corner wide, keeping my rifle pointed down the side of the building. It was mostly bare concrete, painted white with few windows. I spotted someone rounding the corner at the far end, going in the other direction to get to the back of the building. He was in a big enough hurry I wasn't able to squeeze off a shot.

I sprinted to the far end, once again taking the corner wide, keeping my aim down the side of the building as it came into view. A steel door just at the corner was closed. Plenty of windows on the back gave me pause, but only for a second. I was going to run by too quickly for a real danger from within.

Guessing the guy I was chasing was already around the last corner, I sprinted toward it. I slowed slightly as I stepped out from the wall and took the corner wide.

Down at the far end, just near the body of the man I'd shot from the other direction for trying to point his rifle at me, three armed men stood huddled, pointing toward the front of the building. They were making a plan.

Sorry, dipshits. The time for planning was before the first shots were fired.

I pulled my trigger. All three died.

No more armed men on the admin building's perimeter.

I took a hard look across the empty spaces between me and the other buildings, the nearest a few hundred yards away. Nothing except a few d-gens, most of them running, frightened by the gunshots.

More trustees had to be around, and I knew they'd be coming soon.

As I ran down the side of the building, I carefully rounded the corner to the front again and didn't see any dangers. I had some time.

Running back into the lobby, I saw Sienna and Lutz were out of the Mercedes.

Sienna pointed at an elevator against the back wall and then an open staircase up to the second floor.

I ran toward the stairs.

She shouted, "Double doors at the top. You can't miss them."

I bounded up. Lutz and Sienna followed.

Once on the second floor I immediately spotted the doors on one side of a nicely appointed waiting area. More office doors opened off the waiting room. A hallway led away from one corner. Panicked voices came from that direction. I crossed the lobby and took a look down the hall just in time to see a closing door at the end beneath an exit sign.

Office workers fleeing? Probably.

Back to Workman's double doors, I bet on speed and surprise. I ran and hit the pair of doors dead-center with my shoulder and bounced back.

The doors shuddered but didn't break.

I backed up and took another run.

The doors burst open, but I stumbled, fell, and rolled, coming up on one knee with my rifle pointed at Workman's empty desk chair. I spun around and saw the office was empty, though a closed door on one side might hold danger.

I ran over, kicked it, and as it flew open, I leveled my rifle inside. A plump, middle-aged woman with puffy black hair cowered in a glass-door shower stall. No Workman. *Damn!*

"Where is he?" I growled.

Holding her hands over her face, the woman pleaded, "Don't shoot me. I'm just the receptionist. Please."

"I won't ask again."

"He…he ran out the door when…when…"

I had all the information I needed. I ran out of the office, past Lutz and Sienna, and down the hall toward the exit sign, toward the back stairs.

I flung that door open to see two empty flights of steps. I bounded down. Workman couldn't be far.

I burst through the door at the bottom of the stairs and saw people running across the grass trying to get as far from the admin building as they could. I aimed my rifle, pausing as I scrutinized each target. None matched the description of Workman Sienna had given me.

Next guess, back out front. I ran down the side of the building toward the front, hearing a familiar sound as I went.

With my rifle up, I rounded the corner and caught a glimpse of a silvery coif of hair blowing in the wind as it raced away from me on the other side of the parked cars. In the second it took me to understand what I was seeing, a big man on a blue and white hover bike rose up and disappeared behind the boughs of an oak.

"Bastard!" It was Workman, awkwardly huge on the bike. He was getting away and I couldn't shoot because I couldn't see him for the trees.

Chapter 69

Slinging my rifle over my back, I dragged a ragged piece of a hover bike off the top of another that looked to be in one piece. Knowing Workman was getting farther away with each passing second, I gave the bike a quick look for damage. Scratches and chips, nothing else. It was a military model, built a bit more rugged than the cop bikes. I figured I'd chance it. I started the engine, checked the fuel, and spotted Sienna running toward me as she hollered, shaking her finger in the direction Workman had escaped. "That was him! That was Workman!"

"Got it." I looked into the destroyed lobby. I didn't know if Lutz's Mercedes would be going anywhere soon. "You have a car?"

Sienna nodded and pointed, I guess to wherever it was parked.

"You should get out of here. You don't want the blame for any of this falling on you."

"What about your partner?" she asked.

"Nobody gives a shit about Lutz." I pushed the throttle, and the bike floated up. "Because Lutz doesn't give a shit about anybody. Get your car and go."

I shot up to thirty, forty, then fifty feet. I was drifting southwest and climbing. Just because Workman started out fleeing in that direction, didn't mean he kept going that way. If it were me fleeing, I wouldn't have.

I scanned the sky as my bike clawed for more altitude.

I saw no buzz bike.

The century-old oaks stood like giant broccoli florets on thick trunks under sprawling hemispherical crowns. Most were separated by plenty of space to fly a hover bike through. It was a maze that stretched for nearly a half-mile in each direction, and he was staying down between the trees to keep hidden.

He was proving wilier than I'd expected.

But every choice comes with a list of pros and cons. On that cop bike—a bad choice of the two who were left—he could maneuver between the widely spaced oaks if he didn't go too fast. That meant he couldn't get far away from the admin building very quickly. Once he got out of the oaks, he'd either have to make his escape across open fields or over the treetops of the pine forest where the trees were too densely packed for his hover bike to fly safely through.

That meant I had an excellent way to catch him.

I flew in a lazy spiral, going higher and higher. The white stone and glass buildings of the admin complex all came into view among the oaks. I saw Sienna's training compound a half-mile to the south, and I saw the rows of cottages another half-mile to the east. No shiny blue-and-white bike with an old man on top, though.

I'd leveled off at about three hundred feet and continued in circles. I spotted the employee parking lot. People were running toward it. Some were in their cars, already on an exodus down an eastbound road. I didn't see any of Blue Bean's pickup trucks driving toward the admin complex, though I saw some in far away fields, parked near bands of d-gens hard at work.

Lutz's black Mercedes wasn't on the road below me. I wondered if the SUV was stuck in the lobby—maybe it wouldn't be moving again under its own power. If Lutz wasn't such a 24/7, two-faced prick, I might have felt guilty about it.

I hadn't yet spotted Workman, and I started to worry. How long had it been? A minute, three? Could he have parked the hover bike and disappeared into the forest in a car? Could he be holed up somewhere close by with a gang of trustees? Could he be hiding in one of the other buildings, or even in the woods?

The list of possibilities was long. But would a man running for his life—as he surely had to think he was—with a bike under his ass, flying away from danger, second-guess himself into abandoning his buzzing savior for another plan?

A flash of movement across my peripheral vision answered that question.

He was indeed a wily bastard.

The river's surface flowed along ten feet below the high banks. Dense pines on both sides of the river grew to a height of fifty or sixty feet, making the river a near-perfect getaway route. Any hover bike flying along close to the water's surface would be invisible from anyone flying over the forests until they were directly over the river. The only flaw—rivers snake across the landscape in every direction.

I spotted Workman because he'd just zipped down a stretch of river that ran for a quarter-mile directly away from where I'd pinned myself in the sky. My position gave me a full view of that section of the river's surface.

I throttled up to max speed and raced to the spot where I'd seen him for that fleeting second.

I kept my altitude. In moments I was over the river, slowing so I could follow its course.

I looked up and down the course of ruddy water, paying particular attention to the lengthening shadows thrown off the pines on the banks. That's where I expected a sneaky man to fly.

Almost immediately, I was rewarded when I spotted him hugging the bank, flying low and slow at a speed that allowed him to maneuver the cumbersome cop bike along the river's winding course.

Too bad my military bike had been stripped of its armament before being sold into private hands, I could have strafed Workman for an easy kill. He'd never have seen me coming.

Flying down from above and shooting at him with a pistol was a plan that would work only through luck. Hell, Goose Eckenhausen had missed a whole car when he tried to shoot me earlier—at least, I think he missed. The problem was that the air was turbulent enough to make a steady aim impossible. And it was impossible to match speed and course with only one hand on the controls.

Following him until one of us ran out of gas was a wager I didn't want to make.

I needed a better alternative. I looked down the course of the river and an attractive possibility presented itself.

With no idea how Workman's plan of escape would change once he saw the shelter of his tall pines go away, I figured I'd not give him any time to think about it.

Chapter 70

The forest ended at an expanse of soybean fields, which looked to stretch for miles to the south. Through that flat, cultivated ground, the river flowed straight out of the forest for half a mile before cutting a long snaking path for as far as I could see. But I didn't need to see that far.

Making a judgment on how long it would be before Workman's hover bike passed out of the trees, I peeled off my course over the river and dove down a long circular turn that sent me over the forest. By the time I reached the edge of the pines I was just above the treetops, still descending, and still turning my bike back toward the river.

At a meager altitude of five or six feet, in the danger range of ground clutter, I was flying parallel to the line of trees, perpendicular to the river and heading toward it.

I throttled back. My timing didn't have to be perfect, but reaching the river early would ruin my surprise.

Seconds ticked. Ground slipped by beneath me.

And though I was watching for it, anticipating it, I still felt a little surprise when Workman flew out of the forest. From my perspective so close to the ground, I didn't see his bike, which was flying above the water but below the top edge of the bank. I only saw him, looking like a man soaring magically across the landscape.

I accelerated toward him, coming from the side and a little behind. He was less than a few hundred yards in front of me. I was closing the gap quickly at over thirty miles an hour.

A handful of seconds passed as I zeroed in.

He looked to his right, surprise on his face. Maybe he'd caught sight of a blur in his peripheral vision. Maybe he sensed something. Maybe he was skittish, being suddenly out in the open and looking around for threats.

None of it mattered except to give me the satisfaction of him having just enough time to see a hover bike careening at him—just enough time to have the shit scared out of him, but not enough time to do one single thing to avoid it.

The shroud on one of my forward fans collided with his shoulder. He came off the bike, cartwheeling through the air. His bike pitched up, thrown off kilter as it zipped into the air over the soybean field. Mine went into a flat spin with one of the fans jammed against a bent shroud.

I wrestled for control, throttling up, hoping to grab some altitude to avoid hitting anything on the ground.

The landscape blurred by going sideways with the spin. I saw forest, then field, then forest, then field again. Then dirt and sky.

Oh, shit.

With the fans' lift out of balance, the bike bucked forward. By throttling up, I'd made my problem much worse.

I throttled all the way down and leaned back as far as I could to try and balance the bike.

The software in the bike's control system did its best to keep the bike stable as it dropped, and miraculously—luckily—settled it into the soybeans without putting a scratch on me.

I hopped off the bike and stumbled toward the riverbank before falling from dizziness. I shook my head, gave it a moment to clear, jumped back to my feet, and ran. I scanned across the fields as I went, looking for workers or trustees. None. Good luck for me.

At the top edge of the bank, I stopped. I was probably eight feet above the water. The river was wide—nearly twice as wide as it had been back in the forest. That meant shallower. Probably.

Workman was sitting on a sandbar in water about six inches deep, two-thirds of the way across. One of his legs was bent in the wrong direction at the knee. He was conscious, and his right forearm had all of his attention. A broken twig of white bone protruded from the skin halfway down from the wrist. Blood oozed around it.

I made the educated guess he was going nowhere soon.

I ran upriver about a hundred yards, scoping out the sandbanks and deep currents as I went, mapping out a path to get to him that didn't force me to spend too much time in deep, fast water.

When I found my spot, I slid down the muddy bank and sank in water over my head. I swam across a channel twenty feet wide while being washed at least forty feet back downriver before I was able to climb onto a sandbar out in the current. I got to my feet in water just above my knees and moved toward Workman, careful with each step as the current tugged to get my legs out from beneath me.

The water became shallower as I followed the sandbar downstream, angling across the width of the river as I went. Then it was back into a deep but narrow channel. The water was moving particularly fast, and it was difficult climbing onto the sandy bar on the other side. Only one more waist-deep channel had to be crossed after that, and then I was on Workman's sandbar, just a few dozen feet away.

Splashing through the water, breathing heavily from the effort, I stopped in front of him. "You're a greedy bastard."

He looked up, surprised, as if I'd just materialized out of the air when my words hit his ears.

"What's your password?" I asked him, indulging a sudden inspiration to have Workman compensate me for ruining my life.

He was confused. His nose was bleeding. He may have had a concussion along with his other injuries.

"Your password," I demanded. "For your computer. Tell me."

He found some lucidity, and holding his broken arm with his good left arm, he asked, "Why?"

I grabbed a finger on the hand at the end of the broken arm.

He howled.

I hadn't even twisted or yanked it. All it took was that little bit of movement. I knelt down in front of him. He was sobbing and going on about his busted bones. I slapped his face. "Back to me, dumbass. Look at me." I slapped him a second time. "Tell me."

"Tell you what?"

"Your computer password."

Shaking his head, as though he couldn't discern the purpose of my request, or couldn't reason out why his password was worth all the violence I'd perpetrated to get it, he blurted it out.

I smacked him again and made him repeat it twice more before I was satisfied he hadn't made one up just to get me to stop. I stood up and took a step back.

He looked up at me, with tears on his face and asked, "Why?"

"Because you tried to destroy my life to save yourself a few bucks."

"I don't even know who you are." He shook his head as his face turned to a sad grimace. "My arm."

"I'm Christian Black, the Regulator you tried to fuck over."

322   Bobby Adair

I saw recognition on his face, just before he guessed what was about to happen.

I pulled out one of my pistols and shot him twice in the head.

Chapter 71

Having wrestled the bent shroud back to a roughly round shape, I freed the fan blade to spin normally, and my hover bike flew as if nothing had happened—pretty much. On it, I raced back to the admin building. Time was a factor, so I pushed the throttle all the way forward and maxed my speed.

Once over the complex, I took two passes—one wide circle and one tight circle—looking for any threats that might have materialized in my absence.

It looked much like it had when I'd flown away, except the d-gens who'd been frightened by the gunfire were calm again, back doing much of nothing. No trustees were rushing toward the admin complex in their pickups. No men were milling around with guns out looking for perpetrators to punish. The bodies of the dead lay where I'd left them. The flow of employees' cars out of the parking lot near the residence compound had slowed to a trickle, and the parking lot was near empty.

It didn't appear that any of Blue Bean's employees wanted anything to do with the massacre at the admin building. It didn't seem that any of the trustees charged with work camp security were motivated to charge into a situation where they might be gunned down. And why would they—they had nothing to gain by it and everything to lose. Eventually, some law enforcement agency was going to show up. No prisoner with half a brain would want to be an armed inmate standing amidst the bodies around the admin building when that happened. That would look like guilt to any law enforcement-type racing onto the scene to answer the call that had to have gone out.

No, the trustees wouldn't be coming, but who would?

The police weren't already onsite, so that meant whatever police presence had been around to investigate my crime from the night before was gone.

Realistically, the nearest assistance might come from a nearby town with a population large enough to support a sheriff and a deputy or two. I couldn't think of one close by, so that left Houston with its sizeable police force. I might have thirty minutes, or even an hour to work with. Ideally, I wouldn't need that long to put Workman's computer password to good use.

I parked my hover bike in the grass near a tree behind the admin building where I'd have easy access to it out the building's back door. I assumed when the authorities arrived, they'd be coming up the long drive in front. If they arrived before I finished what I was doing, I'd spot them and be able to make my escape undetected.

After hopping off, I raised my rifle and scanned the area for threats. I ran to the doorway that opened up to the back stairs and let myself in. I climbed cautiously, listening for the sound of people in the building. Despite the deductions I'd made while flying in, I could easily have been wrong.

I heard nothing. The building seemed to be abandoned.

I took a moment to switch out the magazine in my rifle, guessing that if things got hairy upstairs, I might not have a second to do so then. The one I was removing had three rounds left. I loaded the only full magazine I was carrying for the rifle. I cursed the sticky-fingered trustees again for stealing everything from the Mercedes. Running through a quick count on my pistols, one was full, the other had just eight rounds. I switched my pistols right to left and left to right, putting the full pistol on the right since I was more likely to use that one first.

At the top of the stairs, I hurried down the hall, peeking in through office doors that were still open. At the second-floor waiting room, I looked across to see Workman's office doors ajar. After the way I went through them earlier, they weren't going to close again without repair.

I crept into the waiting area and snuck a look inside.

What the hell?

Sienna and Lutz were sitting in the chairs facing Workman's desk with their backs to the door. They were alive.

The situation had *trap* written all over it. I retreated across the waiting room and into the hall.

Get the hell out? Maybe.

Go kill the knuckleheads hoping to shoot me in the back? Bingo!

I didn't like running from a fight.

Having given the offices off the hall only a cursory glance on the way through a moment before, I went back and did a fast but thorough check. All were empty.

Going back to the waiting room, I very quietly crept along the wall and checked each office directly off that space. Again, no one lurking there to put a bullet in my back.

My ambushers weren't very good at what they did. They had to be waiting just inside Workman's office on each side of the door.

Right, left, both?

Why take a chance? I had a full magazine in the rifle I could spare to save myself from a shot in the back, and I was all but finished killing folks for the day.

I took up a position in the lobby, looking through the office doors with Sienna and Lutz directly in front of me but way on the other side of Workman's office, still sitting and facing the other direction. They weren't aware I was in the building.

I pointed my rifle at the wall just to the left of the double doors. Because of the angle to the wall beside the door from where I stood, none of my bullets would hit either Lutz or Sienna. I fired ten rapid shots in a wide pattern across that wall and immediately fired another ten into the wall on the right. Anyone behind either wall had to be dead or wounded, and I still had ten rounds in the rifle, just in case.

With the pop of my shots still echoing, with Sienna screaming and Lutz cursing, I ran into the office, letting my rifle hang in its sling and drawing my pistols.

Once through the door, I spun, looking for the ambushers I was certain were there.

They weren't.

Not one body.

It made no sense.

I was sure it was an ambush.

I turned on Lutz. "What the hell?"

Lutz was out of his chair and facing me. "What the hell yourself! I damn near pissed my pants."

"Is there anyone here?" I demanded. "Ambush?"

"No," Lutz told me. "You fucking killed everybody already."

"Not everybody." I crossed over to the restroom I'd kicked the door in on earlier. It was empty. I glanced over at Sienna. She hadn't moved. "You okay?" I resisted the urge to bring my weapon to bear on Lutz.

She nodded.

I hurried around Workman's desk, and I gave Lutz a once-over glance for a weapon. He wasn't holding one, didn't have a pistol stuffed in his belt, but he did have an extra big bulge in one of his baggy pockets. I laid my pistol on the desk, told Lutz and Sienna to sit, dragged Workman's phone over in front of me, and dialed Ricardo's number.

He picked up immediately. "Who is this?"

I put the phone on speaker. "Christian Black here. I've got the dipshit with me, and someone else. A bystander."

"Lutz the dipshit." Ricardo laughed. "I like that. Why are you calling? What do you need?"

"I'm in front of a computer full of information about accounts I think are loaded with money. I suspect there'll be information on offshore accounts, illegal tax-evasion shit. Maybe more stuff."

"And?" Ricardo asked.

I logged into Workman's computer as I spoke, pleased that he'd given me the correct password. "I've got a quick, do-it-now-or-forget-it deal."

Intrigued, Ricardo asked, "What's that?"

"I've got access to the computer. I can give you the password. I can give you the IP address, any network details you need in order to find it from the outside. Can your hacker — what's her name, Blix — get in and download all the account access information we need to drain the accounts? The clock is ticking. It'll all have to be wrapped up in the next six to twelve hours."

"How much money are we talking about?" asked Ricardo.

"Millions is my guess." I looked at Sienna. "That sound right to you?"

"Tens of millions," she answered robotically.

Something was wrong here, very wrong. I casually laid a hand next to one of my pistols. I told Ricardo, "Tens of millions."

"What's the split?" he asked.

"Half for me," I answered. "Half for you to split with Blix."

"Three ways," answered Ricardo. "A third for you. A third for me. One-third for Blix."

What did I care about the split? A third of whatever Workman had in his accounts was way more than I'd need, and probably enough to set me up for a good many years. "Deal."

"Will you be at this number?" Ricardo asked.

"Maybe ten more minutes," I told him. "Then I need to be gone."

"Okay," he said. "I'll have Blix call you in a minute."

"Ten minutes," I reminded him. I looked at a clock on Workman's desk. "That's it."

"The phone will ring," Ricardo assured me.

I hung up, looked at Sienna, and asked. "Why didn't you leave?"

"We thought it best," Lutz answered for her, "that we all leave together, get back to Ricardo's, plan our next move." He looked out the window as if expecting to see something, didn't, and looked back at me. "Maybe talk about a more equitable split of Workman's money."

Sometimes the things Lutz says are so far outside my reality I can't help but stare, dumbfounded.

"It's true," Sienna said, though it didn't sound at all true the way she said it.

Workman's desk phone rang. I picked it up. "Yes?"

"You were expecting my call?" asked Blix, like there was no time pressure at all.

I put the phone on speaker. "I assume Ricardo explained the situation?"

"Yes."

"You know the time constraint."

"I do."

I smiled. "Tell me what you need."

We spent only a few minutes of my ten-minute allotment while I answered questions and she got connected.

She asked, "Can you see the mouse moving on your screen?"

"Yes," I answered. "You're doing it?"

"I have control of the computer," she confirmed.

"Anything else you need from me?" I asked.

"No," she told me. "You can hang up and—"

"Oh," I interrupted. "One more thing."

"What's that?"

"I've seen a few surveillance cameras around. Can you access Blue Bean's security system and erase any record of me, Lutz, or Sienna Galloway?"

"If I can get access," Blix told me, "I'll erase everything."

"Perfect. I'll talk to you later today." I hung up.

Chapter 72

Everything important to me was taken care of. All I needed to do was leave. I spun around in Workman's chair, just for the hell of it, and to get a quick look down the long driveway. It was still empty, but the sky behind was glowing orange and the clouds smeared across the horizon were turning red.

Had the whole day already passed?

I realized, circumstances and time had given me the opportunity for one more quick thing.

I spun again in Workman's chair to face his desk. I tore a piece of paper off a tablet, rifled through a few drawers to find a pen, and I started writing.

"What are you doing?" Lutz asked.

"Insurance," I told him.

I slid the piece of paper across the desk to Sienna. "Take it."

She hesitated, glanced at Lutz, and then leaned forward to pick it up. "What is it?"

"The combination to a safe in my house."

"Why?" she asked.

Lutz opened his mouth to speak—in fact, got most of a syllable out—before I shushed him back to silence. I'd come to a conclusion about what to do with him. "You're a liar without an ounce of loyalty to anyone or anything."

Lutz shook his head but didn't seem at all displeased.

"I've thought a lot about killing you this afternoon. I don't know what part you had in making this situation go to hell, but I'm sure it was significant. Nevertheless, it's your lucky day."

"Yeah," Lutz told me sarcastically. "Sounds like it."

"Don't screw me again," I told him, looking into his eyes to let him know I was serious.

Lutz shook his head. "I was—"

"I don't want to hear your voice again unless I ask for an answer."

Lutz slouched in his chair, unconcerned.

To Sienna, I said, "I'm a fugitive now. I'll have to cross the border, maybe go to one of the failed states where the law can't reach me. I'm not sure where, but I am certain going back to Houston will be a mistake."

I pointed at the piece of paper in her hand. "I would like to ask of you a service for which I'll pay."

"What's that?" Sienna asked.

"There's a safe in my house. I need the money in that safe."

Sienna looked at the computer. She'd heard the deal I'd just made with Ricardo and Blix.

"In case they cheat me," I told her. "Lutz can take you to my house to get the money. He'll protect you in case any low-life Regulators are there waiting for me. No harm will come to you. I guarantee it with Lutz's life." I turned to Lutz. "Do you believe I can provide that guarantee?"

He nodded. He knew about *Oxido Negro*. He knew about *Oscuridad*, my nicknames from south of the border. He knew what I could do to him.

Sienna took a moment to consider the situation as her eyes drifted down to look at her hands. "How much money?"

"Enough to help you start a new life," I told her.

"I don't understand." She looked up at me. "It's your money."

"The order of the day seems to be the three-way split," I told her. "One third for dipshit, here. One third for you. A third for me. You hold onto mine, and I'll contact you eventually and let you know what to do with it."

"And for that I get a third of your money?" she asked, shaking her head. She didn't believe.

"Right now the money is worthless to me," I said. "I'll never be able to get it. I'm paying you because I don't want to have to go back to Houston."

I turned to glare at Lutz. "If I don't give him something, he won't be able to keep himself from trying to steal some of yours or mine. I'm cutting him in so you won't get hurt and so I won't have to kill him. Besides, he needs money to get himself set up wherever he runs to after a warrant comes down for his arrest. Are you still planning to tell the truth about what happened?"

Sienna was reluctant to answer.

"It's okay," I told her. "It doesn't matter, not to me. I was doomed from the moment Workman called in the tip, I just didn't know it until earlier this afternoon. Lutz is slow. He'll figure that out, too. It doesn't matter what you tell the police when they ask. Even if Lutz and I get off on killing all those d-gens, consequences will come for killing Workman and the others. The police will investigate. Some of the blame will land on Lutz even though he didn't pull a trigger. He'll need to get out of town."

"This needs to be done quickly, then?" she asked.

"As soon as you leave here," I told her. "Go straight to my place." I turned to Lutz. "After that, you should leave town, immediately. Take your cash and go." I figured I'd better dumb it down for him. "Do you understand what's going to happen? Do you understand what I'm asking you to do? Do you understand I'm buying you a chance at a new life in Canada? Don't go down to Mexico, okay? You won't last a month down there."

Lutz nodded.

"I want to hear you say it."

"I understand."

"Thank you, Lutz." I turned back to Sienna. "Thank you, too."

I reached out a hand to Lutz. "Give me that phone I bought for you." I gave Sienna the number from the phone. "Any problems, call me. You two should go. Sienna, take your car. Lutz, leave yours. Don't ever come back for it."

He grimaced and said, "But it cost—"

"Doesn't matter," I told him. "The only place that Mercedes will take you to is prison. Besides, there's enough money in your share from my safe to buy another wherever you're going. You'll have plenty—" I stopped talking as a rumble grew suddenly out of nothingness, like an earthquake falling from the sky.

Shit!

I'd stayed too long.

Chapter 73

Helicopters had come for me, and I had a lot of blood on my hands.

Hate flamed in my eyes for Lutz because when I looked at him, I saw on his face that somehow, the helicopters were his doing.

I did a quick guestimation. With my military model hover bike's speed, maneuverability, and range, I could get away. I just needed to get to it.

I jumped to my feet, sending Workman's chair bouncing off the glass wall behind me as I took up my pistols.

"Don't." Lutz said it in a peculiar, satisfied way that caught my attention enough to spend a precious second of my escape window pausing to listen further.

"Four helicopters," he spoke in a voice that wasn't his. It was confident. The nasally quality was gone. He didn't sound like a dipshit. "They're all FBI. One on each corner of the building. At least two dozen shooters. Former Special Ops, not like the yokels you killed today. You won't make it out alive."

The scope of Lutz's lies, the sudden change in his demeanor, the presence of the FBI, didn't make sense to me, and I was usually one to put the pieces of a mystery together in a snap.

"Sit down," Lutz told me. "We need to talk."

I didn't sit.

"I'm FBI." He said it like I didn't have two loaded pistols in my hands.

Snap!

All the pieces fell into place. At least enough of them did.

Rotor wash was beating the enormous windows behind me. Vibrations shook my feet through the floor. Men were rappelling to the ground. I was screwed.

Only one choice to make—die in a firefight, or hope I'd find a way to escape before Texas strapped me into an electric chair somewhere down the road.

Bad odds don't bother me. I can deal with those. Zero odds, I hate.

I hauled back, ready to pitch a pistol at Lutz's face.

Seeing my windup, he dodged to his right.

Guessing in which direction his reaction would take him, I threw the pistol where I figured my target would be.

The butt smashed his nose and blood splattered out.

"Damn!" Lutz shouted as my pistol clattered on the floor. "The bet at the office was that you'd shoot me when it went down. My money was on you being smart enough not to."

"I still have one pistol," I spat, "and the blood of a dozen on my hands." That last one wasn't an exaggeration but an estimate. "What difference does one more make?"

"If you believed that," said Lutz, "I'd already be dead. You haven't killed me because you want me to tell you why I just admitted I was in the FBI despite the risk. You want to know why I didn't let you go outside to die."

"I've been in worse situations." If there were indeed four helicopters—and it sounded like there could be—and they had just dropped former Special Ops shooters from the FBI outside the perimeter of the building, then my boast had probably been a lie.

Lutz smiled, his teeth red with blood from a smashed nose he seemed to have no regard for. "Sit down."

I didn't. I was angry. "I'm thinking about shooting myself out of shame for getting duped for seven months by a dipshit-snitch bastard like you."

"You got duped because I'm so goddamn good at what I do." Lutz didn't sound like he was bragging, so much as reciting the score of a baseball game. "I'm so good you can't stop believing the lie I sold you even though I'm sitting right here telling you it was a lie, even though two dozen FBI shooters are outside, waiting for me to tell them to come or not. I've got your life in my hands right now, not Lutz the dipshit Regulator you think you worked with, but Lutz the undercover FBI agent who's a lot smarter than your arrogant dumb ass."

"How will you do that?" I asked. "Tell them to come or not."

Lutz moved a hand to his shirt.

I pointed my pistol at the mess of his nose, threatening him to be careful. It was still a valid threat. What difference would one more murder make?

"No danger." Slowly, he unbuttoned his shirt to reveal a little mic taped to his chest and a dangling wire running down his belly. "My boss is on the other end in one of the helicopters."

I adjusted my aim at the microphone, which was conveniently placed over his heart.

"Don't," said Lutz.

"Don't?" I asked.

"I see the look in your eyes," said Lutz. "You're planning. You still think you have a hope to get out of this. If the mic goes dead, they'll come. Why don't you sit down? We need to talk about a deal."

I hate losing. I hate it more than the idea of dying. Backwards? Maybe. But losing is failure I have to live with, dying isn't.

I sat down and laid my remaining pistol on the desk, trying to unravel the mistakes that had gotten me to where I was. "What I don't understand…" I shook my head as I thought about it. "How long were you a Regulator in Houston hoping I'd show up?"

"You live in a self-centered little world, don't you?" said Lutz. "That's probably why it was so easy to fool you. You think you're always right. I only needed to fool you the first time. Once you decided I was a dipshit, I could have worn my FBI badge on a chain around my neck, and you'd have never figured it out."

"Try that on your next case," I told him. "I'm sure it'll work out fine."

Lutz looked over at Sienna. "Why don't you leave? You don't need to be here for this." Lutz glanced at me. "She didn't know anything. She was just a bystander."

Sienna got out of her chair.

"Raise your hands," he said. "Walk slow. You don't have anything to worry about. You didn't do anything wrong."

Sienna silently left Workman's office.

"How'd you manage the hook up with me in Houston?" I asked.

"I was there working other cases," said Lutz. "I spotted you on that TV show, Bash. A video drone picked up one of your kills. I'm good with faces. You looked familiar. I ran you through our facial recognition software and voila, Christian Black. My partner at the time had an accident—"

"I'll bet."

"—and I contacted you about the opening."

"So this whole seven months, you've what, been waiting to catch me breaking the law in FBI jurisdiction so you could bust me?"

"No," said Lutz. "It was all about information, at first. I was hoping you'd open up to your new dipshit buddy, maybe brag a little bit and tell him some things FBI Lutz could use against the cartels down in Mexico. I'll bet you've got a head full of nasty intel. You were down there long enough to learn a lot."

I shrugged. No sense in revealing anything at this point.

"But we're past that," said Lutz.

"Why?" I asked.

"We got tired of waiting. We decided we wanted more. Our requirements changed. You weren't forthcoming with any helpful nuggets. Pick one."

"So you set me up," I guessed. "You made all this happen. This wasn't a sequence of shitty coincidences." Then it hit me, the possibility I'd killed the wrong person. "It wasn't Workman who called in the tip. It wasn't Goose Ecken-fuckin-hausen. It was you."

"It wasn't me." Lutz reached for the mic on his chest and yanked it off. The wire came loose from whatever it was attached to. He laid it on the desk. "Just you and me now."

"They won't come in?" I asked.

"They know you're being civil," said Lutz. "They'll give us some room."

"So it was you who called in the d-gen tip. How?"

"It wasn't me," said Lutz, "but I did arrange it with a buddy."

"So you set me up," I accused. "All the people I shot, they were your fault."

"You shot 'em," said Lutz. "Don't pin it on me. I just gave you the opportunity."

"You egged me on. You told me a hundred times to kill Sienna. Why?"

"I needed you to be guilty of a capital crime, so I could get you to deal."

"You're a dirtier cop than you ever were a Regulator," I told him. "Is that how the FBI works? Dirty agents breaking the law to do what? Catch lawbreakers?"

"No," said Lutz. "The FBI isn't dirty. They've got their rules. They play by them. Me, not so much."

"And they don't care?"

"They turn a blind eye to results."

"I'll bet." I crossed my arms. "Well, you got me. I've committed at least a dozen capital crimes." I drilled Lutz with a hard look. "But I killed the wrong people."

"No you didn't," said Lutz, shaking his head. "Workman was corrupt. He was guilty of plenty. And those trustees, you can bet they were all guilty of a lot more than they were in prison for. No loss. Not in my eyes. Not in the FBI's eyes, at least that's true as long as you're willing to deal."

"Fine," I told him. "What's the deal?"

"All this," Lutz waved a hand at the helicopters. "All those d-gens you killed. Everybody you murdered today, it all goes away. Hell, even that little cybercrime you just committed with Ricardo's hacker bitch, that disappears, too."

"And the price for all this exoneration?" I asked, flatly.

"Don't say it like that," said Lutz. "This is what you've been working toward since last night. This is fucking Christmas day for you. You risked everything. You paid big money. You killed people so you could be an innocent man again, an upstanding citizen. I'm making it happen."

"What do you want?" It wasn't a question I needed to ask. Christian Black didn't have anything that would interest the FBI except for one thing.

"The Camachos."

There it was.

"If you wanted the Camachos dead," I asked, "why not just hire me to kill them? You apparently know who I was. You apparently know what I did down in Mexico."

"No," said Lutz. "We want you to lead us to them. Nobody at the FBI would trust paying a thug like you. We don't buy contracts to have people killed."

"You kill them yourselves," I snapped.

"Don't get self-righteous," said Lutz. "Don't forget what your résumé looks like."

I felt like I needed time to think about the deal on the table but I didn't. It was a one-option deal, take it or die. Sure, I could sit behind Workman's desk and fantasize about killing Lutz and shooting my way out, but that was just a delay. My only way out was to take Lutz's deal.

"This is your new start," said Lutz, trying to convince me to say yes to what I was certain was a postponement of my death. "This is the end of an episode in your shitty black life. Take the deal. Help us put two nasty psychopaths in a hole, and save some American lives."

"Yes." I was seething over being conned by dipshit Lutz as I silently dredged my memory for clues about him from all those months that should have tipped me off about what and who he really was, but I was too angry for any to come to mind. None that mattered, though. I really had no choice. "I'll do it."

Better to try tomorrow than die today.

The End

Christian will be back!
Be sure to get the free ebook prequel to Black Rust,
Black Virus, on Amazon.

Other Books by Bobby Adair

Black Rust series, Prequel and Book 1
Audiobook coming Fall 2016 on iTunes & Audible.com
A best-selling post-apocalyptic series, new in 2016. The Black Virus prequel (short story) tells the beginning of the story, when Christian Black was young and the virus was just taking hold of society. Black Virus (ebook) is FREE on all platforms.

Slow Burn series, Books 1-9 (Complete)
Audiobook available on iTunes & Audible.com
A best-selling post-apocalyptic adventure series (with some zombies!).

The Last Survivors series, Books 1-6
(1-5 complete as of June 2016)
Audiobook available on iTunes & Audible.com
A futuristic post-apocalyptic tale with a Games of Thrones medieval feel. Collaboration with author T.W. Piperbrook.

Ebola K Trilogy, Books 1-3 (Complete)
Audiobook available on iTunes & Audible.com
Another best-seller. What happens when a pandemic takes over the world? An American college student finds himself in Uganda and in the midst of a sinister terrorist plot to weaponize Ebola.

Dusty's Diary: One Angry Man's Post-Apocalyptic Story
A short story by Bobby that he used to blow off steam after the seriousness of writing Ebola K. A little raunchy and rough around the edges, Dusty finds himself stuck in a bunker after the zombie apocalypse.

Let's Keep in Touch

Like my Facebook Page or **subscribe to my email list**. I like to keep in touch, and I swear, I won't SPAM you or sell your email address. No, really…

Newsletter: http://bobbyadair.com/blackrust-subscribe/

Facebook: http://www.facebook.com/BobbyAdairAuthor

Did You Find a Typo?

Gosh, I hope not! Although I think Black Rust is the cleanest book we've put out to date, there is a possibility you might find a mistake. If you don't mind, please visit our typo reporting page…this form automatically puts any corrections in a spreadsheet for us so we can update the next version of the book.

http://www.bobbyadair.com/typos

Bank Some Good Karma! Write a Review…

And if you're so inclined and liked Black Rust and want to share that with the world, please leave a review. Or if you think maybe the next book could use a few more F-words, a little more romance, maybe a flying saucer, or more cowbell (Christopher Walken reference), please put your comments in a review and let me know. Reviews really help authors find new readers (and pay the rent and buy dog toys) in this new world of ebooks. My dogs thank you for that zombie-foot dog toy and all the squeakies that distract me from writing. Thanks for reading!

smarturl.it/BR1-Amz

Made in the USA
San Bernardino, CA
01 March 2017